THE HOUSE OF DRACULA

By the same author

Dracula's Children
Tales from the Shadows
Tales from Beyond
A Quiver of Ghosts
The Brats
The Partaker
The Fantastic World of Kamtellar
The Cradle Demon

Books containing tales of Clavering Grange
Tales from the Haunted House
The King's Ghost
Tales of Darkness
Tales from the Other Side
Ghosts from the Mist of Time

The House of Dracula

R. CHETWYND-HAYES

WILLIAM KIMBER · LONDON

First published in 1987 by
WILLIAM KIMBER & CO. LIMITED
100 Jermyn Street, London SW1Y 6EE

© R. Chetwynd-Hayes, 1987

ISBN 0-7183-0668-6

This book is copyright. No part of it may be reproduced in any form without permission in writing from the publishers except by a reviewer who wishes to quote brief passages in a review written for inclusion in a newspaper, magazine, radio or television broadcast.

Photoset in North Wales by
Derek Doyle & Associates Mold, Clwyd
and printed in Great Britain by
Biddles Limited, Guildford and King's Lynn

Contents

		Page
	Draculain Genealogical Table	6
	Introduction	9
I	Caroline	13
II	Marikova	77
III	Karl	123
IV	Gilbert	155
V	Louis	183

Draculain Genealogical Table

Count Dracula (1147-1896)
=

Three Vampire 'wives'

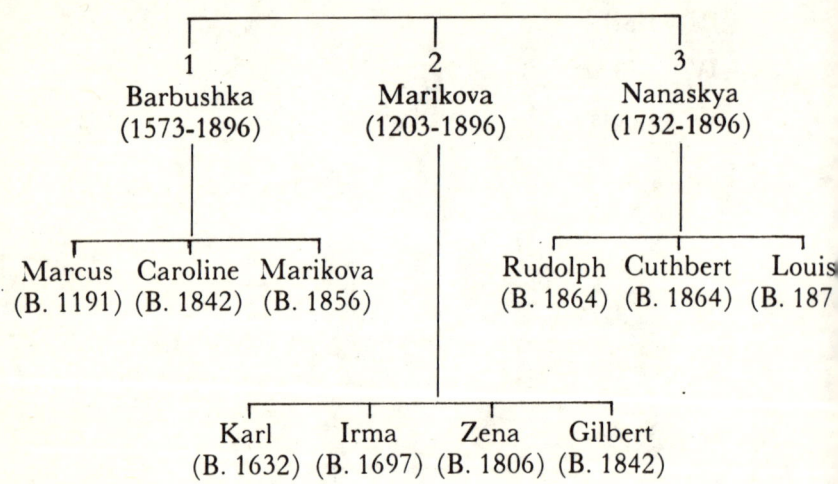

Count Dracula
Second Generation Vampires

Third generation Vamlings mated to humans (Humes)

Mocks
Fourth generation – Mocks mated to humans

Shadmocks
Fifth generation – Mocks mated to Vamlings

Maddies (female)   Shaddies (male)

Sixth generation Mongrels (Genetic Composition unknown)

Madvams (The pack)

Notes: It would seem that the offspring of a shadmock and a human is considered to be free from vampire blood and can therefore be designated as one hundred percent hume.

Introduction

Shortly after the publication of *Dracula's Children* I received the following letter, which with the writer's permission, I am reproducing in its entirety:

Dear Mr Chetwynd-Hayes,
 I do not usually read the kind of book that you write, having a preference for light romance, a style of literature that soothes, whereas yours is inclined to have an opposite effect. But a friend of mine, who knows something of my family history, pressed me to read *Dracula's Children*.
 You can imagine my amazement when I realised your late night visitor, the collector of the *Dracula Papers*, was my uncle and that his father, who was so impressed by the outstanding beauty of Countess von Hentzen, was my grandfather.
 Most – if not all – of the *Papers* came from my attic where they were dumped after my grandfather's disappearance. His name was ... Well perhaps not. I have no wish for a visit from the pack. But I must stress that although my uncle did track down quite a few of the 'family' himself – and paid the price – the documents were actually written up by my grandfather – whose disappearance in 1976 so worried us all. He did not tell you about that.
 But the reason I am writing to you is this: I have in my possession papers which deal with five more of Dracula's children.
 May I suggest we do a swop? You bring back to me those now in your possession and I will give you those in mine. Where any of them came from originally I have not the slightest idea.

I need hardly say I have no wish for my *real* name to appear at any time, although you may quote this letter in part or in full.

Yours sincerely,
B.L. Bransom (Mrs)

I visited the lady and we had quite an exciting time comparing our respective manuscripts, all of which had been crudely typed, corrections (such as they were) being done with a ball-point pen and in some cases pencil.

I am going to be honest: the following four stories are very freely adapted from the original manuscripts, for I have felt it wise to update the period – in particular the last which I have written under the title 'Louis' – as there was a distinct danger that the characters might well have been recognized, had I not done so. I have also taken liberties with appearance, age, background and in one case – sex.

When Mrs Bransom states she has no idea where the manuscripts came from, she is of course referring to the narrative, as there can be no doubt in my mind the entire two hundred A4 pages were typed by one person – her grandfather – as were the original *Dracula Papers*. I have already started a hunt for the letters exchanged between Mrs Hilda McCarthy and Miss Liza Russell (See 'Louis' page 183), but have had to practise great discretion, not wishing to attract unwelcome attention from a certain source.

However, I have great pleasure in presenting this further proof of the existence of this most remarkable family before the public, but cannot too strongly stress the danger in attempting to track them – or even a single member – down.

I am convinced the pack is a grim reality that must not be ignored.

Lastly. Is this the end of the story? Did Count Dracula sire more than eleven children? As he and his original 'wives' walked this planet for around seven hundred years, it is more than probable. Mrs Bransom assures me she has no more manuscripts tucked away. But somewhere, in attic, closet, under floorboards, or in a rarely disturbed library, there could well be bundles of dust-grimed papers that reveal the existance of other *vamlings* who bow to no being save the High

Lord Marcus who holds eternal court at Wittering Grange.

A last lastly: I have been asked – do I believe in the hidden world? One word will suffice as an answer. Yes.

I

Caroline

PART ONE

SIMON

God was very angry with Simon.

Divine wrath was manifested as a rumbling roar that banished sleep, then reinforced its dire message by several savage flashes of lightning that briefly turned the bedroom into a brilliantly lit cavern. On one such occasion the Supreme Being let rip with a mighty explosion that took place just beyond the window and made the house tremble down to its very foundations.

The reasons for this dread display of celestial displeasure were manifold. Firstly Simon had refused to eat his wheaticles which were guaranteed to turn him from a five stone weak little boy to a man resembling Hercules who according to Nanna had performed a lot of back-breaking labours back in olden times. Then there was the little matter of drawing pins on Nanna's chair that only he – Simon – and God knew about.

Looking dead at the dog that barked at him.

What a pity it was that God did not understand he hadn't intended to look dead at the dog, but he had been frightened at the time and the dog dropped dead almost before Simon realised what he had done.

Then only yesterday he had looked big at the bunch of flowers the almost grown-up girl was carrying and when they became so large they hid her face, she dropped them and ran away.

And Nanna, even though she did not know about looking dead and big, had warned him what to expect.

'He sees all,' she had announced, pointing a quivering finger ceilingwards. 'There's nothing – *nothing* – He doesn't see. And He don't forget. Mark my words, one of these days you'll hear from Him.'

And Simon – shaking in his bed – was hearing from Him. Roaring and rumbling across the face of heaven; spitting fire before drenching the earth with a torrential downpour that threatened to drum its way through the roof. An impromptu prayer expressing repentance seemed only to further inflame the divine rage, for it was followed by a salvo of thudding roars that had Simon burrowing down under the bedclothes.

Then Simon whispered, 'Go away. You've rumbled and roared enough,' and almost instantly thunderclaps grew fainter, lightning lost its ability to do more than illuminate the window frame, then ceased altogether. The rain slowed its pace until it became nothing more than a soft patter on the window panes before retiring to the mist-shrouded cloud-valleys that had given it birth. Silver moonlight painted a soft outline round the window curtains. It would seem that God had to be told what to do, not implored.

Now to get out of bed and look down upon a rain-washed world that basked in silver light, where the lawn glittered like a diamond studded crystal green floor, while beyond a line of beech trees shook their heads sadly and shed gleaming tears as though they were racked with the grief of repentance.

Simon eased back the curtains and extended his view so as to see more clearly the old house which stood beyond the tall privet hedge that bordered the left hand side of the garden. A thick, well-trimmed wall of a hedge that did not permit so much of a glimpse of what stood on the other side.

Only roof and chimney stacks if one stood well back and looked over the top – or viewed the scene from an upper window. Nanna thought the house was empty, or maybe just occupied by a caretaker, and was it not fortunate that someone had cultivated this tall hedge which so adequately divided our well-kept garden from the over-grown wilderness next door. But when Satan was doing his very worst and planting temptations left, right and centre in a restless brain, Simon found he could not concur with this statement, for would it not have been exciting to explore the riotous garden, not to mention the house itself, were it indeed uninhabited?

Now the wet roof had temporarily acquired silver slates and deep red glistening chimney pots, and the top half of three moon-glazed windows that had something in common with half-open tear-filled eyes.

Simon forgot the angry God – who was now busy being angry somewhere else – and began to concentrate his attention on the moonlit scene. There could be no doubt that the world of night had a certain magic that was missing from the harsh world of day.

A magic hard to define. Something to do with the way that light gradually blended with shadow and started to produce ... Ah!

He had seen, or rather observed it before, but up to that moment forgotten what he had seen. This act of forgetfulness might be yet another reason for the God's anger, for – as often stressed – to be absent from one's mind was the result of laziness.

Yet, was there not, on occasion, a voice that spoke at the very back of the mind, that said slowly and with great emphasis: 'Pay heed to all that happens in the golden garden of childhood, for it is so easily forgotten in the burning years of adolescence.'

Now, he concentrated on what he saw, and decided in no way would he forget, no matter that a thousand years pass, and his ego be transformed into the soul-blinding aura of an astral emperor.

A woman in white drifted from the tall hedge.

A statement of fact that could in no wise be disputed.

A tall silver-beautiful woman attired in a long white gown that covered her from neck to ankles and threatened to engulf her long-fingered hands. Hair as black as midnight, enhanced by glittering moon diamonds. The eyes were bright, the teeth so white and dazzling. The voice that whispered in his head gentle, soothing and so different from the roaring of an angry God.

'Come out and play. You must. Bathe your hands in moonlight. Chase cloud shadows and listen to the breeze-rustled trees as they whisper secrets that must never, but never be repeated.'

Simon liked this idea very much for he had often thought how exciting it would be to go out and play when everyone was fast asleep in bed. The trouble was – how to get out. The front and back doors were firmly locked and bolted and the keys tucked under Nanna's pillow.

'Climb down the clinging vine,' the voice instructed.

That was certainly a possibility, although Simon had never before considered climbing down the sweet-smelling, tough-branched vine, which covered the entire rear of the house and actually surrounded his bedroom window. He raised the bottom sash and looked down. Yes, there seemed to be plenty of footholds, and the lady was whispering in his head again, telling him not to fear, she would make certain he did not fall.

So, attired in bright blue pyjamas, bare of foot and slightly agitated of mind, Simon clambered over the window sill, wriggled first one foot, then the other, then very slowly made his way down to the garden below.

A fresh, warm breeze took him into its gentle embrace; soft damp grass made a quite comfortable carpet beneath his feet, while moonlight created wonderful silver-tinted shadows that undulated across the lawn, and indeed could well be chased if one was of that turn of mind.

But the lady in white stretched out her hands and he ran to her, aware of the need to love, be accepted, then rejected, caressed before being hurt, become lost in the cold mist that seemed to surround her person.

Her cold hands gripped his and the clear voice grew louder as she lowered her head.

'What a nice little boy you are! I've been looking for someone like you for a very, very long time. How fortunate it was that the thunder woke you up.'

Simon knew he must not allow this beautiful lady to remain a moment longer under a misapprehension. He looked up into her pale face and whispered what *he knew* to be the truth.

'That was not thunder, but the voice of God being very angry with me.'

Her laugh reminded him of church bells heard across a sleepy countryside, while her cold lips brushed his cheek.

'No, little man, that was the voice of my father being very

angry with me. I had not thought about him for such a long time.'

Then she led him towards the hedge.

*

Thelma Martin was regarded by most men as a cool blonde, and indeed it cannot be denied she had almost ash-blonde hair, a pale flawless complexion; a combination that created the impression of an almost frozen don't-you-dare-touch Aryan beauty. Her face was comprised of flat planes and straight lines, as though it had been chiselled from a block of white marble, then expertly tinted by a master craftsman. Her pale blue eyes were slightly slanted; her lips well-shaped, although rather too thin for popular taste; nose straight, modelled perhaps by that deity whose decision is final, on the one possessed by Venus de Milo; chin-line a miracle of perfection.

Tall for a woman, her figure hinted at angularity, while still retaining an attractive outline: it was not without some justification she had been labelled the goddess of frustrated desire.

The lady was a widow, the late Albert Martin having given up the ghost some five years after their marriage; the death certificate boldly stated cerebral thrombosis, but there were those who maintained the goddess had wrung him dry, then discarded him like a worn-out dishcloth.

Nevertheless she did not lack suitors, every one prepared to face a similar fate, and that cheerfully.

And she had a small son; also blond, but an aloof, withdrawn child, not at all helpful to those wishing to scale the glittering iceberg and sacrifice themselves on the altar of frustrated desire.

*

George Vernon admitted to thirty-six, looked forty-two in a favourable light, had more superfluous weight than his sparse frame had been designed to carry, a round red face and scanty matching hair. Small watery blue eyes surveyed the world with guarded amicability and he radiated a kind of resistible charm.

He presented Simon with a box of liquid centre chocolates, and was disgusted when the little brat regarded the gift with scant interest, then put it to one side with a murmured, 'Thank you very much, but Nanna says I mustn't eat sweets. They're not good for the teeth.'

A veritable chip off the old iceberg. Acted and talked like an old, old man who had been educated in the worst kind of public school. George went into action without any further preliminaries.

'How would you like me as a new daddy?'

Large grey eyes regarded him with disconcerting gravity. Then:

'Not very much.'

This was in the nature of a set-back. Even a little blister like this one generally gave a favourable answer. Or at the very worse – don't know. He assumed a hurt expression and asked:

'Why not?'

'Because I don't want a new daddy.'

A little wretch ripe for brain-washing. Get him word perfect so he can relay the message to the goddess. Screw your face up into a tragic oh-aren't-I-a-funny-man grimace, then pat the little sausage on the shoulder, while saying in a loud voice:

'Oh, come, come, you'd love a new daddy, particularly old George. Someone to buy you all you want. Take you out for long car rides.'

'Nanna says I have too much already and am taken out far too often. She says I'll soon be spoilt beyond redemption.'

'The old moo isn't so far ... Well, if I became your new daddy there would be no need for a nanny. And I would be able to look after your mummy.'

'Which mummy?'

The question demanded thought. More, it clamoured for consideration. George had a simple mind that had been equipped with a direct thrust and parry defence system and nothing much in the way of investigatory apparatus. The concept of Simon having a courtesy father was quite acceptable, particularly as George was a candidate for the role himself, but under the circumstances an extra mummy had to be ridiculous.

He endeavoured to explain this indisputable fact.

'You have only one mummy, the beautiful lady who looks after you. Who …'

'She doesn't look after me. Nanna does.'

George mistook a glimmer of light for a flash of intelligence.

'Oh, you mean your nanny is a second mummy. I see …'

'No, I don't. Nanna is just someone who is paid to look after me. She says it's not enough.'

George was not discouraged, but continued his thrust and parry exercise.

'But you have only one mummy, the beautiful lady who pays your nanny to look after you, and sometimes takes you out to tea, and kisses you goodnight. Now, when you are alone together, I'll give you a pound if you'll …'

'She's my daytime mummy. I like the night-time one best.'

One could say George reeled from a stomach blow and was forced to pause while he regained his breath. Eventually he released a deep sigh, then followed it up by a reasonable question.

'How can you possibly have a night mummy?'

'Because she only comes out at night.'

George produced a laugh.

'That's interesting. And where does this night-time mummy come from?'

'The hedge.'

'Hedge!'

'Yes. The tall one that's between our garden and the one next door. I think she may live in the old house that everyone imagines is empty, but she comes out of the solid hedge. And has taken me through it. And neither of us was scratched a bit. Wasn't that marvellous?'

George came to a conclusion. There was madness in the family, hopefully on the father's side. In fact, after making full allowance for children's imagination, the little blister must be well on his way round the bend and tied in a complicated knot on the other side. George had seen the hedge and knew no solid body could come through it, not without a certain amount of personal damage. However it might be well to play all future dialogue by ear.

'I would like to meet this night-time mummy of yours. Is she as nice as your daytime mummy?'

Simon put his head on to one side and stared at George through narrowed eyes, looking not unlike his mother when she was in a contrary mood.

'Much better. I see more of her, mostly every night and she thinks I'm the best little boy that ever was. I'm beautiful, heart-quickening, fang-baring and exceedingly drinkable. My daytime mummy never says anything like that, and Nanna says I'm the most horrible little brat she's ever seen and that includes Lord Dunwilliam's son who once put a live snake in her bed.'

George nodded and spoke without thinking. 'She has a point. But you have to put up with the rough if there's to be any hope of ever reaching the smooth.'

'And,' Simon went on, 'my night mummy wouldn't like to meet you at all, because she doesn't think I should talk about her. She doesn't want intruders. But I had to tell someone or burst.'

George had just stifled a yawn, for as everyone knows infantile fantasy – with the exception of fond parents – has only a limited appeal, when Thelma Martin entered the room. She frowned at George, gave her son a questioning glance as though making certain he was the same offspring she had seen put to bed the night before, then spoke with her customary beautiful, if somewhat cold voice.

'George, why are you here so early? You know I don't really come alive until twelve-thirty.'

'Thought I'd try to beat the rush. I mean you're usually surrounded by odds and ends. Bankers on the make, bored virgins popping around for coffee and inspiration, old hags starved for a bit of scandal – best come early and take a chance on you being a bit frosty.'

Thelma sat down, crossed her legs and pretended not to know the devastating effect this simple action had on her self-invited guest, then proceeded to rub pink cream into her long slender hands.

'I'm sure, George, your waspish remarks are very clever, but really I'm in no mood to appreciate them so early. Simon, shouldn't you be out walking with Nanna? I seem to remember seeing her in hat and coat ten minutes ago.'

Simon nodded. 'Yes, but she needs lots of time to finish

herself off. Brushing, doing things to her eyebrows and polishing her shoes with a handkerchief.'

'I thought only I did that,' George observed quietly. 'Just goes to show how instructive nannies are.'

Thelma began to paint her finger nails. 'Well, Simon, trot along like a good boy and tell Nanna I said you must have your constitutional now before the weather turns nasty.'

'OK.'

'And don't use that awful expression.'

Both watched the young boy leave the room and once again George spoke without conscious thought.

'To think I'm aspiring to be his step-daddy.'

'Don't hold your breath,' Thelma advised.

'But I was about to say if that happy position should ever be mine, I would get rid of that nanny. No one has nannies these days.'

'Indeed they do.'

'OK. Maybe the royal family. But, angel, you may be regal, but not ...'

'Most single parent career women now employ a child-minder, which is just another name for a nanny. But really I have no wish to discuss the matter further. Amelia is a competent person and I'm quite happy to leave Simon in her hands.'

George was quite prepared to worship his divinity, but he had quite firm ideas how far one should allow a woman to express an opinion without being subjected to masculine correction. In consequence he raised a small flag of rebellion.

'How do you know she is a competent person? Apart from tucking the kid up each night and giving him a maternal kiss on the forehead, you have only the slightest idea how the woman is rearing him. By rights he should be at school.'

Thelma blew on bright red finger nails. 'By rights Simon's upbringing or the lack of it, is none of your business. But if you must know, Amelia has a perfectly respectable degree and is quite capable of imparting basic education until Simon is old enough to enter a prep school.'

'Oh Gawd!'

'You are being extremely objectionable this morning.'

'That's because you haven't offered me a cup of coffee.'

Thelma sighed deeply, then shaking both hands drifted rather than walked to the doorway.

'You'd better come into the kitchen. And make the coffee, being so much more better at it than I am.'

George sprang to his feet in one effortless movement. 'I'm chockful of husbandly virtues. You should try my casserole. Six hours in the making, but worth every minute.'

'I believe in eating out whenever possible. Food should be cooked by experts. That is to say food fit to be eaten.'

'Rubbish.'

The kitchen would have graced any showroom window, being a glorious display of stainless steel, wood-pattern plastic, equipped with the latest deep freeze, micro-wave oven, hot plates and double sink unit. George looked around at the rows of metal cupboards and smiled.

'Plenty of artillery, but little in the way of ammunition.'

He knew how to use the complicated coffee-maker and soon had a delicious smelling dark brown liquid bubbling in a glass bowl. He filled two grey earthenware mugs, added milk and brown sugar, then swung himself up on to a waist high cabinet.

'The boy shouldn't be alone for such long periods,' he stated. 'Has too much time to feed his imagination. If you will forgive the purple prose.'

She took up one mug, tasted the contents, then frowned.

'Too much sugar as usual. Are you still on about Simon? I do wish you'd mind your own business. He is a happy self-sufficient little chap and really most practical. Amelia told me only the other day, he washes behind his ears every day without being prompted, and I do not know any other little boy who does that.'

'He also dreams up a night mummy,' George said.

'A what?'

'A night mummy who comes out of the hedge. The tall one which divides your garden from the one next door.'

'What utter rot.'

'That's what I say, but he seems to believe it.'

Thelma shook her head. 'No, I mean what rot thinking for one moment Simon believes a woman comes out of that hedge. Why, you can't even see through it.'

'That's as may be. But your son has still managed to imagine or invent a lady who comes from that hedge and flourishes under the appellation of night mummy. Which could be some kind of reflection on your more concrete role of daytime mummy.'

Thelma emptied her coffee cup and slammed it down on to the plastic surface.

'Are you sure you're not making all this up?'

'Cut me throat and hope to die. Ask the young perisher yourself.'

'Please, I hate what Albert used to call slack language. If you mean Simon, say so. I will certainly have words with Amelia on the subject. After all it is not my place to interfere with her training programme, and what you have just related may be part of that programme. I don't pretend to understand child psychology.'

'You mean what to do if he's going round the bend?'

Her eyes flashed a shaft of anger and it seemed that he could hear the cracking of melting ice. His rather grim amusement was that of a man who persists in prodding a sleeping cobra. Her voice sliced the air.

'I find your remark in the worst possible taste.'

'A child is a child is a child. Any kind of behaviour is acceptable from one's offspring – or so I am given to understand. A fond parent corrects so far is possible. Does anyone live next door?'

Her cold beautiful face was marred by the faintest outline of a sneer. 'How you do change the subject. Not so far as I know. The place does not look lived in. But I understand the milkman has seen someone looking out from an upstairs window. Why?'

'Night-time mummy could come from there. Maybe not through the hedge, but by other means. Put that up to Amelia – if you don't feel like tackling the job yourself.'

'I think it's about time you went. Even you must have something to do.'

'I haven't actually.'

'Well I have. And your company is beginning to bore.'

He got up and stretched, then grinned ruefully.

'Funny. I set out with the intention of impressing you with

my sterling character, but finish up raising your ire. I don't know why I want to marry you. You must be hell to live with.'

'You can find your own way out?'

'Yes. I just follow the beaten track.'

*

Thelma watched her would-be lover from the drawing room window and toyed with the words 'Why not?' before erasing them by two more 'But why?' She possessed the two most important assets that life can offer – health and wealth. A small son ranked about sixth in essential priorities.

She had turned and walked back into the room when the door opened and Amelia Dunlop entered. She could have been a well preserved thirty-five or a well-worn fifty. Tall, lean, sharp featured, particularly the nose, which had reminded some imaginative observers of a shark's fin; deceptively mild blue eyes and a lusciously rich, full mouth that pouted obscenely, suggesting its owner had been denied a long sought-after lustful kiss. She wore a blue serge jacket and skirt that contrasted with a plain white shirt. Thelma thought that if her looks did her justice, she would be the chair-person of an all women board of directors.

She said, 'Ah! Amelia! Just the person I wanted to see.'

The use of Christian names did not mean anything like intimacy existed between the two women, in fact Thelma could not remember how the practice had come about. She rather thought the first overture had come from the older woman and she had never summoned the courage other than to reciprocate. Now she waved her to a chair, then after a quick glance in a gilt-framed mirror, seated herself opposite.

'I would like to discuss Simon for a few moments, if that is agreeable to you. Although you are engaged as a nanny, over the years you have taken on the duties of governess. And ably so I might add. But I am beginning to think it might be time we at least thought about sending him to school. I mean – eight – going on nine …'

Amelia Dunlop managed to make a shrug an act of aggression.

'That's entirely up to you, Thelma. But I thought we had agreed that the kind of individual tuition that I can give is so much more satisfactory than just being one member of a large class, more than likely passed over by a harassed teacher.'

Thelma raised her right hand, then lowered it gently on to her right knee.

'And that is still true. Still true. And I'm sure – even certain – that Simon is streets ahead of any schoolboy of his age, anywhere. I really do. But shouldn't he be mixing with children of his own age? Being – well – taken out of himself? I know that is a trite expression, but … Look, Amelia, have you noticed if he's getting – well – a trifle fanciful?'

Amelia twisted her over-full lips into a grotesque red ring.

'No…o…o, Thelma, I can't say I have. That is being perfectly honest. If he had I'd say so. But he hasn't, so I must deny it. As for him mixing with other children. That can be a disadvantage. Many a genius has been hand-reared – if I may be permitted the expression. On the other hand – look what a public school did for the poet Swinburne.'

Thelma had not the slightest idea what a public school had done for Swinburne, but hated confessing ignorance to someone, who after all was an employee, so nodded gently and said:

'Yes, indeed. But, I must get back to his being fanciful. A friend – someone has told me he has acquired – invented – another mother.'

Amelia came dangerously near simpering. 'Well, of course I …'

'No, not you. Some woman that comes out of the hedge.'

Amelia screwed up her face, until her eyes all but disappeared, then pursed her thick lips which had the effect of giving her a pig-like appearance.

'Woman come from hedge? Not possible, Thelma dear. Too thick entirely. Just not possible.'

Thelma's smile was rather strained. 'Precisely. That is just my point. Simon has become fanciful. He has adopted a non-existent woman who comes from a completely non-come-from-able hedge. We – that is to say you – must put a stop to it.'

Amelia quickly erased a puzzled expression and nodded with a grim air of determination.

'That I will. Of that you may be sure. Yes, indeed.'

Thelma got up and hastily inspected her hair from the reflection in a wall mirror. 'Well, I'll leave the matter in your most capable hands. I mean you are the child psychology expert. Me, I have an appointment to sit on a board at ten-thirty. Must fly. Let me know how you get on sometime. Then we can recap on the go-to-school-keep-at-home problem. Bye.'

And she drifted from the room. Beauty on the wing. Motherhood in retreat.

*

Amelia Dunlop was not at all certain if she liked Simon. To dislike a child, and one in her care into the bargain, must be the ultimate heresy, but in the small hours, when sleep had become an absent friend, she had reluctantly to admit this was so.

In some respects he was too bright by half, in others seemingly very stupid. He asked so many questions that often Amelia had difficulty in supplying what one might call adequate answers. At times she was inclined to believe the child watched her from behind a veil of deceptive innocence and actually derived amusement from her attempts to impart information. Certainly after weeks of apparent inability to absorb a particular lesson he would suddenly become word perfect and furthermore fire a barrage of questions that had tested Amelia's not unlimited fund of knowledge to the limit – and beyond.

Now – she had to deal with an imaginary mother who came out of a very solid hedge.

She began the afternoon with a particularly fierce battle over the reign of Henry VIII. Simon would insist that the much married monarch had made seven trips to the altar, although history states emphatically there were only six such royal mishaps. Amelia stretched herself to the fullest extent, and even went so far as to name names and quote dates, not to mention the individual means used to dissolve five of the unions.

But Simon remained adamant.

'Seven,' he said for the eighth time. 'Seven.'

Miss Dunlop began to commit the ultimate offence. To wit: lose control of her temper.

'You're just being silly. Silly and contrary. Your mother will have to be told. I just can't teach a child who refuses to be taught.'

'Seven,' Simon continued to insist. 'Bessie Blount.'

'Elizabeth Blount was only the king's mistress.'

'She had a little boy. She must have been the king's wife. Six and one makes seven.'

The logic of ignorance that had no business coming from the brain of an eight year old. She decided to use it as a means of tackling the extra mother problem.

'Simon listen to me very carefully. You really must stop using your imagination to such an alarming degree. You really must. Nice well brought up little boys just imagine nice well regulated things and never, but never tell terrible lies. For example …'

Amelia paused, took a deep breath, suddenly aware of an unexplainable quickening of her heartbeat. She took the plunge.

'Inventing an extra mummy who comes out of the hedge.'

'My night-time mummy. I didn't invent her. She's as real as chocolate pudding.'

'That is absolute wicked nonsense. You know it is.'

He created a nasty little sneering smile and said:

'I've told her about you and told her what room you sleep in, and I think she somehow got up to your window and watched you get ready for bed.'

'What?'

'Yes, I think she must have. Because she wanted to know where that scar on your tummy came from.'

Fear and anger blended and made her grab a small arm.

'Who is this woman? How could she get up to my window?'

'I think she sort of drifts up. And she's my night mummy.'

No one had seen Amelia minus her clothes since the far off days spent in a girls' boarding school, not counting of course the hospital staff when she had her appendix removed five years before. But it would seem as if some woman had been spying on her, aided and abetted by this super-sweet little monster. She wanted to shake him until he gave her the plain truth and completely erased the ridiculous thought that he knew something perfectly horrible, even if he did not understand what it was he knew. A complicated mess-up that should never have originated from her normally tidy mind and she would never forgive him for so disturbing a placid existence. The good lord above and the bad one below knew life was too brief for complications.

The day before yesterday she had been seventeen. Yesterday twenty-seven. Today ...

'You've only one mummy. One only. The beautiful lady who ...'

'Pays you to look after me. Uncle George explained. But there is the night-time one.' He looked up as a dazzling smile transformed his face. 'Please – don't go to sleep tonight. Come out and meet her. I know she would like to meet you. She said so.'

Now she did shake him, even while her brain, superbly trained by the Child Psychology College, screamed that this was not the way to extract information from infant minds.

'What are you talking about? There's no woman who wants to meet me. There can't be. It's you. Strange, introvert – they warned us of your kind. Others have come to grief ... Never thought I'd come across one. That I didn't ...'

Her hands fell away from his frail shoulders and she became aware that he was crying. Sobbing to be exact, and pity – for how could he help being so different? – made her clutch the trembling body and cry out: 'I'm sorry ... sorry ... I didn't mean to hurt you. It's just I can't understand.'

Presently the sobbing ceased, the small head came up and a soft small voice tried to explain.

'My night mummy is frightened too. Of her dreadful father. Sometimes he becomes very angry and roars across the sky. You see, Nanna, it's not God being angry with me when the thunder roars. It's Him. The big Him who is angry with His children when they try to forget him.'

Amelia knew she should be angry herself, for this last statement must be bordering on blasphemous slander. But way at the back of her mind there dawned a dim understanding. The boy had been told a kind of parable. It was clearly her duty to see this woman, whoever she might be, if only to tell her to keep her side of the hedge.

'She wants to see me in the garden?'

Simon wiped his eyes on the sleeve of his jacket.

'Yes. Tonight. Because the moon is full and she likes to bask in moonlight and get a moon tan.'

'You're making it all up again.'

'No, I'm not. She's awfully white but after she's moonbathed for a little while, her skin goes sort of grey.'

'And am I to understand you have been creeping out at night to meet this – person?'

'Yes. You won't be angry?'

'It would seem too late for me to be angry. Well, how do you do it?'

'I climb down the vine. It's getting a bit loose now. Do you think Jenkins the gardener can tighten it up – or something?'

'There will be no more climbing down vines. Good grief! If you had fallen I would most likely get the blame. You will stay in bed, young man, while I go and have words with this woman. Do you understand?'

He nodded his head very slowly, then, shook it gently.

'I understand what you say, but I don't think she's going to like it.'

'Then she must dislike it.'

'Maybe if I wave to her from my window she won't be so angry.'

'You will do nothing of the kind. Bed means sleep. Not looking out of windows.'

She prepared a return to Henry VIII, then paused:

'Listen, Simon, I hope for your sake this lady turns up. I'd hate to be standing around in the garden while you are giggling under the bedclothes.'

'She'll be there. So long as there is moonshine.'

Amelia cut the lessons short that day, for her mind kept wandering in shady side roads and she was unable to even consider cramming knowledge into a brain that rejected or digested according to the current whim. When she returned to her own room, the setting sun was casting long shadows across the garden. She looked at the tall privet hedge and decided that to expect anyone to come through that was like the fiction that depicted Father Christmas descending a modern chimney.

'The little wretch is having us on,' she muttered. 'Imagination gone wild must mean – I don't know – something.'

At six o'clock Thelma rang to say she would not be home

until late; be staying with a friend. Amelia wondered if the friend was male or female and could not quite smother a little white flame of hate, which always flared up when she was reminded of Thelma's blatant sexuality. This was often reinforced by the knowledge that the other woman looked upon her with a certain amused contempt.

She allowed Simon to watch television until seven-thirty, then supervised his bath before dispatching him to bed at nine o'clock. When she was tucking him in she asked the last question.

'Now, Simon, tell the truth. Does a lady really come into the garden at night?'

He smiled sleepily. 'You'll see her for yourself. Very soon now. I don't think I'll sit up to wave at her. I'm much too tired. Tell her I'll try to see her tomorrow.'

And with that Amelia had to be satisfied.

She saw no good reason why she should spend hours in the garden waiting for this woman to appear — always supposing she did — so she sat by her bedroom window and watched the moonlight gradually creep over the green lawn and create a host of ghost-shadows that lingered under flower clusters and at the very bottom of the hedge. Presently she noticed little streaks of white mist that came drifting from that same hedge; seeping from tiny leaves, slowly whirling round until it resembled white candy floss, before rising up to become a solid pillar.

Amelia felt an ice-cold shudder glide up from her feet and threaten to do something dreadful to her heart, as the pillar trembled and gradually turned into a tall woman dressed in a long white robe. Amelia's first coherent impression was that of a study in black and white. Black long hair, matching thick eyebrows, dazzling black eyes. The rest white-white; skin like snow on a mountainside in moonlight. Teeth — rather large — again dazzling white, the canines inclined to be pointed. The general effect — if one could forget the unique way she had come into being — was that of death-style beauty. Amelia began to giggle hysterically as the thought crept into her brain; beauty that would look well when framed by a polished walnut coffin.

White, cold, dead beauty standing in a pool of silver

moonlight. But the woman was not dead, even though the life force that activated her might be that which makes the maggot wriggle and assists its purpose – to carry out the work of decomposition.

A commonplace, no-nonsense brain becomes surprisingly imaginative after it has digested the information that a woman had been formed from a pillar of white mist.

A soft, caressing voice spoke in her head.

'Will you come down or shall I come up?'

'I'll come down.' Amelia spoke to the room in general. 'Don't come up.'

No ... in no way must that creature come up – as it would appear she had done once before. Drifted up like the mist from which she had been formed and watched her – Amelia – undress. Last Tuesday that must have been, when the curtains had been left in the laundry basket. If she had turned at the wrong time she might have seen death-beauty looking in through the bedroom window. Corpse-face pressed against the glass.

Now she was trotting down the stairs to meet that creature on the lawn, because it was her duty – and Amelia had been trained from early childhood to be strong on duty – but mainly because she couldn't do anything else. She had to go out and be dazzled by silver moonlight and be more frightened than any respectable body should be.

All because of that little brat who was either fast asleep in his bed or waving happily at death in the garden. She had always known he was different from any other kid she had ever known or had dealings with. His eyes were beautiful grey clear pools that watched but revealed nothing. Sometimes she thought there was an adult lurking behind those eyes, mocking, pretending to be a child, even if at times he allowed the mask to slip.

She had reached the hall acutely aware that apart from the boy she was alone in the house.

'No business,' she spoke quite loudly as she fought with an obstinate bolt, 'no business at all to leave me here alone. Oh, my God!'

The door seemed to spring back of its own accord, doing its very best to knock Amelia off her feet. She clung to it, panting like a very old person who has run very fast in a short while and is now holding back that fatal heart attack by pure force of will.

The woman in white stood dead centre of the lawn, immediately to Amelia's front, some thirty yards away. She was so still, even her hair did not move in the breeze that disturbed the leaves of the hedge; and there was an indefinable suggestion that she might at any time disintegrate back into swirling mist.

Amelia heard the voice in her head again.

'Come to me.'

She must walk through the doorway, then over the narrow cement path, on to the soft springy grass; walk so slowly, but perhaps not too slowly or that creature might think you don't want to come near her – and one doesn't – one would rather not. Then smell! Damp loam. Rotting wood. Crumbling bones and coffins. Decaying ... decaying ... something that would never cease to be.

Now she was quite near and it must be time to stop, hold one's breath, close the nostrils.

Now the soft voice could be heard by the ears.

'So sorry about the aroma. The family have decided to try another form of nourishment and it is upsetting that which remains inside. After a while you will not notice it, but it might be more comfortable if you were to move down wind.'

The creature was trying to sound commonplace – just like you and me – but it didn't work. She looked more blood-congealing close-up, than from a distance. Amelia was so frightened she was very near wetting her blue serge knickers. She walked past the creature and took up a position about six feet further on. The smell abated quite considerably. The soft voice spoke again.

'Where is the child? I am hungry for a sight of him. He is a very important personage – do you realise that?'

Amelia thought it wise to nod, the power of speech having temporarily deserted her. It was so horrible to have to hear everyday style speech come from between those thin black lips. The voice continued to explain, although there was now a hint of impatience.

'We need him. Most important that he be reared under our

supervision. In fact he is to become an honorary member of the family. The pack will keep an eye upon him. Diabolo! This woman is a peasant! There will be no way of using her.'

The face took on an expression. Savage, unbridled rage. The black eyes seemed to have a tiny red flame burning deep down. The voice was no longer soft, but harsh, domineering, carrying more than a hint of menace.

'The boy must not be moved from here. Stay ... stay ... until we can make arrangements. You understand? Speak, woman. Speak or I will tear the fingers from your left hand.'

Amelia croaked a reply. Freely translated it was: 'I understand. Boy not to be moved.'

'There's a glimmer of intelligence! It's not quite a beast! Beldaza be praised. But let us put a little lock of fear on its substitute for a brain.'

The creature turned her head and whistled softly and instantly a low dark figure came loping from the direction of the back gate which opened on a rear passage. It wore a long overcoat and a broad-brimmed hat that did not hide the grotesque dog-like face. Amelia whimpered when she saw the long pointed jaws, the wet round nose and the black, red-tinted, deep-set eyes. The tall black and white woman made a strange coaxing noise and called: 'Bimba, come to mother,' and the dog-face being fawned, rubbed his wet nose on her left leg, while making a growling sound.

Then she bent her head and whispered into one tapering ear and Amelia all but fainted when she saw the hideous head come round and stare at her. The eyes grew brighter, the growl deeper, then the creature came loping over to her and Amelia became as a sinful man on judgement day.

It could have been a deformed human being, only there was an animal smell. That of a dog on a hot day and the black lips were obscenely wet. After a while Amelia accepted that it couldn't stand upright.

The other creature-person, her of the white skin and jet black hair, said with the merest hint of a chuckle, 'Now Bimba has your scent. Should you ever dream of telling of my – unorthodox life-style, or the kind of staff I employ, then will Bimba come looking for you. And no matter where you hide, he will dig you out within seven days and seven nights.' She paused for a moment as though to determine the effect of this threat, before adding: 'There are others of his kind. They hunt in packs of four. Officially they are called madvams. You may go now.'

Amelia walked back past the creatures – for in no way could she now regard either as humans – controlled the impulse to run before reaching the cement path. Then she stumbled forward a few paces, almost fell over the doorstep and finally collapsed in the kitchen.

She recovered consciousness some ten minutes later.

When she had garnered a meagre store of courage that enabled her to look out of the doorway, the garden was empty. Both creatures had vanished.

Amelia did not sleep well that night.

*

'Why won't you tell me what happened?' Simon demanded. 'I saw you out there with my night mummy and that funny looking thing.'

A terrible fear sprang from the morass of her mind. The irresponsibility of extreme youth. He would tell Thelma or one of the men who were always hanging round her. That George person for example. But surely no one would believe the truth; accept that a creature that looked like a woman could come into existence from a pillar of mist, or she had a pack of dog-like beings waiting to do her bidding? But she must lie to the boy. Lie convincingly. Try to stop him going out there, only, would not that thing come into the house?

'The lady likes you very much, but she says you must always do what I tell you in future.'

He shook his head and giggled. 'No. You must do what I tell *you*. Or that lady – my night mummy – will be very angry with you. Did she tell you who she is? Her real name?'

'No. We did not find time to exchange names.'

'She told me. It is Princess Caroline Karlvina. She made me repeat it several times so I would not forget it. But I have never seen that thing that looked like a dressed up dog before. What is it?'

Fortunately the door opened before Amelia could answer

and Thelma entered the room. She wore a magnificent silver mink coat that covered her from neck to a little above the ankles, and Amelia was reminded that Leopold von Sacher-Masoch was excited by the mere sight of a beautiful woman dressed in fur. At that moment, such was the effect of carefully suppressed fear, she too felt a wave of desire flood her being, while the strength seemed to drain from her legs.

Thelma opened the coat, shrugged it off and allowed it to drop to the floor. Amelia coined an unusual phrase. A pool of mink. Simon's mother still wore a silver lame backless evening dress, proving that she had not been home since the previous evening, a fact that at that time endowed her with a kind of vulnerable sexuality. Amelia thought – and the words helped her to escape for a while from the cavern of fear – You have to pay for your beauty, my lady. You have to give men whatever it is they want, for their burning regard keeps the flame of passion undimmed, so that your lovely body has become a strangling chain of flesh.

'Amelia!' The emotionless voice spoke and fresh fantasy flowers unfolded in the hot house of her brain. 'What are you and Simon doing up so early? Good heavens, it's barely five-thirty. Even the milkman isn't astir yet.'

'I couldn't sleep,' Amelia confessed.

'And I heard her bumping about,' Simon added, 'so thought I might as well get up too. Mummy, where have you been?'

'Here, there and everywhere.' She sank down on to a plastic covered chair. 'Amelia, be an angel and pick up my coat. I'm not fit for anything. And since you're here I might as well have a cup of tea. I'm parched.'

Simon watched his mother for a little while until she frowned and said, 'You mustn't stare, darling. It's rude and disconcerting.'

'Nanna went out into the garden last night and met my night mummy.'

Thelma displayed a flash of interest. 'Oh, yes, how did you get on? I did wonder.'

Amelia busied herself with the electric kettle and kept her face well hidden from both mother and son.

'Oh, all right. She came into our garden – from the back gate …'

'She didn't,' Simon shouted. 'She didn't. She came out of the hedge as …'

Made brave by desperation, Amelia turned to face him. 'You mustn't make things up, Simon. I've told you about it before.'

His mother nodded her golden head. 'Yes, so have I. Go on, Amelia. What did she want?'

'Oh, she takes an evening walk and sometimes sees Simon at his window, then strays into our garden. That's all.'

Simon widened his eyes and blew out his cheeks. 'Crikey! What lies! She pours out of the hedge and last night had a thing that looks like a dog in a long overcoat with her.'

Thelma now scowled and stamped her foot. 'Simon that's enough. Now upstairs with you. This instant.'

'But she's lying …'

'Upstairs – now.'

The boy still muttering shuffled from the room, then slammed the door behind him. Thelma shook her head. 'Really, he hasn't been taught self control. My mother used to say that's the first lesson a child should learn. However, we all have different standards and you are the child psychology expert. Now, coming back to that woman. A hell of a cheek *straying* into our garden and chatting up my son when he should be fast asleep. I hope you told her to keep to her side of the hedge. She does come from next door, I take it?'

'Yes, I believe …'

'Must say I'm surprised. The place doesn't look lived in. In fact I wouldn't have thought it possible. The windows are broken in some places. Still, perhaps some of it is habitable.' She yawned, then stretched. 'Think I'll have a few hours shut-eye. What with one thing – and another – it's been a hard night.'

She took the mink coat from the chair back where Amelia had put it, slung it over one shoulder, then ambled to the door. When her hand was on the handle Amelia called out:

'Thelma.'

The beautiful face looked back over one bare shoulder.

'Yes.'

'You won't worry about that woman who comes into the garden, will you?'

'Of course I won't worry, silly. That's your chore. But I must say I don't cotton on to the idea of any woman mooching about without a by-your-leave.'

'But you won't …'

'Won't what? Come on – I'm near dropping.'

'Won't sort of look out for her?'

A silvery laugh that had a slightly contemptuous element and Amelia shivered even as she flinched. 'You are really a silly old thing, Amelia. Really you are. Why on earth should I look out for some woman who has the cheek to wander in my garden? If she becomes a nuisance I'd telephone the police. Good night – or rather – good morning.'

She left the door open and Amelia sat down to have a good cry. She felt much worse afterwards.

*

George Vernon ran up the front steps and pressed the bell button then whistled his appreciation when the nifty little maid opened the door. Hardly was he in the hall than he made a grab for her, which she neatly avoided, then poked the handle end of a feather duster in the direction of his face.

'Keep your hands to yourself,' she instructed. 'Or keep them for the missus.'

'No luck there so far, Jenny,' he confided. 'Anyone else been sniffing around since yesterday?'

She grinned. 'Not that you'd notice, but she came home with the milkman this morning. And I don't expect she slept on a park bench.'

George sighed. 'What is it I lack, Jenny?'

'Youth, looks, personality and sex appeal. Otherwise you're fine. Do you want to see old Blubber-Lips?'

'No, *thank* you. Is the glorious Thelma still in bed?'

'She was the last time I looked in. Why don't you pop up? Never know your luck.'

'I lack the courage. Be a good girl and bring me a cup of coffee in the lounge. I'm not unwound yet.'

She did a charming little mock curtsey and placed a pointed forefinger under her chin. 'I delight to oblige a guest, sir. You take two lumps of sugar, if my memory is not at fault.'

He raised his hand and before she had time to dodge

slapped her rump with a resounding whack. She squealed and ran for the kitchen, there to stop in the doorway rubbing vigorously, while glaring at George with pretended anger.

'That's goodbye to your coffee. Oh!'

She disappeared into the kitchen and George turned and grinned sheepishly at Thelma who was approaching from the bottom of the stairs.

'Look here,' he began, but she raised an impatient hand.

'If you must molest the maid, George, do it when she's off duty. That's almost every evening and every Sunday. I gather Jennie is hung up on pin bowling – or whatever they call it – and that will make a nice secondary hobby for you. Now go away, I'm still whacked.'

'You've got to listen, Thelma, just because I indulge in a bit of nonsense with the girl, doesn't mean ...'

She did not jerk away when he laid a hand on her arm. 'George, I'm not the teensiest bit interested as to why you have a weakness for presentable little maids. I understand Oscar Wilde couldn't resist stable boys and he was a genius.'

'You look very beautiful this morning, Thelma.'

'I know. I looked in the mirror the moment I got out of bed. Surprisingly really as I feel about a hundred and one and fit for nothing at all. It's absolutely wonderful how my body refuses to give in to the ravages of time. It's not as though I take care of myself. Eat, drink, smoke and lots more far too much. Go to bed at all hours, that's when I go to bed at all.'

George squeezed her arm. 'I'd like to look after you.'

'Don't be so soft. You can't look after yourself, let alone me. Your job in life is to amuse women like me, cheer us up and occasionally call us to account. But as a husband! I'd be smothered by constant regard.'

They entered the lounge and Thelma at once flung herself down on a sofa, while George strolled over to the window and stood looking out on to the garden. Presently Thelma's voice came to him as a kind of sleep-misted dream.

'Amelia! Silly baa lamb. Getting all worked up about some woman who comes into our garden.'

George exclaimed, 'Ah! Then someone did tackle her?'

'You could say so. But she was most insistent that I did not sit up looking for her. The woman I mean. As though I would.'

'Who is she?' George asked.

'Damned if I know. I mean, Amelia never thinks of asking about simple essentials like that. Simon will probably know. I gather she lives next door.'

'Be an idea if you called. Should, you know. The new neighbour. That kind of thing.'

'But the place is in such a shambles. Not a thing has been done since old Sinclair died. I mean she may be living out of saucepans.'

'Then you can offer to lend her some of your chinaware.'

'She's got a hope. Of course while I'm there I can give a hint that it's polite to ask before you stroll round other people's gardens.'

'Let's go now.'

'At the break of day? Have a heart.'

'It's twelve-thirty. Almost lunch time. The mysterious night lady will probably offer us lunch out of an iron saucepan.'

Thelma sat up and giggled, now completely relaxed, her eyes sparkling with mischievous humour.

'I say, it would be a bit of a caper. I'll wear what I've got on. You can be my intended for the nonce. Have you a card?'

'I never need one. Everyone knows me.'

'I've got some somewhere. Amelia will know. Push the bell button.'

In fact Amelia answered the bell as the cook had sent Jennie out to buy some more coffee, a fact that reinforced George's belief that the house was not well run. Indeed it could be said the house was not run at all. It bumped along under its own inefficiency.

'I've got some cards, haven't I, Amelia?'

'Yes, in the small left-hand drawer in your bureau.'

'Get them for me, there's an angel. We're going visiting.'

Amelia looked dutifully surprised. 'Indeed. Where?'

'Next door. To see Simon's night mummy.'

Now Amelia took on an expression of terrified astonishment and seemed to shrink visibly into a being that had lived – or who is preparing to live – an eternity in some cold valley of fear. She gasped:

'Not there, madam,' thereby revealing an inner feeling of subservience that up to that time had always been concealed.

Thelma raised an elegant eyebrow. 'No need to go ga-ga, angel. We're just going to pay a social call. Welcome her to the neighbourhood, such as it is. Lawd sakes, chile! Unscrew that face, the world's not coming to an end.'

As she turned Amelia stretched out a hand and spoke with a voice that imperfectly relayed the rising flood of terror. 'You mustn't. You don't know what she is.'

Thelma gave George an expressive glance, then made a face at Amelia, while saying in an extravagated over-patient voice:

'And what is she, pray, Miss Know-All?'

'I can't ... I mustn't tell you.'

'It gets curiouser and curiouser,' George quoted, 'and we still don't know what it is all about.'

Amelia clasped shaking hands to her face and seemed to be near a state of total collapse; a condition that increased Thelma's astonishment, and George's concern.

'I think there's something really wrong, Thelma. I really do. Shouldn't we send for a doctor or something?'

'Certainly not. If she's ill she must go to a hospital or a nursing home. I can't bear the mere sight of ill people. Never mind the visiting cards. I want to visit the woman next door before the urge to do so wears off.' She turned to Amelia. 'For heaven's sake, Amelia, pull yourself together and practise some self-control. If you have a valid reason why I shouldn't see this woman, I am willing to listen. Otherwise, go to your room, lie down for a little while, then when you have recovered, return to looking after my son. Where is he now?'

'Upstairs in his play room, but ...'

Thelma ran from the room; George followed more slowly and looked back when he reached the doorway. He made a gesture denoting helplessness before disappearing into the passage.

*

A large wrought-iron gate stood open, the path which led to the house was flanked by bushes that had not been trimmed for many a day so that now their branches all but blocked the entire path.

'Suffering hangovers!' Thelma exclaimed. 'How the hell does she or anyone get in?'

'Perhaps there's another way in,' George suggested.

'How can there be? A bloody great wall backs both this property and mine. A thick privet hedge on both sides – hells bells! We've both looked. So, if there's to be a surprise visit, you George must be a trail breaker.'

George manfully pushed his way through the interwoven branches, while Thelma followed a few feet behind. Whippy twigs and slender branches kept springing back, forcing Thelma to raise her hands, palms turned outwards so as to shield her face. When they were about twenty yards along the path, one long thin branch whipped back and slashed savagely across the young woman's palms. She emitted a squeal of pain and began to wring her smarting hands.

Instantly George came back, his face wearing an almost comical expression of alarm, then asked in a plaintive voice:

'What happened?'

Thelma glared at him before unclasping her hands and holding them out for his inspection. Two deep red weals ran across each palm under the long fingers.

'Look at those. Look. All because of your carelessness. You knew I was just behind.'

'Better your hands than your face,' George pointed out. 'Might have been your eyes.'

'Thank you! Could have been my throat, or me boswam. If you had been more careful none would have been in danger and neither would I have had two ruddy great tramlines across my hands.'

'I'm very sorry. Really I am. But I thought …'

'Never mind what you thought. At least we're almost there. Push on and keep well to the front.'

'That's only possible if you keep well to the rear.'

They came out on to a wide cracked cement path which lay in front of three marble steps, that in turn led up to a door which was mainly bare, weather-worn wood to which a few traces of flaking green paint still clung. On either side large sash windows also displayed signs of neglect, while those on the upper storeys gleamed dully as though reluctant to reflect light.

'What a dump!' Thelma expressed her disgust. 'I can only suppose who ever this woman is, she hasn't had time to get the builders in. I can't remember when the place was last looked at. Probably not in my time.'

'No sign of a bell button,' George observed. 'I suppose I'd better bang on the door.'

'You do that,' Thelma answered shortly, examining her hands with some concern. 'I hope I'm not going to be scarred for life.'

George ran up the steps and without hesitation knocked on the door several times, then stood back.

'All I'm doing is hurt my knuckles. That door is so damned thick. And I'm certain no one can hear my futile efforts in there.'

'Oh, for heaven's sake! Use something – a stone or a piece of wood. Honestly you've no sense at all.'

George descended the steps, ambled dejectedly along the cement path, then came running back when Thelma with a snort of exasperation, went up to the door, removed her shoe and banged on the bare wood with the heel.

She looked down at her faithful attendant and shook her head.

'If you want a job done, do it yourself. OK. Come on up. I can hear someone coming.'

George slowly ascended the three steps, looking rather unhappy, for he had not been all that keen on paying this uninvited visit in the first place, now he was most certainly against it. He did not like the atmosphere the old house seemed to exude. And this was not entirely the result of the run-down appearance of the place, but rather as though it contained either people or some unexplainable object that emitted an evil influence.

Thelma tapped her foot impatiently.

'Come on ... come on ... Hell, those footsteps seem to go on forever.'

But to George's aroused imagination they seemed to be getting remarkably louder, as though some heavy person was stamping his feet with increasing violence. Then the door opened and a slight youth with an oval, almost feline pretty face surmounted by a thick profusion of black curls, bared dazzling white teeth and said in a cultured soft voice:

'Visitors who somehow got through and now come

knocking on our door! How nice. And what can I do for you sweet things?'

Thelma looked upon the young man with an appreciative eye and said in the low seductive voice she reserved for these occasions:

'I am from next door and would like to meet the lady who lives here.'

He raised a slim eyebrow while caressing his upper lip with a delicate forefinger.

'Now that is a question, beautiful one. I suppose she lives here in the accepted sense of the term, although live is a word we rarely toy with. But come in, darlings. Since you made it here, inside you must come. There's the beginning of a poem there. I must toss it around sometime. But ... please ...'

He stood to one side, made a low bow and waved them into a gloomy dingy hall with a white, well-shaped hand.

There may have been dust on the floor, there was most certainly cobwebs festooning the ceiling. Suddenly a beam of sunlight high-lighted a large frosted window and the hall became a place where floating dust motes formed glittering elvin pathways that spanned the room from wall to wall.

The youth watched Thelma with a strange intensity. 'Let me introduce myself. Andrea de Villefort. Prefixed by a rather silly little title. Count Andrea de Villefort. I understand I had a human ancestor who sent an innocent young man to languish for fourteen years in the Chateau D'If. There has been a curse on both sides of the family ever since.'

'And I,' Thelma said rather loudly, for she was not at all pleased to find she felt absurdly nervous in the presence of this youth, 'am Thelma Martin. And this is George. My fiancé George Vernon.'

Andrea de Villefort bowed again, twice in fact, a deep obeisance in Thelma's direction, a rather curt jerking of the shoulders for George.

Then his eyes brightened. 'But you keep clasping your hands, beautiful lady. Can it be you are hurt?'

Thelma turned her hands palms uppermost and revealed the single purple weal that ran across each. 'This was done by the overgrown shrubbery in your pathway. I am fortunate my face or eyes were not injured.'

He stared at the weals with wide-open eyes and drew in his breath sharply. 'Indeed, madam, you are indeed protected. Intruders have been blinded in one eye. Others have been tripped and strang... But what am I saying? My imagination took flight when I saw the injury done to those so beautiful hands. Allow me to kiss them well, madam.'

Thelma pulled her hands back. 'Thank you that will not be necessary. There is little discomfort now. Can I prevail upon you to inform ...'

'My aunt, madam. The Princess Caroline Karlvina. She is resting at the moment, but if it be your wish I will enquire if she can receive you.'

'I will be grateful.'

He reached out and opened a door. 'Then perhaps you can rest after your trying journey along our front pathway. Be so kind as to step into this room.'

The room into which he ushered them was not very large and painted completely black. Black walls and ceiling, the latter however relieved by clusters of silver stars. George sat down on a hard-seat chair and looked around with wide open eyes. 'It looks like a coal cellar with holes in the ceiling,' he commented. 'Look, Thelma, let's get the hell out of here.'

She gave him an amused smile. 'No fear. I think this so delightfully kinky. Really I do. Did you notice how that precious number drooled over my hands? And the way he looked me over?'

George sighed deeply. 'And that really turns you on. I've a feeling we're playing silly buggers in a lion's cage. And that pretty lad has some very sharp claws.'

Thelma shivered with pretended ecstasy. 'How delicious!'

Heavy footsteps again came into being; trudged ponderously down what must have been bare stairboards, then turned abruptly into a soft-foot tread that terminated when Andrea appeared in the doorway.

Thelma trembled when he smiled at her. 'My most gracious aunt is quite prepared to see you, but begs of you to excuse her if she appears to be a trifle – how shall I put it? – shop worn. She has had a tiring night.'

'Who hasn't?' Thelma nodded her agreement. 'Lead on and the devil preserve the wrong.'

'I'm not all that happy,' George complained.

'You never are. This could be a glorious adventure.'

'It could be a short cut to the nearest lunatic asylum.'

The stairs they mounted were innocent of any covering save that of dust and there could be no doubt that Andrea's feet started to make a loud trudging sound when they were about halfway up. This phenomenon worried George very much, but Thelma merely giggled and said, 'How quaint!'

But she did cry out in alarm when they came up on to the landing in time to see two well-nourished rats scurry away.

'Squatters,' Andrea explained. 'But the house is large enough for all of us.'

He tapped on a door which although grimed by the accumulated dust of many years, had a small coronet painted on one panel; and when a sound which could be translated as an invitation to enter made itself heard, turned a brass handle and gently pushed the door open.

Thelma entered with a reluctant George close behind.

Simon would have recognised the lady who lay upon the vast bed.

In the light that came from the uncurtained window she looked ill, for the extreme pallor was tinged with grey and the large dark eyes seemed to be the saddest that George had ever seen. She looked very young, at the same time mature, embalmed in an eternity of experience. Sometimes it seemed as if there were lines round her eyes and mouth, at others her face appeared as unlined as that of a sixteen-year-old. She eased her slim body up and gestured imperiously to her nephew.

'Place a pillow behind my back. That's not right. Push it further down ... come on, boy ...'

'Still ... still,' Andrea snapped. 'How can I do anything with you moving all the time.'

The princess twisted round and struck him across one cheek with a resounding slap. Instantly he jerked back, hand held to his cheek, while his eyes seemed to be spitting fire.

'You dare again!' he hissed the words. 'One day and you'll go too far and I will ...'

Now the woman was sitting upright and she no longer looked young, but old beyond time itself.

'You'll do what? Listen, unlicked cub, with one hand I could claw liver and heart from your puny body and leave you screeching for a thousand years.' Now she radiated raw appalling power and the youth backed away, jerking his hands outwards as though trying to repel some invisible but tangible object. The princess raised her voice to a shriek.

'Down on your knees, cub, for the power is upon me and I cannot control it if there is the slightest opposition to my will.'

Reluctantly, but with great dread etched upon his beautiful face, Andrea sank to his knees and lowered his head. George shrank against the doorpost and watched the scene dully, not really understanding what was taking place or fully believing the evidence relayed by his eyes.

Then Thelma wiped moist lips on the back of a trembling hand and made strange cooing sounds that had much in common with a pigeon pursuing a reluctant mate. Even her golden hair reflected rainbow colours, or so it seemed to a bemused George as his desire to possess her flared up, but it was no longer tender, blended with the need to protect, but harsh, fired by the urge to use her simply as an object of pleasure.

But the dramatic scene displayed signs of coming to an end. The woman on the bed gradually relaxed, a softer light came into her eyes, the impression of raw energy faded away, then she smiled gently and said in a wondrous soft voice:

'My poor Andrea! Did I frighten you and come near to hurting you? I am sorry, but you mustn't speak rudely to your poor auntie. I cannot always control that which my dear father passed down to me. Now, get up and come give your auntie a nice kiss.'

Andrea's vast sigh of relief completed the return to what passed for normality in that place, and he jumped up and after grabbing the Princess Caroline, clamped his mouth to hers in a most unnephew-like kiss. Then he turned and bowed to the two visitors.

'You will forgive this little family – how do you express it? – this little family tiff?'

George murmured (most unconvincingly), 'We quite understand.'

'I think,' Thelma gasped, 'I think it was one of the most pulse-stirring experiences ever. Really I do.'

'Ah!' Andrea now did take one of her hands in his and kissed the palm. 'You understand the joy that comes from hurting and being hurt, then soothing, even if it be only expressed by word of mouth, the harsh or soft word, or the advancement and retreat of fear. You should be one of us.'

'I would like to be.'

The princess slowly clambered from off the bed and put on a red dressing gown with a vast golden dragon embroidered on the back, then sank into an armchair. Her voice had regained a little of its former harshness when she spoke again.

'So, you came to see me. Why?'

'I understood from my young son and his nannie, you had paid several visits to my garden. So I thought I should come to see you. But your front path is rather discouraging.'

'You got stung, did you? We do not welcome strangers, but you as the mother of that amazing boy have to be an exception. I am sorry you were hurt.' She looked up at her nephew. 'When you visit me again, you must come by another path that Andrea will show you. Now, to an important question. Who was the boy's father?'

'Why, my husband of course.'

'You lie. That lad was never sired by the commonplace Albert Martin. Never ... never. Now, who was he?'

Thelma blushed, something she had not done for many years.

'Well, if you insist on knowing.'

'I do. I most certainly do.'

'Well, one night ... It is rather wicked actually.'

'Of course. All interesting experiences are. Go on.'

'I was travelling through France in the year 1977. Late at night, it being my intention to spend the night in Rouen. Just as a really ferocious thunderstorm made the night absolutely hideous, my car broke down. The chauffeur proved to be completely useless and just sat there looking helplessly through the windscreen. But I spotted a lighted window some hundred yards away and decided to make a bolt for it. So, I wrapped myself in a tartan rug and ran up the horrid little dirt road, getting awfully wet in the process. When I reached the building with the lighted window, I saw from the board in the front garden it was the residence of the local curé.'

The princess intervened. 'The house of a godly man! How strange, not to say surprising.'

'If you will kindly allow me to continue. I knocked on the door and it was opened by a tall, dark and very handsome man in a cassock. He gave me one look, then stood to one side. "You must come in at once, madam," he said. "You are soaked to the skin, as indeed I was myself an hour or so ago. This is the second violent storm this evening."

'The cottage consisted of two rooms down and two up, and the priest – for such I assumed the man to be – conducted me into the largest where a great fire was blazing and a number of men's clothes were hanging on chairbacks to dry.

'The priest bowed and said, "Alas, madam, I cannot offer you a change of clothes, only a large dressing gown. May I suggest that you remove your wet clothes, put on the dressing gown, while I prepare a bowl of hot bouillon."

'The dressing gown fitted me where it touched, but the priest was pleased to say I made a charming figure, then sat on the opposite side of the fire and talked of much that I have now forgotten, while I thought how wasted was this handsome, cultivated man in the rank of an ordinary parish priest. Presently he yawned, so did I, then he said, "There are only two sleeping chambers, madam, I am in one – the first at the top of the stairs. May I suggest you use the other?"

'I went upstairs and took charge of the second room and found it was furnished by a narrow bed, a chest of drawers and a chair. I removed the dressing gown and crept naked – as is my usual practice – into the bed and was soon asleep.'

'The story has little point so far,' the princess remarked.

'Ah! But now I come to the important part. I woke suddenly. The way one does sometimes and felt remarkably refreshed. I lay thinking about my host, what an extraordinarily handsome man he was, when a sudden thought came into my head and just wouldn't go away.

'I thought how delightfully exciting it would be to seduce a priest. A real Roman Catholic celibate priest.'

Andrea gave vent to a roar of laughter. 'Bravo, madam. If you must commit a big sin, make it a holy one. How did your priest react?'

'Well, he occupied a monstrous large double bed and when

I crept in beside him, he grunted, then said something very strange. Strange for a priest, I mean.'

'And what was that?' the princess demanded.

'The devil always rewards those who watch and pray.'

'Am I to understand that the gifted boy is the son of a French priest?' the princess demanded again.

'Will you kindly allow me to continue, Highness?' Thelma insisted.

'Very well, but come quickly to the point of this ridiculous story.'

'We spent the night together and the holy man was extremely active, the result I assumed of years of – well – self denial, and frankly I was so worn out it was quite late when I woke next morning. My host was nowhere to be seen.

'Later I found my car and chauffeur – who had found refuge in the inn – and continued my interrupted journey.

'Alas, my wonderful adventure resulted in an embarrassing termination. Three months later I found I was in an interesting condition. I was preggers.'

'So,' the princess began, 'the boy is …'

'Please, madam. I am coming to the point you requested. Deciding that the priest should bear his share of the guilty secret, I returned to the village and drove straight to the curé's house. The door was opened by a tallish elderly man attired in a long black cassock. I asked for the village curé. "That is me, madam," he said. "No, I don't mean you. The other. Much younger." "There is only one priest in this village, and that is me. And has been for the past ten years."

'After I had explained I had taken refuge in the house on April the fourth and had been received by a tall, youngish priest, the elderly man chuckled.

' "It is really very easily explained, madam. On that evening a certain nobleman of my acquaintance also took refuge in my house and as he was soaked to the skin, I insisted he wear one of my cassocks. Then I was called away to the sick bed of a dying woman and did not arrive back until late next morning, by which time my guest – and it would seem you, madam – had departed." '

The princess leaned forward, her body shaking with excitement.

'The nobleman! Did you find out his name?'

'Yes. He – the father of my child – was Count Conrad von Holstein.'

Both nephew and aunt released a cry of joy and Andrea said:

'The finest blood line in the hidden world. No wonder the boy is – what he is.'

'But you managed to pass the boy off as the son of your late husband,' the princess remarked gently, her appearance once again that of a young and beautiful woman, whose strange grey complexion enhanced rather than detracted from her beauty.

'Yes. I had to seduce poor Albert who for months afterwards went around with a dazed expression. He insisted we get married at once when I displayed signs of a premature confinement.'

'Think,' the princess whispered, 'the son of a count of Holstein – and a catamado! The world is ours.'

Andrea shook his head and looked rather anxious.

'Yes, but a catamado! Will we be able to control it.'

'It's worth trying. Reared by us! Think of it. A hand reared catamado!'

Thelma creased her forehead into a perplexed frown. 'A catamado!'

'A rare and wonderful being,' the princess replied. 'Well nigh indestructible, it gradually develops extraordinary powers. A fully mature catamado – in every sense of the word – can control the elements, can heal wounds in a matter of seconds, negate the effects of every known and unknown poison and sustain life under water for a long period. They do of course self-destruct eventually, but that is only after a very long life.

'But they lose very little by destroying the earthly body, for they inherit a secondary body that is even more unique than the first one. My late lamented father, may his ashes rest although his soul still rides in on the north wind –'

'Count Dracula,' Andrea whispered. 'Her father, my great-uncle.'

' – maintained that a catamado can with practice so condition the secondary body, it will exist on this plane for long periods, if not forever. So one could say it had never been away.'

'And my son is one of these ... these creatures?'

'Yes, and I need hardly warn you to keep the knowledge to yourself. Every government has a secret department which has only one function. The extermination of what they call – The Bizarres. Members of my illustrious family. First generation vampires, vamlings and in particular – catamados. One is born on an average once a century, and should word of its existence reach authoritarian ears, the blood squad – so they are called – go into action. Fortunately our own beloved pack can often match them for underhand, cold, ruthless conduct.'

'Does Nanna – that is to say – Amelia know?' Thelma asked.

'She knows your son is special and I am someone to be feared, so it was necessary for me to chill her essential fluid, thus ensuring she does not wag a hinged tongue. Sooner or later she will have to be erased.'

George raised his head and looked upon the Princess Caroline Karlvina with increased horror.

'You mean you will murder poor old Blubber Lips?'

The princess gave him an even colder look, then addressed Thelma. 'Will you take full responsibility for this – this object you have seen fit to bring with you? He does not strike me as the type who can keep a locked mouth. Must I send a member of the pack to visit him as well?'

'He is a fool, but harmless,' Thelma spoke with complete conviction. 'Leave him to me. He'll do as I say.'

'That is well, but should he cause trouble you will be held to account. Now, you have our permission to withdraw. Andrea will show you the way out – and in. However, always request permission for an audience before entering my territory in future.'

Thelma performed a perfect curtsey and began to back from the room, then nudged George who refused to bow and went ambling down the passage with hands pushed firmly in his trouser pockets.

'Wait!' the princess called out and Thelma froze into immobility. 'The important item. The boy – the glorious catamado – is to report here three afternoons a week for special instruction. Only Andrea and I are capable of helping him to develop his special powers.'

'It will be as you say, Highness.'

'And make certain the peasant woman who looks after him remains at a front window when he is absent. A member of the pack will be stationed in the street opposite. The merest sight of him will have a most salutary effect on the woman. That is all.'

Andrea conducted Thelma and George round the house, then helped them clamber through a skilfully disguised hole in the tall privet hedge. Before leaving he kissed both of Thelma's hands.

'My word,' Thelma said with evident ecstasy, 'aren't they simply exciting! So kinky, blood-chilling and loin-warming. Know what I mean?'

'No,' George replied, 'I don't understand what you mean. I think those two are some kind of dangerous crooks. And if you allow Simon to go to that ... that ... place, then you're not the person I thought you were. That's all I've got to say.'

Thelma sucked in her breath, ground her teeth, then stamped her right foot, all signs that she was about to lose her temper. She even went so far as to repeat her companion's name three times.

'George ... George ... George ... You are mildew. All blue and mildew. You hang on to antiquated ideas and judge the entire world by them. Yes, you do. I mean, you didn't trouble to listen to what the princess said. My son is someone special.'

'Seducing a priest!' George muttered. 'Absolutely disgusting.'

'I did not seduce a priest, but a marvellously degenerate nobleman.'

'You thought you'd seduced a priest. That's the same thing.'

'George, are you going all puritan on me?'

'Of course not, but there are limits.'

'Only to fools and cowards. Think, the princess is a daughter of Count Dracula?'

'Rubbish. Balls and balderdash.'

'You're more than mildew. You are – at least half – decomposed.'

'If you let Simon to go to that house, I'll take some kind of action. I mean that.'

'You'll do nothing of the kind. Do you hear me?'

'My conscience ...'

'Piffle. Put it to sleep. I did mine years ago and I can honestly say I've never missed it.'

'I love you, Thelma, even adore you, but you sometimes shock me out of my mind.'

'Do I? Well, listen, you ain't seen nuttin' yet.'

*

Simon was sent to the princess's house by means of the skilfully disguised hole in the hedge, three times a week, and absolutely refused to tell his mother what had taken place. George stayed away for three entire weeks, then came back with lowered head and sad eyes. 'I'm despicable,' he said. 'So weak. Weakness is the greatest crime.'

Amelia became more terror-stricken by the day and Thelma had to push her to the front window so she could gaze down upon the pack; three seated in a black, box-shaped car, one leaning against the bonnet looking up.

One Tuesday afternoon she said to Thelma, 'I think I am going to slip out of my mind and go somewhere far, far away.'

Thelma looked at her thoughtfully. 'It would certainly solve a very large problem.'

Two days later Amelia went quietly mad. Not violently mad. That was not her way, but in a manner, that had she been in full possession of her senses, she would have approved.

She stood in a corner, with her face to the wall and refused to speak or move. Were she forcibly removed, she took the first opportunity to return to the corner and stare intently at one particular spot on the wall.

She had been standing in this position for the best part of six hours before Thelma decided something really must be done.

She summoned a doctor, who in turn summoned the mental health officer, who to Thelma's rage between them decided that as Amelia could not under any circumstances be described as a danger either to herself or the general public, she could not be committed to an institution.

'But she can't remain here,' Thelma insisted. 'I mean she's only an employee. This is not her home. And I will have to employ someone else to look after my young son.'

'You have a problem,' the mental health officer agreed. 'Has she any relatives who would be willing to care for her?'

'Not so far as I know.'

The mental health officer shrugged. 'This is the position as I see it. As the lady is in your employ and domiciled in your house, full bed and board being part of her remuneration for services rendered, you must be held responsible for her welfare, until such times she can be accepted into an institution of one kind or another.'

'And how long will that take?' Thelma asked.

'Oh, a year ... two ...'

'This is outrageous!'

'I can see it might seriously inconvenience you. Why not take advice on the matter?'

So Amelia remained in her corner, leaving it twice a day to visit the bathroom, eating her meals standing up and sleeping so far as anyone knew on her feet. Once Thelma thought she would get a reaction by locking the bathroom door – she did. Amelia merely returned to her corner, squatted down and deposited a very large stool on the recently installed fitted carpet, plus a medium size pool of urine.

Of course Thelma exclaimed again: 'This just can't go on.'

George did his best for the afflicted woman, arranged for a tall table to be placed in the corner which enabled her to eat from a standing position without too much inconvenience. Simon viewed his preceptress's predicament with lively interest and was clearly puzzled when his questions received no response.

It must be assumed he acquainted the princess with Amelia's condition when he next visited her house for special instruction.

One week after quietly slipping from her mind, Amelia disappeared. She was standing in her corner when Jennie turned the lights out, but when Thelma came home around four o'clock next morning, there was no sign of her. Later cook said she had heard the front door close around three o'clock next morning, followed by the gentle purr of a slowly driven car. Even the police when summoned, could not decide if this car had anything to do with Amelia's disappearance. But whatever the truth of the matter, pathetic Amelia Dunlop, with her obscenely pouting lips, was never seen again.

But one of her shoes and her handbag were found on a cross channel ferry some three days later. In the handbag was fifty-six pounds seventy-two pence, the missing lady's passport, two handkerchiefs, a set of keys that fitted every lock in Thelma's house and an expensive diamond ring. A deposit and current account in the local Westminster Bank yielded the total sum of thirty-five thousand, three hundred and fifty-two pounds and forty-nine pence.

Thelma was heard to state that she had never been so misled by anyone before. A poverty-stricken dependent had bloody well no business leaving such a sum that was far more than Thelma had possessed in ready cash in her entire life.

A coroner's court came to the conclusion that Amelia Dunlop had most likely taken her life while the balance of her mind was disturbed.

George wept a few sincere tears of remorse, Thelma said, 'Well that's that,' and Simon giggled in a rather nauseating fashion and instantly paid an unscheduled visit next door by means of the hole in the hedge.

PART TWO

GEORGE

I am going to write down everything that happened since the day poor Amelia disappeared and then maybe I'll begin to believe what I saw, heard and experienced.

To begin: I am George Vernon, a very ordinary sort of chap, who is hooked on Thelma Martin, which is something I can't help, although there are times when I wish I could. Being in love can be pure hell, particularly when the goddess of your choice can on occasion be a cold-eyed, frozen voiced, silly bitch, who loves nothing better than dishing out verbal barbs when the mood so takes her.

The trouble is, being so damned beautiful, she's absolutely spoilt by men. I know that if I can't stand the pace there's a few hundred candidates willing and eager to take my place. Well – ten or so at any rate. How her late husband coped I just can't imagine. I believe he was as simple as a ten-year-old who still believes the world is a wonderful place to live in, which it would be if everyone were nice to each other. And everything would only remain normal and not suddenly erupt into a confusing and terrifying sea of conjecture. And that shows my state of mind when I start using words like that.

Thelma has a son. Nice-looking little chap, I thought when first laying eyes on him, and indeed so he was. Blond like his mother, with her eyes, but deep as the Atlantic; you never knew what he was thinking, but were pretty certain it was about you and not very complimentary at that.

Poor Amelia, the nannie who looked after him before she disappeared, was a poor slob of a woman, ugly as could be – with great pouting lips and eyes like boiled gooseberries – was chosen for the job because she was cheap, could provide Simon with an elementary education, and make Thelma look even more gorgeous in comparison.

I suppose we would have soldiered on if it hadn't been for that woman moving in next door. Princess Caroline Karlvina she called herself, a cold mad piece of churchyard salad if I ever saw any. I know that last statement takes a bit of working out, but it's the only way I can express the effect she had on me. And the nephew! When I first saw them together I didn't know if I should spit or shudder. Kinky, obscene and devilish. Probably a mixture of all three. And even then that princess creature was talking about wiping out poor old Blubber Lips and hinting I'd be for the chop if Thelma didn't keep me in order.

And keep me in order she did, which is proved by the fact that I did nothing when Amelia was supposed to have thrown herself off the cross-Channel ferry. Let's not beat about the bush. That lot next door and the things that look after them, somehow got the poor cow on that ferry and either made her jump overboard or threw her themselves.

And let me face another fact. One day they'll get me. I know too much and am not all that inclined to keep it to myself.

Particularly what I know about that so called boy Simon.

The catamado.

The most awesome, terrifying, dangerous and wondrous being to ever walk upright under the sky.

The princess told us what he was (not that I believed her at the time) and why she wanted him, which to my mind is not too clear. When he arrives at full maturity he could wipe her lot out and the pack into the bargain. But the Dracula family – and I've come to believe they do exist – have some kind of potential that the princess only hinted at, and it would seem the vast fund of power that is a catamado's birthright, can help ensure that potential comes into full flower. That's my theory at any rate.

One good thing from my point of view had come out of all this: Thelma had taken to treating me much more kindly and even displayed occasional signs of affection. When she first slipped her hand into mine I almost fainted. To be frank I have a kind of hand fetish. Some men are hung up on breasts and buttocks; for myself one of the great pleasures of this life is the sight and feel of a fairly large, well-shaped, white feminine hand. When that lovely member is part of the woman one loves, then the pleasure is doubled.

Of course a little voice way back of my mind told me this was merely an inducement to keep me happy and less inclined to talk about what I had seen and heard. As I said earlier it worked. This is the first time I have dared to record what took place after poor old Blubber Lips disappeared.

Simon went to that house every Tuesday, Thursday and Saturday for 'instruction'. He never talked about what he had seen, taught, or what took place there. But I did notice an awesome maturity that gradually came into being. He had always been strange – now that strangeness became more pronounced. One day I shouted at him because he had ignored his mother's enquiry as to if the princess had enquired about her and he gave me the kind of look that a lion reserves for a gazelle that has wandered into its line of vision. Then he said quietly: 'How fortunate you are that they have taught me how to control looking dead.'

And the hair stood up on the back of my neck, for I had a feeling I had just escaped death by a fluke.

Thelma, from being the essence of sexuality, the careless

discarder of men when they first displayed signs of boring sentimentality, changed before my eyes into a dreamy worshipper at the shrine of Princess Karlvina and Count Andrea de Villefort. I all but wept when I saw her crawling through that hole in the hedge, knowing she would not be allowed into that awful house unless by invitation.

On the rare occasion that we were *officially* invited to take green tea and wafer thin sandwiches, one of those awful dog like creatures turned up carrying a gigantic card on which was described:

*H.S.H. The Princess Caroline Karlvina and
His Excellency The Count Andrea de Villefort,*

Requests and demands the presence of:

Madam Thelma Martin and Escort

for green tea and conversation at 4 post meridian.

On receipt of this piece of arrogant nonsense Thelma would become wildly excited and proceed to prepare herself for the event hours before we need depart. On one occasion she took three showers, drove Jennie to distraction by changing her hair style at least four times. I was ordered to go home – which had become a dormitory as I only slept there and that most reluctantly – to put on my very best suit and generally make myself worthy of the event.

Having done all this beautifying, we then had to crawl through a hole in the hedge, which meant me carrying a clothes brush in my jacket pocket. When we arrived at the house that smarmy nephew always answered the door, insisted on kissing the palm of Thelma's left hand, as though he were tasting it before taking a good bite.

I found the princess was a great name dropper, only I had never heard of the names before. She would say, 'What a pity you can't meet the Lord Marcus. He's the present head of our family.' Or: 'The Khan of Moncola represents the family in Asia. Even those who sit on padded chairs in the Kremlin bow their heads to him.'

I began to tire of this perpetual boasting and said with heavy irony, 'I will look forward to seeing one of your illustrious family in 10 Downing Street.'

My sarcasm was completely lost because she said calmly, 'That will not be long delayed. There is a Draculain in the present cabinet.'

And I had to wonder who it could be.

Then came the day when the princess collapsed.

It is important to realise on the afternoons we were invited to tea, young Simon was not present, it being one of the days when he did not report for special instruction. I can remember there was an altercation between Andrea and his aunt because she had been rather greedy and eaten – for her – a vast number of thin sandwiches. Andrea had been kept quite busy running to and fro fetching fresh supplies.

'I will eat what so pleases me,' she stated, 'and I will not have a mere cub telling me otherwise.'

'For your own good,' he pleaded. 'You know the digestive trouble ...'

'Ears!' she barked. 'F and B's listening.'

'Please yourself,' and he stomped from the room in a fine old temper.

I must say up to that time the princess had eaten very little – at least in our presence – and I was surprised to see her cramming black pudding sandwiches into her mouth. But hardly had her nephew departed than she emitted a loud cry and fell back in her chair.

Did I mention her exceptionally white skin had a greyish tinge which young Simon said was due to moon-bathing – a piece of nonsense if there ever was. Now she turned black. In a matter of seconds her skin became gleaming black, looking for all the world like highly polished black leather. Then she began to croak and I shouted for Andrea, who came on the run and all but passed out when he saw the state his aunt was in.

He did not hesitate, but grabbed Thelma and spluttered in her face, 'You will do anything to save the princess? Yes?'

'Yes ... yes ... I suppose so.'

'Please listen to me. She cannot die, but can be seriously incapacitated. The digestive juices have been over-activated to deal with an over-abundance of blood sausage sandwiches. The vein fluid has been seriously affected and she may become a helpless vegetable for many years if drastic action is not taken. You understand?'

Thelma nodded. I could only watch that shining black figure in the chair, aware that my stomach was threatening to misbehave. Andrea without asking further questions stepped up to Thelma and tore the sleeve from her left arm.

'Kneel down beside my aunt,' he ordered. 'But now – at once.'

Thelma sank to her knees and the count gripped his aunt's head in his right hand, her lower jaw in his left and literally pulled her mouth open. He removed his hand from her head and inserted a forefinger into her mouth and gently rubbed the gums over the eye-teeth. Instantly the two eye-teeth grew longer; in fact as I discovered later slid from sheaths until they dimpled the chin. Then Andrea gripped the head again and extended the mouth to its fullest extent.

'Madam,' he shouted, 'place your upper arm over my aunt's mouth ... now.'

Before I could protest Thelma obeyed this monstrous order and laid her lovely rounded arm between black lips, only to give vent to a piercing shriek when the long teeth sank into the white flesh.

I shouted my rage and horror and moved forward, only to shrink back when Andrea's burning gaze all but paralysed me.

'Don't worry,' he said. 'After the initial pain Madam will not be hurt. She is now giving my aunt much needed natural nourishment. You, fetch the catamado. The boy. He has the power to heal and make good. Then the woman will not be drained.'

'Drained!' I exclaimed.

'That is what I said. The longer you linger the more essential fluid will your mistress donate.'

I raced to the door, began calling Simon's name long before I reached the hedge, the memory of Thelma's white arm clamped between those awful lips while long fangs were driven into her flesh, drawing off her life's blood, was a goad to drive me through a brick wall.

I certainly enlarged that damned hole in the hedge – a

ridiculous means of entrance if there was one.

I tore down our garden path still calling Simon's name, stumbled into the house and found the little wretch seated in the dining-room drawing pentagrams on a large sheet of cartridge paper.

I grabbed his arm with the intention of dragging him to the princess's house. But the moment my fingers encircled his arm, his head jerked round and never had I seen such a look of rage on any face before.

His eyes from being blue were now green; a blazing fiery green such is sometimes found in wild animals. He spat at me and it seemed as if my hands had suddenly burst into flames, so that I screamed in agony and dashed around the room like a madman. I do not suppose the pain lasted longer than a few moments, but it seemed like a lifetime. But just as suddenly as it had come, it went and I was shrinking back from Simon who hissed words at me.

'Don't ever ... ever ... lay hands on me again.'

Memory returned and I again thought of Thelma's blood being drawn into that gaping mouth and I shouted at Simon:

'Do what you like to me, but your mother needs you. The princess is ill and your mother's blood is ...'

He raised one small slender finger. 'I know sufficient.'

'Then come quickly.'

He tilted his head on to one side and said quietly:

'It is not necessary for me to leave this room.'

'But ...'

'Quiet.'

He seemed to be listening for some little while, then he jerked his head and sat upright.

'I have cured the princess. My mother will feel no ill effects from her donation. You may return to them now.'

I stared at him with wide-eyed astonishment. 'You can cure ... from a distance?'

He returned to drawing pentagrams.

'It is a small matter. Go now.'

I slunk from the room and once outside doubt tormented my mind, so I raced back to the hole in the hedge, then lumbered my way back to that decrepit house and finally into the large room.

The princess was sitting upright looking much the same as usual, while Thelma sat smiling in her chair as Andrea kissed two small pink marks on her upper arm.

'This is the second time you have suffered hurt in the confines of this house,' he said softly. 'We must think of means of recompensing you.'

Princess Caroline gave her a gracious smile. 'Yes, indeed. You served most adequately in an emergency. Think of a favour that you would like me to grant you. The death of an enemy for example. The crippling of a too ardent admirer. If it is not in my power to grant it, I will permit your son to do so.'

We left soon after that charming offer and on the way back I said to Thelma:

'Look, this is getting too much for me. I'd like to stay and look after you, but I can't see how I can. Simon is now a miracle worker, you seem to be wrapped up in the princess and that ... Andrea. I never thought I'd live to say this – but I do think you and I had better part company.'

I swear she was near tears. 'But you can't mean that, George. I'd be lost without you. I mean, you're so ordinary and they're so ... so tremendous.'

A wave of irrational happiness flooded my being, together with a need to torment; take a small measure of revenge and expand my badly deflated ego.

'But you must see my point of view, Thelma. To me black can never be anything but black. *Dracula* is a horror novel I've never read; and little boys of Simon's age mostly play football and only have the power to be a bloody nuisance. And there was that business of you giving blood to the princess – the way it was done. To me that was horrible. And I can't dismiss the idea that you actually enjoyed it.'

'Don't be so silly.'

'No. I mean it.'

In fact I was beginning to convince myself. Although a chap can love or intensely desire a certain woman, even in the midst of the deepest infatuation, he becomes aware of the lady's defects, certain traits of character and little foibles that would normally irritate, but now can be ignored. When some more intense emotion takes over – such as fear – then those defects stand out, like rocks when the tide recedes.

So long as I lived my desire for Thelma would remain undimmed, but now the instinct for survival which no one can ignore forever, was threatening to claim the greater part of my conscious thoughts.

I went on, talking slowly.

'What I would like you to do is cut the princess and that house right out of your life. And Simon, well, I think some kind of mental treatment is in order, for it would be fairly hair-raising for a grown man – anyone – to be what he has already become, let alone an eight year old boy.'

She sighed deeply and maybe swallowed an angry retort, but at that time she was most anxious that I did not leave her.

'The princess has explained a catamado …'

'Please these words mean nothing. A catamado, daughter of Dracula … I only know there's an atmosphere of evil about that place and Simon can learn nothing good there. The way that woman turned black – and the fangs which slid out from her gums … and you put your arm across her gaping mouth without the slightest hesitation … I can't get that memory out of my mind.'

'George, don't leave me. Please.'

I deliberately did not answer until we were back in the house and I was seated in the most comfortable chair the lounge could offer, for such a change of mastery was a bit much to take in one go.

Without being asked she poured me a triple gin and tonic, which I drank cautiously for I needed what few wits I have clear as daylight for the next few hours. Then I said:

'If I don't leave you, there can only be one alternative. You must move in with me. At least for the time being.'

She shook her head several times and now she did cry; shed a few tears and I was beginning to feel like the worst kind of rat, but the horror I had witnessed that afternoon clung to me like a damp shroud. But when she said: 'I can't … not now. The princess … Simon … don't you see I'm hooked? Like I've been all my life, only this is the worst of all.'

And she sank down upon her knees and laid her golden head on my lap and cried like the child she really was.

A woman's tears often wash away a strong man's resolution, and heavens above knows I am far from being a strong man. I stroked her hair and gabbled baby talk and that was the limit of my comforting procedure (having had little practice) save for:

'Stay here if you must – do what you wish – I will never leave you.'

She looked up at me with tear-bright eyes. 'You promise. Really and truly promise?'

'I promise on my life. No matter what – I will never leave you. Except to go home to sleep.'

She reached into my pocket and took out a clean handkerchief she knew I kept there and used it to wipe her eyes.

'There will not be any need for you to do that – unless you want to.'

Moses suddenly allowed to enter the promised land – after so many had been before him. Offered the crown that had lain so long in the gutter. I wondered if my desire had been so long denied, so that now full realization would fall far short of that experienced in dreams. Also doubts had to be banished.

'There's no need for you to do this. My promise had no strings attached.'

'No ... no ... I want you to stay.'

'Why?'

She hesitated too long and I began to wonder if it were necessary for her to manufacture a reason for this sudden change of heart, for when I had pleaded for this privilege, she had mocked me and stated that I would never physically attract her. But now she raised her head and looked up at me with an intense stare that I found to be disconcerting and said:

'Because I now realise you must be a man in a million. Any other man I know would have run for his life, had he been faced by half what you endured. You have accepted terrible knowledge and merely asked for another cup of tea. Surely you are entitled to any poor privilege I can grant you.'

That made sense to my prosaic mind and had a ring of sincerity and I was quite prepared to take advantage of the offer. After all, she had given herself to others who had done nothing to deserve the pleasure. I had given her years of devotion and received nothing but slights and on occasion insults.

My ego was now sitting up and taking nourishment.

So it was that I fetched three full bags from my flat and ignoring Jennie's knowing smirk, deposited them with an air of grim determination into Thelma's bedroom.

That night I joined a naked Thelma in the large double bed and left it some two hours later.

To be honest I have never been what you might call a sex maniac. I can take it or leave it, derive more pleasure from preparing the meal than eating it. And let's be honest, I'm all for a plain no-nonsense menu, which means kinky side dishes are apt to turn my stomach.

Thelma jumped out of bed, switched on the overhead light, so I was permitted to gaze upon enraged, glorious beauty, and pointed to the bedroom door.

'Out of my bed. There's no place there for an innocent boy who only knows how to play with himself.'

This of course got me going and next instant I was out of bed and roaring back at her.

'And I've never found it necessary to bed down a practised whore before.'

She threw an alabaster figurine at me, which fortunately just missed my head and shattered against the wall. I hastily withdrew from the room and suffered the humiliation of being seen by Jennie, slinking into the spare room. There I spent the remainder of what could be described as my unsolemnized wedding night. However around six o'clock next morning I was awakened by a tapping on the door, which presently opened to reveal Thelma looking particularly appealing in a light blue negligée and wearing a repentant smile.

'I'm sorry,' she said. 'It was – well – I'm not used to unsophistication ... Can I have another chance?'

Instantly my frail wall of resentment crumbled and I allowed myself to be drawn from the spare room back to the double bed where whatever common-law relationship we had entered into was consummated.

I became as Christian when he lost his burden and journeyed forth into my own mind, knowing, hopefully the flame of love would burn as brightly as ever, but the chains of infatuation must fall away. Also between the hours of six and nine o'clock in the morning I ceased to be afraid of Thelma

Martin, which had been a formidable barrier between us, although up to that time I had not been aware of its existence.

When I finally rose and went out under the noonday sun, I strutted across the surface of the earth with the arrogance of a man who has sipped from the cup of immortality.

That afternoon I descended from the heights of Olympus after I had glimpsed another facet of the bizarre.

A walk in the garden, a prolonged study of that tall hedge – then disquiet, mind disturbance, the inability to find a rational explanation: forced to remember what had taken place a few days earlier.

One part of the hedge had become a packed mass of giant leaves, as though cabbages had in some way mutated and replaced the former privet. A neat rectangle some six feet high by four wide on which was spread a spider's web that could have been three feet in diameter.

The owner-tenant lurked at the very top. I estimated he was the size of a soup plate.

From below there gradually emerged a green caterpillar. Possibly a three foot six length of undulating green flesh that raised a round red head that was not enhanced by gigantic blue eyes, that surveyed me with seemingly insatiable curiosity.

A distant relation, the size and thickness of my arm, complete with a black fur coat, came slowly out into the sunlight, its dazzling violet eyes horribly grotesque, but not without an element of repellent beauty.

A column of ants the size of well developed mice, went marching across the lawn and I – suddenly sick with horror – stamped on them, then swallowed bile when armour-clad bodies cracked and grey fluid seeped into the earth.

Black terror floated through the mists of fever dreams.

Immense termites eating away those props which support the frail structure of sanity.

I heard a voice call out from the endless halls of eternity.

'*Great Dracula, must your progeny always be drawn to the seething septic horror that afflicts the body universe? The only cure is complete destruction; far better the peace of death than the prolonged agony of tainted life, for unless suffering is streaked with joy, then there is no purpose to the very act of creation.*'

I went back into the house, my brain numb, my soul a cringing atom of consciousness that wanted to *know*, but would rather not be told. When I looked out of the window God was looking down at me from a massive cloud bank, but the devil was spread out under every blade of grass.

Thelma had not risen from our bed and smiled voluptuously when I entered the room.

'Your son,' I said, 'is preparing for his O levels. His teachers must be very proud of their pupil. He is enlarging life.'

Her smile widened and she stretched out a hand, but I backed away. 'No, darling George. Not enlarging. Merely doing his homework.'

I found Simon in the dining room, the table covered with A4 sheets of paper on which were inscribed line upon line of hieroglyphics, all written in a neat, well-formed lettering.

I approached him boldly, not without fear, for I knew he could at least do me a terrible injury, but I had to strip the thick veil from the face of truth, no matter that it be my last act. My first question was so direct it astonished me, as I listened to my own voice.

'How soon before you reach full maturity?'

When he looked up I detected a gleam of surprise in his eyes.

'Never. The catamado continues to develop until time fuses into an indivisible whole. But irrevocable laws may demand self-destruction in about ten years of your time.'

'In the meanwhile?'

'I will gradually take to pieces the nest that has nurtured me, before proceeding to insert my spoon into the international pot. The body universe needs the special nostrum that only I can provide.'

'How will you repay the Dracula family for the tuition they have given you?'

'That is a question I have no right to answer. Ask the princess or her nephew. Ah! Listen to and observe a small wonder, that will soon be surpassed by greater events.'

I heard a sound that I can only describe as a growling squeak, and spinning round saw the sideboard slowly rise at the right hand corner, then return to normal with a loud bump. Presently from under the gap provided by means of short legs, there emerged a mouse that was at least the size of a well grown cat. It came out into the room with the confidence that comes to any creature whose size is large, relative to its surroundings.

Simon spoke softly: 'I am planting an image of you in its brain, married to a suggestion that your flesh is ripe cheese waiting to be stripped from your bones. It will be an interesting and instructive experiment to find out what happens.'

I came near to falling on to my knees before an eight-year-old boy, who happened to be a catamado.

Instead, I looked around for a weapon to defend myself, but could see nothing more lethal than a ruler. Then Simon giggled and the giant mouse streaked across the floor and landed on my left shoe, its teeth bared, while it emitted the growling-squeak which did more to undermine whatever courage I possessed, than the actual attack.

I kicked with my unencumbered foot and a soft body crashed against the table leg, transformed the squeak into a shrill scream, but instantly recovered and renewed its attack upon my person. I gasped when pointed teeth sank into my ankle and bent down with the intention of pulling the thing free and smashing its head on the table, when it suddenly rolled on to the floor – dead.

Simon leaned back in his chair and tapped a ball point pen on the table.

'There is always satisfaction in developing one's natural gifts. I have thought *big* before, but not without a certain amount of soul-searching. The same can be said of *Thinking Dead*. But I am delighted the accuracy with which I can hit a selected part of the target. Do you know I can now think-dead one particular ant out of ten thousand?'

'Those monsters in the garden ...' I began, but he quickly interrupted. 'Thank you for reminding me. I will erase them immediately.' He blinked three times, tapped his left foot twice, then nodded. 'Done. The caterpillars I will leave for the time being. They could develop into something interesting. Imagine butterflies with a six foot wing span. Ants the size of elephants might be a bit too much. As yet.'

'You could bring devastation to the planet,' I protested.

He raised his eyebrows in surprise. 'But that is inevitable. Didn't you know that? The means are not important and there are several alternatives. Why not a surfeit of over-large insects?'

'You mustn't even think of such a thing,' I urged. 'The very thought of what would happen if the insect world got out of control, is too terrible to contemplate.'

I found myself looking down on to a child's face made grotesque by a pair of cold grey eyes. The very tone of his voice made me shudder.

'I can do whatever I please. I am a catamado. Immortal, well nigh indestructible. With power that will never cease to expand. At this moment I have only to think you dead – and you fall to the floor – dead. A lifeless lump of flesh and bone. The ultimate is when I can destroy the universe – and re-create it – all in the space of a single heartbeat. No one, no power on earth can stand against me.'

I remembered that Lord Acton had said: 'Power tends to corrupt, and absolute power corrupts absolutely.' How much more must this be true when a child of tender years discovers he has the power of life and death and even the invisible power that judges both heaven and earth cannot bring him to account. For a while a blend of pity and awe coloured my thoughts, then I again realised what he could do and what he would do when that awesome couple from behind the hedge had fully instructed him in developing his as yet untapped potential.

I looked down upon the dead super-mouse and a terrible dread froze my soul.

Truth has a disconcerting habit of revealing its often far from pretty face to a simple person like me, which could be the reason that most not over-bright people finish up wallowing in the manure.

It was revealed to me that the little blister, the super-brat, the menace to unborn generations – would have to be put down. Assassinated or murdered – whichever way you like to consider the killing of a fellow being – only Simon was no fellow being of mine.

But who was going to do it?

Certainly not me, for the moment I raised a violent hand – always supposing I found the willpower to do so – he'd think me dead.

The answer was so simple it hurt.

Surely the only creatures I knew on this unhappy planet who might have a chance of clobbering the little monstrosity, were the princess and the object she called a nephew. And they were engaged in building him up into a power-colossus for some reason of their own. Someone must have a heart to heart talk with them and endeavour to clarify the situation.

I just could not see Thelma doing the job for even her under nourished maternal instinct would baulk at the prospect of her one and only offspring being given the chop.

That I must somehow convince the princess it was not in her interest to continue Simon's tuition and general upbringing.

If she told Thelma of my hard-come-by ultimate solution, that would mean vacate-my-bed-and-house-and-be-on-your-way-rat, but that was only one of the risks I must take.

Now I had to get out of this room without the mini-horror even guessing what I had in mind. When one considered all his other achievements, thought reading should have been a minor accomplishment.

How I managed to crease my face into a reasonable facsimile of a smile, I will never know, but I stood there shuffling from one foot to another, then sidling towards the door, in fact behaving in a manner that would have aroused his suspicion had he been paying me the slightest attention. But he had returned to writing hieroglyphics on A4 sheets of paper and I was able to make an escape without attracting a single glance.

There could be no delay in carrying out my intention, for given time for consideration I would never carry it out at all.

I crawled under the hedge, walked as boldly as my waning courage allowed, then banged on that hard door with a stone.

Andrea opened it and stared at me with a look of surprised enquiry.

'I was not aware my aunt had summoned you to her presence.'

'She didn't,' I replied curtly, for I was in no mood to be ordered around by the nephew; I had to reserve my fund of humility for the aunt. 'But I must see her at once.'

'I thought it had been made clear that neither you or your mistress ...'

I brushed by him and ignoring his protest, made my way to

the room where the princess normally received us. I found her seated in her usual chair, her white, grey-tinged face expressionless as a virgin sheet of white paper; her voice relayed crystallized displeasure.

'What is the meaning of this intrusion?'

I dared to sit down without waiting for an invitation to do so.

'I want to talk about Simon. The boy wonder.'

Princess Caroline cleared her throat while her face was transformed by a deep grey flush. 'Firstly I am not in the least interested in anything you may say. Secondly I must stress the word boy suggests an immaturity – a child. The being known as Simon Martin is not, or ever has been a child in any sense of the word. He is a catamado. The result of a well-preserved ancient blood line exploding –'

'Please,' I began.

'I would be obliged if you did not interrupt. Exploding into a cataclysm that can solidify into an ever pliable force …'

'Can you control it?' I asked.

She stopped in mid-sentence and gazed at me with as near an expression depicting amazement that her face would permit.

'Can we …? We can do almost anything. After all, most of us have centuries of experience to draw upon.'

'Yes, but when that – that thing – has reached full maturity …'

'Again I must correct an assumption. A catamado is fully mature from the moment of birth. He will never be more mature than he is now.'

I released a deep sigh. 'Very well, when you have completed maturing his exceptional gifts. Will you be able to control him?'

'He will have given us the power to walk abroad under the naked sun. Only one other of our kind has so far done this. A certain Carlos Markland …'

'But suppose he decides to think-dead you. Will you be able to stop him?'

The princess opened her mouth three times, but did not utter a word until she called out: 'Andrea. Attend me.'

Andrea entered the room and gave me a look that should have thought me dead on the spot.

'He just walked in, auntie. There was nothing I could do to stop him. We should never have encouraged …'

'Never mind that. Once the catamado has been fully briefed, can we control him?'

Now it was Andrea's turn to look extremely thoughtful, before saying rather weakly, 'Well, the Lord Marcus could erase him from the time channel.'

Princess Caroline shook her head very slowly as though unable to dispel grave thoughts. 'I'm not at all certain about that. A catamado cannot be regarded as a natural phenomenon. If you stopped him being born from one source, he'd just pop up from another.'

'But ... but ... surely he can't do us any actual harm?'

'I can't think of any way he can terminate us — me at any rate — But he might be able to put us out of action for a long time. Or think-big at all the small life in our vicinity.'

'He's thought of doing that to the entire planet,' I said.

Nephew berated aunt. 'Why didn't you go into all this before we started to fully activate a catamado? And I would point out it is only you who gets anything out of this. I can walk in sunlight any time I wish.'

'Anything which benefits one member of the family, eventually contributes to the welfare of the entire family. And that includes mongrels as well as thoroughbreds. As for considering the effects that a fully activated catamado might have on ourselves, I will confess to a certain slackness of mind, but you are equally culpable. I can't think of everything.'

'What must be done?'

'I badly want to be sunproof, but not at the price of a plague of giant insects and a devastated planet.'

'But is there anything we can do?' Andrea insisted.

The princess thought for a while, then said in a quiet, deceptively mild voice: 'The pack might be able to do something. If we act at once, before the catamado becomes alive to our change of heart — if I may be permitted the use of such a hackneyed phrase.'

Andrea released words as articulate sighs. 'Essence of poppy to send the mind into a pleasure-hued oblivion, then very careful dissection, the bits and pieces distributed round the countryside.'

'Even a catamado surely will not survive that,' Princess Caroline proclaimed hopefully.

'Each portion wrapped respectfully in brown paper,' Andrea added as a final inducement. 'With a black X cross on each.'

The princess shuddered. 'Well, that's decided. Andrea, I leave it to you to make the arrangements.' She turned to me. 'Young man, we owe you some kind of thanks for drawing our attention to this oversight. I will think of some reward when I have time.'

'Keep all the grisly details from me,' I pleaded. 'That will be reward enough.'

'And you make certain the mother does not make a nuisance of herself. I'd hate to have you both liquidated. We will endeavour to convince her that the creature she still looks upon as an infant son has been dispatched abroad to further develop his potential.'

Then I left, more than a little relieved that my mission had been so easily accomplished. During the next few days quite a few persons came and went next door, and Simon (so I still thought of him) seemed very occupied in studying large books on anatomy.

He visited the princess's house every day.

Then came the time when I realised I hadn't seen him for several days. I mentioned the fact to Thelma.

'Oh,' she said casually, 'the princess has explained it was necessary for Simon to go to Egypt. Expand his ego or something. I gather he'll be away for some time.'

We did not mention the matter again and I came to the conclusion she was rather relieved to have Simon out of the way. It is quite possible she had grown to be at least a little afraid of him.

Weeks passed and I began to sink into a kind of cosy contentment. With the disappearance of Simon, Thelma did not visit the princess any more (at least to my knowledge) and seemed to enjoy my company.

I even got used to – and in some measure enjoy – her unconventional bed behaviour and it could be said my mind broadened in consequence.

I began to toy with a dreadful word – Marriage.

Then one morning I read the following item in the newspaper: BOUNCING HEAD ON M1.

'The driver of a car that swerved into a bollard on the M1 yesterday, stated he had been unnerved by the sight of a human head bouncing along the left hand side of the motorway. A police spokesman said a breathalizer test proved to be negative.'

I smiled complacently and marvelled at the ingenuity of the human brain.

One week later I heard a shrill scream from the overgrown garden next door and being unable to resist the temptation, crept through the now rarely used hole in the hedge and found Andrea de Villefort in a state of abject terror. He would insist on pointing to a large bush and gasping, 'Arm ... wriggling arm ... still bits of brown paper ...'

To satisfy him I poked about in the bush with a stick, but failed to uncover a wriggling arm, which was just as well for my peace of mind.

Next day both he and his aunt left the house and we never saw them again. I suppose they went to join that illustrious family the princess would boast about and placed their problems in the hands of the great Lord Marcus.

The following Sunday I heard Thelma screaming like a tormented banshee in our garden and when she had recovered sufficiently to talk coherently, gathered she had seen a leg wriggling its way through the hole in the hedge.

Again I investigated but failed to find anything that even resembled a wriggling leg, although I did detect minute shreds of what could have been rotting brown paper.

I managed to pacify my lady – only just – by pointing out the sheer impossibility of seeing a human leg, wriggling or otherwise, and she must have been deceived by a mixture of light and shadow. After several slow walks up and down the garden she did agree this may well have been the case.

All would have been well – maybe – and I would not have been writing this account if I – may the blessed good Lord help me – had not seen Simon's head bouncing across our lawn and making a bee line for the hole in the hedge. I have reason to believe he was doing a bit of self-assembly in the old potting shed.

Yes, I did get drunk, but more or less came back to my very badly shaken senses after Jenny had thrown a bucket of cold water over me. I opened my eyes and saw both her and Thelma looking down at me.

Thelma wrung her hands.

'What are we going to do?' she asked.

I produced one word. 'Move.'

II

Marikova

Derek Wallis lived alone in a four-room cottage that stood alone in the midst of a large wood.

People called him a recluse. A hermit. A weirdo.

He called himself a gentleman in retirement.

To maintain a state of idle solitude an assured unearned income was required. Derek had such an income.

To exist without sight or sound of another human being, supreme confidence that one's own company will not soon or later bore is an essential. Derek Wallis possessed such confidence.

His cottage was equipped with a twenty-four inch television set, a hundred or more video cassettes, and a telephone.

This mass of twentieth century toy-equipment could be regarded as insurance just in case supreme confidence was misplaced and one did get bored with one's own company.

And there were books. Hundreds of books packed on shelves which lined every spare foot of wall space.

And there was a small garden both back and front for him to play with.

Did Derek Wallis trudge every day to the nearest town to buy provisions it may be asked?

The answer is no. When he required to go into town – which was not often – he rang a car hire firm and arranged to be picked up in the lane that bordered the wood. Otherwise the local travelling grocer and everything-that-you-possibly-need left a made-up order as detailed on a list pinned to a tree. Derek fetched the goods in a wheelbarrow. All in all he was a contented if not a happy man.

At forty he hoped to see seventy, at which age – the biblical three score and ten – he assumed – or rather dreamed as he was wont to do – that a nice painless and convenient heart attack would allow him to make a dignified exit while gazing up at the great star lanes through a roof of whispering leaves.

A cat served as tangible company – otherwise what remained of the human race after the postman and the travelling grocer had been deducted, existed for the simple purpose of playing imaginary roles on a glass screen.

So it was that – assisted by modern know-how – a man had created his own universe, or a pleasure prison, where his soul was gradually being transformed into an astral butterfly.

Then one sun-bathed evening a girl with golden hair came to his door on bleeding feet – and his universe exploded. As indeed we are given to understand universes often do.

A rap-tap on his green painted door, a gasping cry in the region of his letter box, then alarm and curiosity forced him to turn a brass handle and face that which had come from – somewhere or the other.

Beauty on the screen or in a picture he could worship. That which one meets in the harsh world of reality, is so often deceptive – or so Derek had come to believe. It rarely if ever passes the close-up test. Possibly the long forgotten gods who had the final word on the matter of physical beauty decided that unblemished perfection would be more than mortal man could endure. Unless viewed in the abstract on a glass screen.

But now the one dreadful, unthinkable and any other adjective you care to think of, miracle occurred and Derek Wallis looked upon flawless beauty and was from that time onward as one dead.

Always supposing he wasn't already.

A wonderful white face, lit by fantastic deep blue eyes and framed by slightly wavy hair. A poet might have described her full lips which were parted so as to reveal gleaming white teeth, but no ordinary man could hope to do so. The flounced white dress had been ripped down the back so that it hung off smooth, white rounded shoulders and partially revealed the left breast.

Derek's soul cried out in anguish – the figure was perfect too – and the bare delicate feet were bleeding and yes – and yes again – here was beauty in distress and he must take it in and comfort and protect it, until someone more worthy arrived to take it off his hands.

Leaving him to die slowly of a disease that up to then he had thought himself immune: Loneliness.

Peerless beauty fainted.

Derek should have gathered it up in his arms and carried it with becoming reverence to his lowly bed (or couch as the poet would have it), but instead – being unversed in such procedures – placed rude hands under armpits and dragged the inert form into his sitting room and deposited it into a deep armchair.

Then he drew up a foot stool and sat gazing upon this miracle of perfection until he was numbed by the wonder of it, then accepted the thought he should be performing some sort of restorative action. All he could think of was a glass of water.

Since forcibly parting those lips could only be likened to sacrilege of the worst possible kind, he sprinkled a few drops on the white forehead, which did have the effect of producing a kind of wriggling movement – so delicious to watch – and the slow raising of eyelids that were fringed with curving black lashes.

For a while the dark blue eyes were without expression; cold pools that could not reflect light; then they came alive; relit a tiny flame of fear. A clear soft voice that held the merest suggestion of a lilting accent, cleared Derek's brain of all emotion save that of wonderment.

'Hopkins. Matthew Hopkins.'

Derek assumed he was being mistaken for someone else.

'My name is Wallis – Derek Wallis.'

'Oh!' She sat up and wiped water from her forehead with the back of her hand. 'I ran so hard and twice they almost caught me, gripped my dress and tore it ... But ...'

'You mean ... someone was about to do you an injury!'

'Burn me alive. Matthew Hopkins and his crew always burn those he is pleased to call witches. But surely you know that. The village cannot be more than ...'

She stopped and looked slowly round the room, took note of the television set, the video, furniture, then as though suddenly understanding had lit a flame in her brain, a joyous smile transformed her face into that of an angel – or so Derek thought.

'Why,' she breathed the words, 'I must have ... I really

must have time-jumped. Almighty Beldaza came to my rescue.'

A man who lives all by himself surrounded by trees and only views the world through a cathode tube, may be stupid, but he most certainly acquires an inner perception that detects far more, than brighter, get-out-and-with-it person can ever hope – or want – to do.

Four hundred years ago he would have sunk to his knees and said, 'I am in the presence of an angel.' Two hundred years later he would have crossed himself most devoutly and said, 'I am in the presence of a she-devil.'

Now without saying anything he knew with an unwavering certainty he was in the presence of the unusual.

As his knees shook rather violently he sat down and wondered how the situation would have been handled on TV.

The girl – well, she looked like one – twisted round and revealed her bare back.

'Is my back scratched?'

It wasn't. Not so much as a mark of any kind whatsoever and Derek groaned when he saw its white perfection.

'Well?' she enquired.

'No. Not at all. Quite unmarked.'

'That is fortunate. I can heal very quickly, but I prefer not to, it uses up precious energy, which I might need at any time. Well, I time-jumped here.' She giggled, an enchanting sound. 'I might time-jump back there and find that mob on my heels.' She paused and frowned. 'I wonder what the pack were up to? They should have been looking after me. I suppose they lost me on the time channel. I'll complain to Uncle Marcus next time I see him. He's my brother actually, but he's so much older I think of him as my uncle.'

Derek was in such a bemused state it did not particularly worry him that he did not understand what she was talking about. Just to sit still and listen to that voice with its undefinable lilting accent was enough to put his ego in bondage for the next thousand years; in the inner, most inner part of his essential being he knew about such things.

This flawless beauty would not only bring about his death, but damn that part of him that could not die as well. But it did not matter. Not in the least. Some memory that related to childhood made him realise he should be offering some kind of refreshment; enquire as to his guest's well-being.

'Can I get you something?'

The question sounded so banal and she was right to treat it with an air of surprised enquiry.

'Get me something? How do you mean?'

'Tea, coffee. Plum cake with icing on the top.'

She laughed. Now a youthful, joyful sound. 'Oh! Nourishment! Well now.' She looked at him with eyes that were brimful of mischievous laughter. 'Let me see. Have you black pudding? Or nice juicy liver? Or a jug of rich health giving primitive but so essential natural fluid? But I tease do I not? So playfully pull the leg and you are so serious and want to serve me.'

Derek was so enslaved by this beauty from the mists of time he was in grave danger of falling to his knees.

'My stock of food is so limited. Visitors are so rare.'

'And my needs so simple. Just liquid. Tea will be marvellous. And ... I wonder ...?'

He was halfway to the kitchen, but now he turned quickly:

'Yes.'

'Have you something I could wear? This dress of mine is all torn and hardly – well – covers me.'

Derek had been acutely aware of that fact ever since she had made such a dramatic entrance, but was at a loss to think of anything in his sparse wardrobe that would fit her. His distress must have shown in his face, for she said:

'Anything will be better than this. Anything at all.'

'I have a spare shirt.'

'That will be perfect.'

'But it will be much too big.'

'We can tie a knot in it, can't we?'

'And a pair of my trousers will ...'

'We can roll up the legs and keep the garment in place with a belt or something.'

Derek decided that clothes took precedence over tea and ran to the bedroom from which he presently emerged carrying a pair of grey flannel trousers, a pink shirt and a leather belt. He ran even faster to the kitchen when the beautiful stranger began to strip off the torn dress.

The black iron kettle was singing on the black iron range when the door opened and she appeared looking more beautiful than before in an over-large shirt, the tails tied in a neat knot in front, the grey trousers bulging in every direction, the bottoms rolled up to reveal enchanting slim ankles and delicate, but still blood-stained feet.

'How do I look?' she enquired, spinning round to display this surely unique attire from every point of view. 'Is it not chic?'

'Eye-exploding,' Derek who had a weakness for playing with words, agreed. 'But it has suddenly occurred to me, your feet ...'

'Are treading essential essence into your nice carpet. Maybe you have a room where I can bathe myself.'

'Indeed there is. Just a tub I'm afraid. I've never got round to installing a shower.'

The girl flinched, but quickly recreated her smile. 'That is all right. Showers never really agree with me. Where is ...?'

Derek pushed open a door and revealed a rather shabby little bathroom; the walls covered with patches where steam had done its worst over the years, the bath tub losing some of its enamel. He pulled two large towels from a cupboard, a fresh bar of soap from a drawer of an old bedside cabinet, then began to back towards the passage.

'I'll leave you to ...'

'How do I obtain hot water?'

'Oh! The geezer. Water heater. It is switched on. Just turn the taps ... like this ...'

He adjusted the taps to tepid, then continued his backing out operation. When he reached the door the girl spoke:

'We do not know what to call each other. I am Marikova. The High Lord Marcus says it's a nice safe name.'

Derek first wiped the palm of his hand on the back of his trousers, then extended it.

'I'm Derek. Derek Wallis.'

She accepted his hand, then leaned forward and kissed him on the left cheek.

'I'm so delighted to meet you,' she said.

*

Marikova had been in the cottage for seven days before Derek began to consider the improbable. Had he been accustomed to the ways of women he would have realised that his charming guest had been running up signal flags that stated although she wasn't demanding intimate attention, she would not object too strongly if it came her way.

Once or twice Derek gathered together a small charge of courage that enabled him to briefly touch her, but the feel of her flesh was not unlike the result of putting a finger into an electric socket, or being burnt and frozen both at the same time.

She giggled after one of these rather pathetic overtures, her eyes mocking, but gentle withal, and Derek received a hazy impression that he was on a slippery slide and he would finish up somewhere exciting sooner or later.

Marikova was no trouble. She bathed once a day, made Derek's bed, which he had surrendered to her (making himself uncomfortable on the sofa), did some light dusting and spent a fair amount of time brushing her hair which as a result gleamed like polished gold.

Her disappearance for long or short periods was a rather unsettling experience. Then he would search the house calling her name, go out into the woods where all kinds of life forms played in mist-haunted glens, but failed to detect sight or sound of her, until suddenly he would find her seated in a chair, or standing in the garden, watching him through the window.

The same question every time: 'Where have you been?'

The same answer every time. 'I've been to hell, sir, to wish the devil good day and he was most reluctant to let me go away.'

Derek knelt beside her and said so softly – and it must be admitted sadly, 'One fine day you will disappear like that and never come back.'

She stroked his hair and nodded very slowly and maybe the same sadness was reflected in her eyes.

'I expect I will for the family will demand I go home and listen to the written words once uttered by our dread sire, and then will have to go and perhaps forget my way back to this lonely spot. Love now while you have the opportunity. Do not spend eternity mourning for what might have been.'

It was then that Derek began to consider the improbable.

He wrote sonnets – of a kind – to this lady and washed her

feet in warm water scented with rose petals and it is pleasant to record he no longer spent sleepless hours on the sofa, but instead spent many an enchanted sleepless hour in his own bed, where Marikova took him into a loving, if rather hungry embrace and gave him a foretaste of either a red-tinted hell, or a centrally-heated heaven.

The improbable had become an achievement.

Marikova sang to him in a low sweet voice as he sank in a cosy nest made from dream-mist and the strange weakness which held his body in its thrall.

> Come die with me and be my love.
> And we will wander down star-lit lanes.
> Ride with the dead on clouds above.
> And know that time and space is ours.

There was much more that he did not remember when she had again departed, but the purple residue of melancholy happiness remained with him for days to come.

The intruders came during one of those periods when Marikova was absent. A tall dark, sardonically handsome man followed by hideous creatures wearing broad-brimmed hats and long overcoats that encased their bent bodies from neck to ankles.

Deformed giant dogs wearing broad-brimmed hats; that is how Derek thought of them when they crowded round the front door. The tall man – without a single knock or a word spoken – had entered the cottage and seated himself in the most comfortable chair. Derek began to protest but swallowed unformed words when the creatures round the door growled and the tall man spoke.

'She has taken essence from you, for it would only take a puff of wind to blow you over. Consume red meat in large quantities, if you would live to donate again. Now, where is she?'

Derek knew it would be a waste of time to pretend ignorance of whom the man spoke, for the cottage was saturated with the aura of her presence, so he answered truthfully.

'I do not know. She leaves me like this quite often.'

The man nodded. 'The urge to time-jump into a more entertaining age becomes at times irresistible. But she should have learnt by now that superstition and ignorance often explode into violence. I will wait for her.'

Now a great fear came to the man who had retreated from those of his own kind, for instinct told him the tall man and those who remained outside were beings who had small claim to be called human. And the tall man closed his eyes and instantly turned into the likeness of a corpse, for he too shared the extreme pallor that made Marikova's beauty so exceptional, although it gave the man a sinister aspect. Three of the creatures round the door squatted on the ground and bowed their heads; the fourth stationed himself by the window and fixed Derek with an unblinking stare.

He got up and crept from the room. The man in the chair did not move, the three dog-like creatures squatting by the front door remained as huddled humps, but the one staring through the sitting-room window blinked and gave the impression it was not happy about this change of location.

Derek went upstairs and into the bedroom that he and Marikova had shared, then looked out at the light dappled tree trunks, the roof of interwoven branches and yearned for the peace that for years had been his. Like other blessings one does not value contentment until it has gone.

The dog-faced creature walked away from the house, then stood looking up at the bedroom window, the eyes bright with a baleful gleam, the round mouth moist, the tapering, hair-fringed ears pushed out into an oblique angle by the broad-brimmed hat.

Derek sat on the rumpled bed, removed his shoes, then lay down and closed his eyes.

The nebulous ghost of a perfume brought a scarlet vision into being when he closed his eyes. A great castle built into the side of a mountain. Bright sunshine high-lighted ruined turrets and gaping window spaces and laid down slabs of shadow in door and gateways. Dust spirals raced over deserted courtyards, but collapsed into writhing grey snakes at the foot of towering walls and those entrances that still retained a stout door.

Then the sunlight was blotted out. Ceased to exist – had

never been – when a vast shadow swept across the mountain and castle like a monstrous black cloak – as a high-pitched scream came into being.

Derek sat up and looked wildly round the room. The scream rang out again – it came from beyond the window, down on the floor of the woods. Derek swung his legs off the bed and reached the window in two long strides, where he again looked down upon the open space that separated his house from the trees.

Marikova was running, pursued by two dog-like creatures, while a voice bellowed from the doorway.

'Catch her! Trip her ... bring her down! But without too much force. She is the Lord Marcus's beloved sister.'

One ... the one to the left ... seemed to glide forward at incredible speed and flung its curved arms round the running girl's legs. She crashed to the ground with a resounding thud, but instantly struggled to break free and even managed to crawl forward a few paces until the second creature seized her arm and dragged her upright.

Derek, the recluse who had been afraid of life, ran down the stairs and raced to the door with the intention of coming to the rescue of his lady. But the third pack member stood on the step, facing inwards, its black lips parted revealing white pointed teeth and a red tongue that was coiled back like a length of rolled raw meat.

A chuckle came from behind him and spinning round he saw the tall man observing the scene with a look of amused indifference.

'It would not be wise to interfere with the pack while they are doing their duty. Don't worry, they won't hurt the little beauty. They protect the family – even from themselves – not harm them. Strange how you both seem to have developed this obsession for each other. Still, that is how little humvams are born. You may well become a humvam daddy before leaf fall time.'

They dragged her in with no gentle hands, great hair-backed paws gripping soft rounded arms; then after a nod from the tall man, they half carried her into the sitting-room. There she was flung into a chair and left to sob without sound, an ability that had amazed Derek on earlier occasions.

The tall man turned to him while still wearing the same

amused smile. 'You too had better sit down, for what I am about to relate may well diminish strength and the power to speak.

'You, Bimba and Carlo,' he addressed the two pack members, 'out! Give warning should there be an intrusion from any sphere. Go.'

They ran from the room like well trained hounds and Derek sat down, for indeed his knees shook alarmingly and cold fear ran like a rising fever along his blood stream.

The tall man shook a protesting finger at Marikova who would have got up from her chair, with the intention possibly of making another futile attempt to escape.

'No, Highness. Do not move. I may only be a mock, but I have the power to have you writhing on the floor in five seconds, whenever it so pleases me.'

She spoke for the first time since her capture.

'Boris, hurt me and the grand council will move against you in full force. Remember who I am. Child of Count Dracula out of Barbushka. Full sister to the Lord Marcus. In direct line to the Draculain throne.'

Boris – for such it would appear was his name – bowed his head.

'I can never forget your status, Highness, but I have a duty to perform that is authorized by a warrant issued by the grand council, that states I am to bring back Her Satanic Highness the Princess Marikova by any means that are in my opinion needful.'

'Why?'

He smiled ruefully and spread wide his hands. 'Because your satanic highness has spent over a century in the sheltered peace of Lord Marcus's court before time-jumping into an age when they burnt our kind at the stake – a fate that almost became yours – then landing by chance in this secluded spot, formed a disastrous relationship with this hume, who will now have to be …'

'No!' Marikova screamed a protest and gazed at Derek with tear-filled eyes. But Boris shook his head and looked as sad as his sardonic face permitted.

'But, Highness, you have left an impression on his brain that only death can erase. The urge to share his madness, longing, with another of his kind will be nigh irresistible. Beldaza forbid, he may even commit his experience to paper, thus forcing the pack to resort to very unpleasant extremes. He will be put down swiftly, that I promise.'

The lovely eyes were filled with tears, although only one flowed down the left cheek. 'But I do not want him to be absorbed. I want to pass eternity in his arms.'

'With the deepest respect, Highness, completely impractical.' Now it seemed as if the tears were dried by the intense glare of rage that turned the eyes into blazing blue pools.

'I will make it practical. I will. And if you touch a hair on my hume's head, I will so worry my brother Marcus that he will have you absorbed just for the sake of peace and quiet.'

Derek thought he detected a hint of anxiety on Boris's face, before he bowed low and said ingratiatingly: 'If Your Highness can think of a way I can safely leave this being alive, I will gladly adopt it.'

'It's so simple. Leave me here with him and I will assure you he will never tell anyone about anything.'

'Gracious, Highness – just not possible.'

'You must make it possible.'

He turned to Derek and began to address him in an irritatingly *reasonable* tone of voice. 'I expect you are rather at a loss to fully understand the situation in which you find yourself. Let me explain briefly. The divine creature that you so ably succoured and took to bed and board is no less a personage than Her Satanic Highness the Princess Marikova, daughter of his late and very much lamented Highness the Sovereign Count Ivlad Dracula, Vampire king of Europe.

'I am Boris Danicova, court chamberlain to the High Lord Marcus, whose duty it is to direct the pack – now on duty in your front garden and return any absconding members of the vampiral family who are considered unable to look after themselves.'

Curiosity – that besetting sin which tradition has it kills cats – enabled Derek to overcome his strength sapping fear and ask a question.

'Where do you come from?'

Boris nodded his approval. 'An intelligent question and one that does credit to your desire for improving knowledge. We come from the avenues of time, having been driven there by centuries of persecution. All time is ours from 1146 – the year the count was born – to the end of time, allowing for a break between 1999 to 2300, which has been declared a barren time-waste due to a regretable blow-up at the end of the present century. But that won't interest you. What else would you like to know?'

'Those hideous creatures ...'

'Yes, the pack. Madvams actually. You must understand the Dracula family are – in one way another – highly sexed and in consequence sired or given birth to many half breeds or humvams, that in turn have produced many hybrids and crossbreeds. The very lowest of the Draculain Table are the madvams, which have only one reason for their existence – protection of the family and the erasure of all those who might endanger that family – anywhere on the time road.'

'And they are to eradicate me?'

Boris turned his face away as though overcome by embarrassment, but frowned when Marikova said hurriedly:

'He has the right to a day's start. By Draculain tradition he has the right to twenty-four hours' start.'

The tall man drew a deep breath, then exhaled slowly. 'You must know that law was only made to ensure the high lords could enjoy some decent sport. The pack only act as hounds when an official hunt is declared; in the present case they are executioners, pure and simple. Apart from anything else a full day's start would only prolong this poor wretch's agony.'

'He would have a chance to live.'

'With respect, Highness, he would not. There is no way anyone can avoid absorption by the pack once they have taken up the chase. One renegade shadmock did keep out of their suckers for six days, but that is a record that has never been equalled, let alone beaten.'

'But he might be the one exception. And he will not talk afterwards if he gives his promise.'

'But I must stress, Highness, he has not left this isolated spot for many years. Suddenly forced to live like a hunted animal, alone in alien surroundings, unable to time-jump, he will soon lose the urge to exist and go down into the pit of oblivion of his own accord.'

Marikova sank down to her knees. 'Please give him the traditional twenty-four hours.'

Boris released a cry of horror and quickly stretched out his hands. 'Please, Highness, you must not kneel to me. Since you make such a point of it I will grant this hume a twenty-four hour start before the pack go into action, on the understanding that your Satanic Highness returns with me to the court of Lord Marcus without further delay.'

She lowered her lovely head. 'I agree. And now I would have a few words with the hume. Words of farewell.'

Boris looked anxious for a few moments, but he eventually nodded.

'Very well. But I would beg of Your Highness to be brief. I must take advantage of the time-ebb which only occurs once every space day. Your Satanic Highness's most humble servant.'

He bowed and backed from the room, a stark contrast, Derek thought, to the manner he had displayed when the girl was first captured. She came to him and slid rounded white arms round his neck. A single tear now slid down from each eye.

'I will never forgive myself for bringing you to the brink of oblivion. Yet, it has been said that no man can escape his destiny and I did not plan the time-jump on to your door step.'

Derek shuddered. He had a very vivid imagination.

'I will keep running to the very last.'

She withdrew one hand from the back of his neck, then began to trace a pattern on the front of his shirt.

'There is a way. You may not like it, but I can think of no better plan at the moment.'

'I am listening,' Derek said, but without any great interest for he was acutely aware the pack were watching him with hungry eyes through the window.

'Well, there is a vampire. A real first generation vampire, not like me who am a second generation – a vamling. Her name is Anne Mellior and she has no connection whatsoever with my family. As you can imagine there is little room for a F.G.V. in your harsh world, so she has disguised herself as a tea-lady in a Kingston collet making factory. I may add her real name isn't Anne Mellior.'

'Anne Mellior,' Derek repeated the name. 'I will not forget. Will she shelter me?'

'For a short time. She is a very resourceful girl and may think of another place you can go to. Remember the Kingston Collet Factory, Richmond Road, Kingston.'

The door opened and Boris entered. He bowed to Marikova and said with a fine air of sadness:

'I much regret, Highness, we must leave now. Time is already beginning to ebb and if we miss the full back-stream, then we'll be stranded for the best part of an earth day.'

Marikova clapped her hands. 'Would not that be a good idea, for then ...'

'Pardon my assumption in interrupting Your Satanic Highness, but I have already informed the Lord Marcus by thought-gram of your cap ... your rescue and he is expecting us to land on the time-dock within the fluid hour.'

Marikova sighed deeply, then drew Derek's head down until their lips met. After a prolonged kiss – which Derek didn't really enjoy – she whispered: 'Please find Anne quickly and don't forget to say I've sent you. Tell her letter following.'

'Highness!' Boris insisted. 'I really must again remind you – time is ebbing.'

Marikova pulled herself free and ran to the door crying with both eyes and making distinct sobbing sounds. From the window Derek watched the take off which did little to resolve his confusion.

Boris took up a position immediately behind Marikova, two members of the pack did likewise on either side. Then on a shouted word of command: 'Forward,' they all broke into a run.

Derek estimated they had covered a distance of some twenty yards before a mist seemed to rise from the ground and completely enveloped them. This cleared as rapidly as it had formed, but the running six figures had disappeared. Derek needed some time before the evidence provided by his eyes could be accepted by his brain, and then a much longer period to fully understand that Marikova had gone and he was a fugitive from the pack.

Now, back in the familiar solitude the bizarre quickly faded to the likeness of a bitter-sweet dream and the memory of Marikova, their lovemaking, became a dull ache that even the fantastic events of the past hour, could not alleviate. He began to look for evidence that Boris and the pack had really existed and soon found the scratch marks on the front door and one talon fragment (in place of finger nails?), which must mean that madvams needed to rid themselves of old talons when new ones grew. Could this mean they were related to the cat family, not the dog?

Away from the house, dust revealed footprints that had been scrambled into piles and ridges when feet had broken into a run. Another twenty yards further on they stopped abruptly, marking the spot where Mary and Boris, plus their grim escort, had jumped into the unknown.

He went back to the cottage and sat in his favourite chair and tried to accept that he must now go on the run. Make the most of the twenty-four hour start and find somewhere to hide, even though Boris had maintained that no one had kept out of the pack's talons – or claws – for longer than six days.

Live today – tomorrow you die. Turn the coinage of time into small change and make the most of every second. Six days would make him a millionaire.

Where to go? Somewhere that would not include four heads turned in his direction, eyes that glowed like smouldering sparks and a raw meat tongue that licked black lips.

Memory slipped back a cog. Anne Mellior who worked in a Kingston collet factory. Anne the vampire. He would have to shack up with a female vampire. Could she be worse than the pack? Surely not.

Hope manifest as a tiny spark. He must leave for the south at once. Catch the first train and hope to reach London before the pack – then seek out this Anne Mellior – only this was not her real name.

It must be recorded as a landmark in the life of Derek Wallis that a few weeks earlier he would not have under any circumstances believed in the existence of vampires. Now he believed in everything, but had faith in nothing.

He fled from one peak of terror to another. Everyday life as personified by railway stations and busy streets had suddenly become mist-haunted and the sky could only be seen dimly through the thickness of a shroud. His eyes which up to that time had only been equipped with straightforward sight, could now see in depth, which resulted in the normally invisible becoming visible.

Black slug-like beings that crawled along gutters and up the side of tall buildings. Those human-shaped things who walked along pavements clad in black that covered the entire figure save for the yellow blazing eyes. Now and again one of them would pounce on a live passer-by and disappear into the thickness of their bodies.

He sat among a massive collection of human bodies as the train raced southwards. They opened and closed mouths, got up, wandered away, then returned and closed lack-lustre eyes. And the *others* crawled between shuffling feet, reared up and tried to sink insubstantial teeth into very substantial necks, then slid into a seated figure, only to slip out when that figure stood up.

And Derek's ears acquired special hearing power so that he detected a continuous low wailing cry, such as one might expect to be sent out by those beings who are only permitted to sip from the cup of life, never drain it.

Then he looked out at Victoria Station that was for some reason clear of alien beings, but by now more than a little weary of train journeys, hired a taxi driver, who for an exorbitant sum agreed to drive him to Kingston.

Even in the restricted confines of a taxi cab he did not entirely escape from the strange world that had been so mysteriously revealed to him, for after a short nap he opened his eyes and discovered something with the likeness of a man dressed in dazzling white, with an ebony black face, seated next to him, staring with wild green eyes, while trying to push a long thin stiletto into his stomach. When Derek released a shrill cry this being merged into the leather-covered seat and was seen no more.

Strangeness put on another mask. The cab driver slid back the glass panel and after slackening speed to not much more than a crawl, said:

'Don't let that experience upset you. It's only a Hibbie-Willy. Can't do any real harm.' Then he closed the panel and drove on at such a speed Derek was propelled forward and landed on the floor.

They arrived in Kingston around ten o'clock in the morning, which meant Derek failed to understand where a number of missing hours had gone to, and stopped at the station. When he came to pay the driver, he could not wait to ask a very pertinent question.

'What did you mean – that thing was a Hibbie-Willy? Have you seen one before?'

The man raised thick eyebrows in real or pretended surprise.

'Don't know what you're talking about, guv. I haven't exchanged a word with you since we left Victoria.'

He drove off and Derek set about finding a collet factory and was misdirected twice before he found it set well back from the Richmond Road. He walked up a broad cement path flanked on both sides with colourful flower beds and came at last to large glass doors that opened up on a red-tiled foyer, where a curved counter stood against one wall. A uniformed porter gave him a strange, calculating look, before asking:

'What can I do to help you, sir?'

'I am looking for a young lady – at least I think she's young – named Anne Mellior.'

The porter nodded gravely. 'That would be our Annie. She's in great demand. Take a seat over there, sir, and I'll see if I can raise her.'

Derek walked to and sank down on to a blue plastic-covered couch and sat waiting with the patience of a man who knows eternity is at his disposal. He might have waited ten minutes or the best part of an hour, but no time seemed to have passed when the girl appeared. Short-cropped blonde hair, thickly marked brows surmounted large hazel eyes; a sweet little nose, a full under lip and an enchanting rounded chin. The tight-fitting blue overalls, emphasised a neat, slender figure. The total suggested a sweet innocent girl who had yet to escape from her teens.

She hurried over to Derek and sat beside him. After a full minute spent in examining his face, she gently took his hands into hers and said softly:

'You poor dear! You must let me help you. I do promise to do my best.'

Fugitive had found a haven. The outcast a kindly companion. The hunted a protector. The donor a partaker.

She peered into his eyes and asked a single word question.

'Pack?'

He nodded. 'I believe the twenty-four hour start is up. They must be on my track by now.'

She shook her head. 'No. You have become time-confused. There's one or two hours yet. But come with me and I'll look after you for a few days. After that – well – we'll have to see.'

Watched by the porter they walked together towards the door and the man called after them.

'Don't worry, Annie. I'll clock off for you.'

She called back over one shoulder. 'Thanks, Harry. I had forgotten.'

Anne allowed two buses to pass, then guided Derek on to the third. The driver-conductor barely glanced at the red card Anne took from her overall pocket, but said in a low voice:

'Black car cruising down Eden Street to the market. They're sniffing the trail of someone.'

Anne sighed and Derek whimpered. She eased him forward until they had reached the long back seat; there gently pushed him into the far corner, where she whispered: 'Keep your head turned inwards for the pack have sharp eyes. Unless your twenty-four hour grace is up they won't touch you yet, but it's not comforting to see their car through a bus rear window. The sight has driven many a hume mad without them knowing why.'

Derek felt dreadfully tired and despite his fear must have dozed off again, for suddenly Anne was shaking his arm, pulling him up from the seat, then steering him towards the exit door. Down on the pavement she had to support him, and he felt shame this should be so, but she comforted him with soothing words.

'Don't let it worry you. The result of mental strain and shock, plus someone being greedy. We're only ten minutes or so from my place, then you can put your feet up.'

Derek felt some relief when he realised the streets were clear of alien beings, although at times a large bird with two necks and matching heads flew immediately above them. Anne laughed softly when he expressed concern and did her best to explain.

'You mustn't be afraid of a night flyer, even though I can't think what that one is doing flying about at eleven in the morning.'

Derek pounded his head with clenched fist. 'I can't understand what has come over me. I keep seeing things like that and I never did before.'

She placed both hands round his arm and slowed her pace to his.

'You've been in close proximity with darling Marikova and so have caught some of her virus. Now you're with me and possibly my near presence is stirring things up again. Soon special sight will become quite normal. The hidden world has many assets that will amaze you.'

Derek turned his head and looked down at her with horrified amazement. 'Assets! To see that dreadful flying thing? Monstrous shapes gliding into people? To be haunted by a white-faced, bulging-eyed horror? You call these – assets?'

She chuckled deep down in her throat, then swallowed a passing fly. 'Of course. It is always an asset to see clearly. A non-asset is when you can't see what is going on under your nose. We of the hidden world insist on seeing everything, no matter how nasty. Then we know what steps to take.'

'And what steps can I take to repel the horror which threatens me?'

'Only you can decide that. And you will when the time comes.'

They came to a tall block of flats that stood in the centre of a well kept lawn. A long black board bore the inscription in large white lettering:

LUCRADA MANSIONS

'How do you pronounce that?' Derek asked, pointing to the inscription.

'Easy,' Anne replied. 'Luck – rada. As Royal Academy of Dramatic Arts. Of course you have worked out the anagram?'

Actually Derek had not realised there was an anagram to be worked out and still had not done so when Anne pushed open the swing doors and preceded him into the green-tiled foyer.

'Push the lift button,' she ordered, 'while I make certain that we've not been followed.'

The lift looked like a lion's cage fitted with amber-tinted mirrors, and when Anne returned (shaking her head) and they had entered, and the iron grid had crashed closed, there came to him a feeling of finality, such as – so some ancestral memory informed him – comes to a condemned man when he mounts the scaffold.

'I saw and sensed nothing untoward,' Anne said. 'They haven't picked up your scent yet. But they will.'

Derek could see his reflection in the mirror walls and decided he looked like a broken down old tramp who had been hitting the meths bottle for ten years. Then with a shock he realised his was the only reflection in the mirror. Anne's was missing. She noticed his dismay and again released a little throaty chuckle. 'Surely you know what I am? And is it not accepted by all flesh eaters we cast no reflection or shadow? You can assume that only a small part of us exists on this material plane, although when you touch me I seem solid enough.'

The lift jerked to a stop and when the doors glided open, they stepped out on to a thickly carpeted passage that was flanked by doors on one side and tall windows on the other. Anne led the way to the left and stopped when she reached a door which had the brass numerals 12A screwed on the centre frame. She produced a key and inserted it into a yale lock, then gestured with her free hand at the number.

'I've never been happy about the number 13, so that's why I've copied the practice that is sometimes used by German hotels and substituted it with 12A. Well, my species has quite enough to contend with without taking unnecessary risks. Come in, this will be your home until we work something out for you.'

Derek liked to think of himself as a gentleman and now began to perform like one.

'Look here, I can't really stay here. I mean – if those things – trace me here, you'll be in the ... the mess.'

She took his left hand in both of hers and pulled him into the flat.

'Don't be such an idiot,' she admonished, while giggling in

a most delightful way. 'I've been fighting off the Draculain henchmen since the year 1860. They hold no terrors for me. If they get too close I spit on them. Honestly, they hate water in any form. Turn a hosepipe on them and the bastards will run like hell.'

Derek was taken for a guided tour of the little flat and a very nice, comfortable living unit it was too. Anne's bed, although wide enough to hold two, could only be described as virginal in appearance, having bright blue blankets and snow white sheets turned down at the top. Derek was given the only spare room which only had space for a two foot six inch divan, but was equipped with a deep sprung mattress and a nice padded headboard.

Anne proved to be an excellent cook and whipped up an appetizing meal for Derek, comprising of lightly fried ham, crispy eggs and mouth-melting fried bread. Succulent coffee and toast followed. Anne contented herself with a glass of dark red liquid that Derek pretended was enriched tomato juice – although he knew it was nothing of the kind.

Afterwards he gave her a hand in washing up and stacking the chinaware in a tall cupboard, before she said most firmly:

'Now, you are to turn in, for you look fair whacked. Me, I must get back to work. I've just been promoted from tea lady to capstan lathe operator and as the sun isn't out I've no excuse for staying at home. Don't answer the door or the telephone. The pack know where I live and I wouldn't put it past them to ring up and see who answers. You wouldn't hear anything because they can't speak, but there's nothing wrong with their hearing.'

Derek had been trained from early childhood to say the right thing at the right time. 'Thank you for your kindness, I will try not to be a nuisance.'

She kissed him on the left cheek (always the left) and said he was cute, then left him alone to enjoy a certain measure of peace, which meant sleep on the narrow bed and dreams that were so free of incident as not to be remembered when he woke. Later he thoroughly searched the flat, starting with the refrigerator.

Bacon, eggs, corned beef, butter and six milk bottles filled with the dark red fluid Anne had drunk at their scrap meal.

These were sealed with red metallic caps which Derek did not even consider removing. Otherwise there was nothing in the flat — unless well hidden — that suggested it was not the living place of a normal young girl. The wardrobe contained a variety of what seemed to be new clothing which ranged from sweaters to expensive evening gowns; shoes of such a shape and design Derek could not understand why the wearer was not crippled; knee-high black leather boots that to his unsophisticated eye looked more comfortable and waterproof.

His conscience, by now liberated by his search among someone else's property, allowed him to turn his attention to a chest of drawers, which resulted in him being soon elbow-high in frilly knickers, bras, black silk stockings and other items of female apparel that he failed to put a name to.

Then the bureau with the locked drawer.

Those that were not locked contained masses of ball-point pens, envelopes, notepaper and a multitude of paper clips. The locked drawer suggested secret correspondence, a diary, photographs ... The longer Derek looked at it, the more essential it seemed that he should in some way get it open.

He was aware that a hairpin in skilled hands will pick the stoutest lock, but although he found a hairpin on the dressing table, no amount of gyrating it in the lock had the slightest effect. Then his eye spotted a letter-opener which originally had been shaped like a miniature sword, but someone had cut off one side of the hilt so as to destroy the marked resemblance to a cross.

He inserted the sharp point just above the lock and applied gentle pressure without actually expecting any result and was therefore more than surprised when the drawer flew open and fell with a clatter on to the desk top.

Stuffed tight with bright blue envelopes, all addressed to:

Ms Anne Mellior,
24 Lucrada Mansions,
Kingston Road,
Kingston, Middlesex. KT12 9HQ.

When he turned one over he saw a gold embossed coronet on the flap and instantly identified this correspondence as being from Marikova. He pulled thick blue notepaper from the first envelope and eagerly – conscience being by now completely stunned – read the scrawling writing.

> My dear Annanova,
> You will shortly be contacted by as nice a piece of grunt-grumble-drinkie-dry as ever placed hand where it no business to be – if I make myself clear. The pack will be hot on the trail, but you need not worry overmuch, having crossed talons with them often before. If the worst does come to the worst, chuck Grunt-and-grumble overboard. I mean, he's very pretty, but not worth a fall out with Marcus and Co. There is of course the ultimate alternative, but that must be your decision.
> Anyway, have fun, and believe me to be your very loving,
> Marikova.
>
> P.S. I exist only for the time when I kiss your feet and what-have-you.

Derek felt sick and became not the first man to wonder at the intricacies of the female mind, no matter the species. He would have sworn on a mountain of bibles that Marikova loved him to distraction, and derived small comfort from the thought that at the time of their dramatic parting, she most probably did.

Now …?

He read most of the remaining letters and found they were chatty, rather spiteful and contained more than a hint that Marikova entertained a strong lesbian yearning for Anne. On reflection Derek seemed to remember reading somewhere that the female vampire had this trait and for that reason mainly partook from a member of her own sex. And Marikova was – how had she described her status? – a vamling. A second generation vampire. And he – Derek had been designated to the role of expendable toy. And if the worst came to the worst, he was to be thrown to the wolves – or to be exact the dog-like creatures called madvams – the pack.

The sick feeling had passed and had been replaced by a dull ache, that was perhaps the physical manifestation of total despair. For what could he do? To go out to be hunted down by the pack was unthinkable. To remain here...? Thrown to the pack should there be no other alternative? But maybe that situation would never arise. Certainly he must never let Anne know he had read these letters and do his very best to please her no matter what demands she might make.

He shuddered. After all he was no longer all that young and a female vampire must have an enormous appetite, unless she so much preferred the left-hand side of the bed, she would have no interest in him at all.

He replaced all the letters in the drawer, then carefully eased the lock tongue under its brass keep, without as far as he could see, making any tell-tale scratches. Then he waited for the day to pass.

Around five o'clock the sun came out and he was able to enjoy it by sitting by an open window, allowing the warm rays to dispel the faint coldness which seemed to be an essential part of this otherwise cosy flat. Presently he fell asleep, for any effort no matter how slight seemed to tire him. When he awoke the clock on the mantelpiece pointed to three minutes past seven – and instantly he wondered why Anne had not yet returned. Had she gone to see someone else – to discuss him? Surely her stint at the factory would have finished at five-thirty?

Suspicion lit the fires of fear and he peered anxiously down into the street dreading to see hideous faces looking up; hoping to see Anne hurrying home, for then would come an easing of suspense, an opportunity to watch her, ask subtle questions, maybe form a favourable opinion. Then he grew tired of watching a street that remained commonplace and went back to his room and lay on his bed.

Thick clouds blacked out the sun around seven-thirty and ten minutes later Derek heard a key being inserted in the yale lock, or rather a sound of someone trying to insert a key, for there was a scratching and several bumps against the door, suggesting a drunken person was unsuccessfully trying to make an entry.

Derek turned the handle, opened the door – and a grey-faced Anne collapsed into his arms.

He first dragged her across the door mat, shut the door with his foot, then carried the inert vampire girl into his own bedroom and laid her on the bed. Her mouth opened slowly and words came seeping out.

'A sun ... storm ... I was ... caught in ... a sun ... storm ... Massage ... must ... massage ...'

She looked dreadful. Her face, hands, arms, from being grey were fast turning black, and she arched her back while managing with great effort to eject a few more words.

'Must strip ... and massage ...'

He began to unbutton her dress, but she brushed his hand away. ' ...No time ... rip ... rip ...'

Derek had little experience in undressing ladies at all, let alone ripping their clothes off, but realising he was faced by an emergency, which as everyone knows is an excuse for almost anything, inserted his fingers into the parting where buttons were married to button holes and jerked outwards.

Buttons flew to left and right, torn material fell away from a blackening body, revealing that this vampire did not wear a bra, only the briefest of knickers and no stockings. For no good reason that Derek could think of the phrase – Ready for Action – flashed across his mind. He did not think it would be at all necessary to remove the knickers, so began to massage the torso, skilfully skirted round the breasts, then descended towards the stomach.

His efforts did not result in any visible improvement, for the flesh continued to take on a darker hue, in fact rubbing it seemed to hasten the decline instead of ending it. Suddenly Anne reached out a trembling hand gasped, 'Needs must,' and pulled his head down and sank long eye-teeth into his neck.

Derek made an interesting guggling cry and mercifully sank into a pit of unconsciousness.

*

He awoke on the narrow bed and at once became aware of a soreness on the left hand side of his neck. Anne was leaning over him, her pretty face transformed into a mask of concern. When he opened his eyes, she released a deep sigh of relief. 'Thank badness!' she exclaimed. 'I thought I'd over drawn. But I was in a bad way, so you will I know, forgive that abrupt partaking. But it had to be.'

Derek felt desperately weak and ravenously hungry, to say nothing of being extremely frightened. He could not dismiss the memory of a pretty mouth being made hideous by a pair of long eye-teeth sliding out from the gums. Eye-teeth horribly prolonged. Could one bite lead to many? But it would seem as if Anne had read his thoughts and sought to reassure him.

'You are a guest recommended by that dear friend of mine, the Princess Marikova. Therefore normally I would never, but never partake from you without your explicit permission. Now, I must do everything to replace the loss you have suffered.'

She looked at him with a wistful expression. 'I suppose as a thorough-bred hume you would not consider a jug of the best AB essential fluid? No? A pity, for there's nothing like essential fluid to replace essential fluid. Look at me now – and remember what I looked like thirty-odd minutes ago. All thanks to your so rich O output. So much more beneficial than the bottled muck they turn out these days. That has lost its natural goodness. But I'm making you some beef tea.'

She fed him right royally, then rubbed his naked body with some clear liquid that did much for his veins for his body sang a hymn of joy, while another more visible portion of his anatomy rose up and demanded attention.

Anne regarded this phenomenon with interest.

'For a hume you have a strong need to dispense happiness to those who need it, but like many of your species, some sub-conscious urge forces you to suppress it. I find that to be very sad. Yet they call us monsters.'

Derek was so embarrassed he could not find the ability to supply a coherent answer, so instead smiled rather inanely and pretended he was more sleepy than was the case. But nevertheless he must have slept for his next conscious action was jumping out of bed, asking: 'Where the hell am I?'

The answer to that question was soon provided by the surroundings and the dim night-light that shed a small circle of light by his bed. He glanced at the clock. Three minutes past three, presumably in the morning. He sat on his bed and yawned, then allowed the sinuous snake of temptation to slither into his mind. Anne's body was no longer black, but an enticing, smooth whiteness. Suppose he were to drift in the direction of her room – sleep dazed – still groggy due to the after-effects of his essential donation – and just maybe explain he was in no mood to sleep alone. He chuckled and began to admire his expanding wickedness and daring.

There did not seem any point in putting on any kind of attire, so he walked naked to the door, pushed it open, then turned left and did not stop until he reached Anne's bedroom. Her door was slightly ajar, the overhead lamp still alight, so that when he entered he was able to see every item of furniture in the room.

The great double bed clamoured for attention.

The sheets and blankets were rolled back, revealing a blue undersheet on which Anne lay. Indeed she was no longer black, but without a blemish, sense-disturbing white. She slept. Eyes wide open, also white without the slightest sign of a pupil. Milk-white marbles. Eye-teeth had again become long fangs that curved down from the gaping mouth and dimpled the rounded chin. Mouth and fangs were coated with blood. A few smears marred the perfection of her breasts. There was even a long streak running down the right thigh.

Derek turned and quickly fled back to his own room where he shut the door and rammed a chair back under the handle. Then he sat down and found he was able calmly to assess the situation.

Fact one: The blood had not been his. He could still walk and indeed felt quite fit and well rested.

Fact two: She had been out – hunting. Had partaken (how easily the word came to mind) from a stranger. Quite possibly the unknown donator was completely unaware he had donated to Anne's well being.

Fact three: Anne was without doubt a no-nonsense-doe (or was it bitch?) vampire.

He sat still, eyes downcast, and mulled over these three important facts. He took them apart, examined their component parts, reassembled them in six various layouts, savoured each word, tasted each sentence, then came to a decision.

He spoke it out loud.

'It takes all kinds to make a world.'

*

Next morning Derek Wallis woke and took certain pleasure from the feeling of unique peace which had come into being some time during the hours of sleep. He had accepted the worst that the bizarre had to offer and could – possibly – allow horror to flow over him, like freezing water over time-smooth rock.

Anne, looking prettier than ever, cooked him a very substantial breakfast, emptied two glasses of O group herself, then filled a vacuum flask with liquid lunch.

'The canteen can cope,' she informed Derek in a confidential whisper, 'but I've a notion they dilute and that's not good for my vibes.'

He faced the prospect of another day spent alone in the flat and decided that his ego had been starved of human vicinity and would soon begin to illusionate, if it hadn't already.

He went out under the noon day sun, as he had many times before, and instantly became subject to an unaccountable dizziness, with sharp pains running down his arms and legs. He staggered to a seat and slumped against the wooden back, aware he was the subject of much curiosity and an element of pity. A motherly looking middle-aged woman sat beside him and peered anxiously into his face.

'Took bad, dear? I must say you don't look right. Gone awfully pale. Yes.'

Derek raised a shaking hand to his head. 'I think it's the sun. I can't bear the strong light.'

'A sunstroke maybe,' the lady suggested, 'although I wouldn't have thought it was hot enough for that. Should get indoors, dear. Yes. Have a little lie-down.'

He thanked her and presently she went away and so did the others when they realised he wasn't going to provide any further entertainment, and it did seem both desirable and wise to make his way back to Anne's flat. He found by keeping to the shade and whenever possible avoiding the direct rays of the sunlight, the dizziness abated and the pains in his arms and legs sank down to an endurable ache.

To reach the entrance to Lucrada Mansions he had to cross a stretch of sun-drenched road, so he did run across it as fast as his aching legs would carry him, to collapse in the foyer, his body a mass of throbbing agony, while his heart beat as though it was trying to break free from his rib cage.

Somehow he got into the lift, pushed the right button and presently staggered into Anne's flat and fell on to her bed, this being nearer than his own. Gradually the excruciating pain passed, his heart resumed its normal beat and he just felt very tired.

Presently he slept.

*

He spluttered back into consciousness when Anne shook his right shoulder; sat up and stared at her with bulging eyes and said very loudly:

'I dreamed I was in my grave and way up above a man with a cross wouldn't let me out.'

She brushed back a strand of hair, then dabbed his moist forehead with a black lace handkerchief.

'Never worry about dreams unless you can feel pain in them.'

'Mental pain?'

'No, that's there all the time. Physical. That which screams reality. And don't we all try to avoid that?'

'Physical pain?'

'No, you sweet innocent. Didn't you realise all secretly long to grasp the stinging nettle with soft tender hands, but will run terror-fed through a mass of dreams to escape from reality.'

'I went out and the sun made my limbs feel as though they were filled with liquid fire. And there's still a strange dizziness in my head.'

Anne's eyes became so sad and the smile that played around her mouth could have been an expression denoting compassion. She leaned over and kissed him full on the mouth, her lips lingering, moving gently, and the liquid fire came back, only now it was in his stomach, threatening to overflow, turn all his senses into a raging inferno.

He jerked his head to one side. 'I love only Marikova,' he said. Anne drew in her breath, then expelled it as a tiny growl.

'The Princess Marikova? She's not for you, little man. Not a princess of the Dracula line. The Lord Marcus will order the pack to rip you apart should he even suspect you have designs on his favourite sister.'

'But Marikova is going to speak to him about us.'

Anne sat down on a low stool and shook her head. 'Bet she won't. Oh, come now, you know she won't.'

Derek would have argued, but he suddenly remembered the letters in the secret drawer and sighed instead. Anne laid a hand on his and looked far more enticing and sweet than he could ever remember Marikova looking. Her voice seemed to have acquired a low, thrilling undertone that made him forget the aches and pains that were the price of walking abroad under the noon day sun.

'You won't throw me to the pack, will you?' he asked softly. 'Not even if the worst comes to the worst.'

Now she placed a hand on either side of his face and looked down at him with bright eyes. 'Never. Not even if every room is open to the sky and the sun never sets again.'

'Then I will love you all the time and Marikova only for part of the time. I think that's fair, don't you?'

'Most definitely. She doesn't deserve even that, and I am speaking about someone who has some claim to be called my best friend. In fact these royal thoroughbreds are all the same. No depth. All over you one day, draining you the next. No, don't get up. Stay where you are while I cook you a nice piece of liver and maybe some chipped potatoes. Right?'

'You're very kind,' Derek admitted. 'Marikova was no good at cooking. I had to do practically everything myself.'

'Never had to do anything for herself,' Anne pointed out. 'Had mocks and maddies to wait on her. Join me in the kitchen when you feel like it.'

Some considerable time had passed before Derek felt like joining his hostess in the kitchen, and there found his meal of fried liver, tomatoes and chips ready for his consumption.

Anne kissed him, pulled out a chair from under a small plastic top table, then eased it forward when he came to sit down, making him realise that if all females had been so loving and helpful, just maybe he wouldn't have become a recluse. The full plate was deposited in front of him; pepper, salt and vinegar stood to one side, knife, fork and spoon waited to be plied, but ... Derek hesitated. He sniffed. He cut a portion of liver and raised it to his mouth, slipped it over lips, chewed ... Spat it out.

A horrified Anne shouted a predictable question.

'What's wrong?'

'Tastes like something that's been dead for at least three weeks,' Derek stated. 'It smells and tastes horrible.'

Anne frowned. 'It does to me – but it shouldn't to you. Perhaps the butcher sold me rotten liver, knowing I would never tell the difference. The meat-eaters often take advantage of us, then pretend to be shocked when they see us drinking essential fluid.'

Derek tried a chip potato. 'That's just as bad. The slimey bitterness of corruption. I've never tasted anything like it before – at least not in this life.'

Anne opened her mouth, started to form a word, then stopped. She watched Derek with a strange intensity, then slowly assumed an air of wonderment. 'It could be possible,' she said after a while. 'After all Marikova did say ... How simply bloody marvellous! How stupendously wonderful! After all these years! Well I'm damned!'

'Have you worked out what turned the liver and chips bad?' Derek enquired. 'I haven't tried the tomatoes yet, but by the smell of them, they're just as bad.'

'I think I have the answer,' Anne replied softly. 'You are turning into a vampire.'

'What?'

She nodded slowly. 'That's the way I see it. Pains in legs and arms, dizziness in the head, can't eat meat-eater's food. You must be going vampire. As you may well have caught the virus from me, that sort of makes me an expectant mother ...'

'I've tried to live a quiet, solitary life,' Derek said bitterly, 'and thought that by not being a nuisance to anyone, nothing dreadful could possibly happen to me. But distressed beauty had to come stumbling out of the mists of time on to my doorstep, then because I dared love an alien princess, a pack of awful creatures were put upon my track. Then I fall into the hands of a lady vampire who contaminates me with a vile ...'

'Hang on a minute,' Anne protested. 'I really ...'

'Vile disease,' Derek went on relentlessly, 'that means I will never again enjoy roast beef and Yorkshire pudding or indeed anything at all that can be described as eatable.'

'Black pudding will stay down,' Anne protested. 'And you've some way to go yet. Actually the complete transformation won't take place until the next full moon. Two to three weeks. The reason you felt ill and couldn't eat liver and chips was the sun. From now on your body won't like direct sunlight. Anyway that's the situation. Can't be helped now.'

Derek pushed the plate to one side and looked helplessly round the kitchen. 'That's all very well, but I'm still hungry.'

Anne shrugged and laid a shapely hand on the refrigerator door. 'There's always black pudding and ... and rich gravy.'

*

Two days later Derek spotted the pack from his bedroom window, and promptly dropped to the floor and crawled behind a tallboy where Anne found him two hours later.

'Hiding from the pack is like hiding from lightning,' she explained. 'If they're tuned in on you – there's no place to hide.'

The courage which is born of desperation finally allowed him to stand upright and once again look down upon the grotesque, a form of reality that had escaped from a nightmare.

Maybe they were not human in the accepted sense of the word, but must have substance which meant some connection with the world of matter. There had to be a way of destroying them: bombarding them with Molotov cocktails for example. Riddling their bodies with machine gun bullets. Blowing them up. Burning them.

Anne who several times had displayed a gift of telepathy, said quietly: 'There would be more – or creatures much worse. It is said in Wittering Grange there are interbred crossbreeds that can lick flesh from bones and boil eyeballs with a single glance.'

'But even they could be destroyed by one means or another,' Derek insisted.

'Yes, if you were very clever and enormously brave, you might destroy an entire pack of Karviles and maybe every kind of mon-breed sent against you, which would mean the Lord Marcus rising up from his bed of contemplation and sending his rage across the cosmos, for he can never forgive anyone who has committed the crime of peace-destruction. Particularly his peace.'

'But isn't the Lord Marcus made of flesh and blood?' Derek enquired.

Anne made a X sign. 'It is not for us to ask of what material the Lord Marcus is formed. He is a phenomenon that cannot be explained in the totally inadequate word talk of meat-eaters. He is neither dead nor alive. He is the eldest son of Count Dracula. Born in 1191 out of Barbushka, the count's number one wife, he exists in every age, save those centuries when civilization lay buried in ashes and mankind was reduced to a few stumbling scarecrows that rooted for food among the ruins. Yet even that catastrophe was put right by adjusting time, so that that period became was-not-but-happened.'

'But every living being is subjected to the certainty of destruction,' Derek desperately wanted to anchor his frail craft to the sand dune of hope. 'Your Lord Marcus would fall before the full force of a machine gun.'

'You just don't understand. Yes, you would kill him today, but he would still be alive in yesterday and tomorrow. You mustn't under-estimate the enormous power that a thousand years of experience generates. Also, power and knowledge leads to the ability to contact other lives, so eventually one being can become the depository of a billion years of experience stretching back to the first great explosion from which the universe was born. That is how gods are formed.'

'But –' Derek would have persisted, but Anne raised her voice and suddenly looked very much like a lady vampire.

'It would be more to the point if you were to concentrate on your immediate problem. The pack down there are already upset for you have set up a new record for remaining at liberty longer than six days. The order implanted in their limited intelligence is to destroy the target in the shortest possible time after the twenty-four hour period of grace has expired. After two days this order becomes more urgent in its influence on the pack's communal psyche. By now they must be in a state of compressed, carefully controlled rage. Would you care to put your head out of the window and take note of the effect?'

Surprisingly, Derek obeyed. Maybe his curiosity was strongest of the emotions that fought for supremacy in his brain, or perhaps it was fear that spurred him to plunge even deeper into the pool of horror, but he opened the window and leaning out looked directly down upon the four figures clustered round the black car. Instantly they all sprang into frenzied action.

They moved out on to the road, stood in a neat row, bowed legs apart, heads well back, tapering jaws wide open revealing the white pointed teeth and red rolled back tongue, while from those gaping jaws there rose up a single high-pitched howl of rage and hunger.

Anne's quiet voice came from behind him. 'You are now the succulent repast laid out before starving men; the blood-dripping haunch dangled before deprived lions; the ripe carrion that the jackals just cannot reach, but will after the expenditure of honest endeavour. Please don't torment those poor creatures further. Pull your brawn-making head in and close the window.'

When he turned Anne was wiping moisture from her chin.

'Forgive me,' she said, 'but I'm only being vampiral. It was the sight of your posterior that did it. Pushing your twin orbs in my direction as though inviting ... I imagined my fangs sunk deep, drinking deep ...! Oh, great Beldaza!'

And she ran from the room, hands clasped to mouth and for the first time Derek realised the terrible strain his continued presence in her immediate vicinity must be, for pretty and loving though she be, the fact remained she was a vampire. Then as an acute pain shot up his left leg the thought exploded in his brain:

'Yes, but in a short time so will I be.'

Question: Did vampires thirst for each other's blood? If not, then Anne would cease to water at the mouth after the next full moon and he ...? Would he lust for her while still dreaming of an adolescent love for Marikova? Could one look upon the vampiral status as promotion or demotion in the Draculain table? How many people leave the streets we know and walk in an alien world?

Anne came back looking grey and haggard, but sad withal as indeed do all life forms when they see their own faces in moon-bright pools.

'What are you thinking?' she asked.

He turned and faced her with a kind of grim determination, that had not been within his power of expression before.

'I was thinking I would never go forth to seek death, but if he came today, I would gladly shake him by the hand.'

'Now, you may never meet him.'

'Then I will forever mourn the loss of a dear friend, for in the final analysis he is the one that will never let us down.'

'You will make a marvellous vampire, for you have the soul of a dreamer. And vampires come from the mis-shrouded halls of dreams.'

'Surely the time will come even for us when we'll sleep beneath the black sky of oblivion?'

She turned from him and went to the window where she stood looking down on to the pack.

'Would you really like that? To be blotted out, never *to be* again? What a waste! Better be a flea on the back of a dying dog than that.'

Another united four-in-one howl rose up from the street below and made the day hideous. Several dogs in the neighbourhood began to bark and one man nearby shouted, 'Shut up, whatever you are,' and instantly barking and howl ceased; was cut off in a second.

Anne spoke quietly: 'In the ranks of the meat eaters are hidden gods. We partakers have to remember that. Divine nectar would be too rich for our stomachs.'

'I am thinking of going back to my house in the woods. At least the end will have more dignity there. There the fire of passion will sink down into the ashes of resignation.'

'The pack will pull you down within five feet of the front door,' Anne stated. 'There's no knocking off at sunset now. Twenty-four hour watch round the clock. They absorb their prey, you know. No trace is left either here or the hidden world. And well – I can't help you to escape anymore. The pack can't harm me, but the Lord Marcus, he can do anything. After all I've got eternity to worry about.'

Again Derek proved he was above all a gentleman of the old school. 'That I quite understand. You have been very kind and to the very end I will never cease to love you most of the time and be grateful all the time.'

She hugged him far tighter than comfort allowed and her eyes did fill with tears, although she did not shed a single one.

'You make me feel simply horrid. I knew you were on the run from the pack before you actually arrived. Marikova wrote and told me. And you were only intended for grunt and grumble, plus donating when the pack moved in. Now I love you more than I love myself, and will mourn you for at least two full moons when the pack have done their best – or from your point of view – their worse.

'What power could have foretold that the Countess Annanova Bulavitch would ever sink to the state of hungering after a miserable hume? Not that you are miserable – well, not in the derogatory sense.'

And it must be recorded that Derek Wallis found time and mental energy to marvel that he, a middle-aged recluse, had somehow succeeded in winning the regard of two highly placed alien life forms, although it might have been more advantageous for his welfare if he had been spared this high honour.

'Romance is all very well,' he said strictly to himself, 'but life and a warm if solitary bed is more satisfying.' Then out aloud, 'I'm tired of being afraid. I'm going to be really terrified and do my best to get back to my cottage. The Good Lord above knows I should never have left it.'

'The hour before dawn would be best,' Anne advised. 'All life is at its lowest ebb then.'

'Including mine.'

'But be under cover by sunrise, unless the sky be overcast. Always supposing you are still ...'

Derek nodded. 'I'm still a functioning life form. Never mind, come what may, I run at dawn.'

*

When the clock chimed four in the sitting room Anne did not want to let him go and at one time seemed about to launch a devastating attack with the aim of putting him out of action. He remembered the old stories and found he still had the power to make a holy cross sign. Anne screamed and afterwards wept tears of shock and dismay, for he did not realise the full effect such a gesture would have on her.

But there was no further attempt to detain him and he left Lucrada Mansions by the tradesmen's entrance at four-fifteen; experiencing both pleasure and surprise when finding that the pack had made no effort to put the back of the building under surveillance, but later decided the instinctive power which motivated them did not permit more than an elementary reasoning process.

He caught the first train to Waterloo that would stop at Nelham around eight o'clock.

Gradually the eerie inhabitants of the hidden world emerged into being, but such was his immediate fear of the pack, he managed to ignore them.

*

The cottage already displayed signs of neglect, rather like a pampered beauty whose attendants have been dramatically removed. Rain had erased all traces that once marked Marikova's and her escort's departure, but the ghost of her perfume still haunted the bedroom, and once or twice it did seem as if her voice called out from somewhere a long way off.

Now to stock up with food, barricade doors and windows and take other – and doubtlessly futile – precautions to keep dog-faced horror at bay. But there came to him the illusory sense of security that is part of that living unit that is saturated by the personality of the person who has resided there for a long time. The nest-syndrome.

Three entire days was he allowed before the pack tracked him down, due no doubt to the fact it took them that long to understand that the prey had returned to the place where the hunt had originated.

He had washed, shaved and was replacing the breakfast china in to the sideboard, when he saw one hideous face pushed hard against the sitting-room window.

His first reaction was one of relief. The suspense melted and reformed as fearful curiosity.

How would the pack set about his dissolution?

How would he meet his end?

For the first day and night they did nothing more than divide their forces between the two main windows and the back and front doors. A war of nerves, or maybe not. Perhaps a period of inactivity was necessary to build their strength after the exhausting chase.

After an hour or so Derek tried a blood-chilling experiment. He walked up to the sitting-room window, made himself comfortable on a chair, then – after pressing his face against the glass – stared directly into the madvam's eyes.

An impression of reddish liquid with a black hole in the centre, nothing more. The creature did not move, blink, or display the slightest sign that he had done anything out of the ordinary. But when he moved to another part of the room the eyes followed him. When he ducked down behind a sofa he heard a low growling which ceased the moment his head came back into view.

Programmed reflex. The overwhelming need to keep the prey in view.

On the morning of the second day a deluge of water descended from the sky and Derek had reason to remember something Anne had told him. The pack were susceptible to water. More, the first drop of moisture to touch their skin resulted in a mad rush for the nearest cover – that inadequately provided by trees – while sending out a hideous chorus of howls that grew louder as the rain continued.

Derek began to fill buckets, a bowl and two large jugs with water and regretted he had never provided himself with a hose-pipe. The rain proved only to be a heavy shower and the moment it ceased the pack came out into the open, shook themselves vigorously and took up their original stations.

They went in action two hours later.

Derek was dozing in his chair when the clatter of broken glass rocketed him back into full awareness.

One madvam had its head stuck through the broken glass of the sitting-room window, another was throwing itself against the door, another had apparently found a ladder for the sound of broken glass came from above stairs, followed by the heavy thump as thick-soled boots landed on fitted carpet.

Derek grabbed the first bucket and threw its contents over the creature who was now half way through the ruined window frame. The effect was electrifying.

A high-pitched howl was transformed into a frenzied scream as the water bubbled on the mottled skin, thick hair-matted hands rubbed in an effort to remove tormenting moisture. Derek managed to empty the greater part of the second bucket over the one that finally smashed the front door and came lumbering into the hall. The contents of jugs and bowl helped to discourage the third that came down the stairs, before he retreated to the kitchen where he turned the tap full on and splashed water over the back door, which raised screams from the fourth pack member who had an arm pushed through a broken panel.

Eventually he allowed the sink to overflow while he stood in an ever-increasing pool of water, which as it spread had the effect of driving the pack from the cottage. They squatted under a tree and wiped each other with bunches of grass, while whimpering in a pathetic fashion that would have aroused Derek's pity had they been other than they were.

The rest of the day and part of the following night was spent standing in ankle deep water, always ready to turn the tap on whenever the pool showed signs of sinking. The pack in their desperation made several charges and even splashed through a few inches of water until the burning agony drove them back.

Finally they stood on chairs placed just beyond the kitchen doorway and snarled at him until he sent a fine spray at them by placing his finger under the tap spout.

Then all four withdrew and began to wander round the house and garden, until one came across a garden fork that Derek had left propped against the tool shed. This was first used as a spear; pushed through the open back doorway, but Derek easily kept beyond the range that would necessitate the pack entering water; then – proving that under pressure madvams could reason – a length of cord was tied to the handle, then the fork thrown with considerable force, in an effort to impale the besieged prey. Fortunately for Derek both fork handle and cord became so saturated by water, the project was abandoned.

When the sun finally set Derek was on the point of collapse as the bitter knowledge hardened into a certainty that the pack would terminate their grim business before dawn.

*

So far as Derek could later estimate the pack launched what was to have been the final attack at three o'clock in the morning.

At that time his full attention was concentrated on the

indisputable fact that a full moon had turned the back garden and the trees beyond into a silver fairyland inhabited by some very grim elves. Or hob-goblins.

When the four figures rushed in through the doorway he threw water over them by means of a plastic bowl that could be easily refilled by dipping it into the full sink, and was shocked to see it was having little effect, due to the thick coating of grease that covered clothes, heads and arms.

Once they had laid hands on him there was little he could do but struggle and scream at the very top of his voice. They dragged him out through the doorway and into the bright moonlight.

Derek looked up at the full moon.

The burning pain began at his feet and raced up his body until it set his brain alight. Then it was transformed into a wonderful, bubbling, sizzling stream that did something extraordinary to his essential being and exploded a bomb in his stomach that released a flow of power-strength such as he had not known for five million years.

His eye-teeth developed an ache that became well nigh unbearable until newly formed fangs slid out from their sheaths. He flung the pack from him and they went rolling over and over, then sprang upright and began to move forward again.

Derek stood upright in the moonlight, hands hanging loosely, fangs bared, curving over his lower lip, dimpling his chin. From his gaping mouth came the roar of the enraged, fully mature buck vampire.

The pack fled.

*

The night was dying when Derek – or the creation he had become – rummaged among the accumulated knowledge that can be contacted in the universal mind by those who know how, and re-discovered the correct way to time-jump. Or time-run.

The starting point was exactly twenty-three yards, two feet and six and three quarters inches from his front door and the jumping off spot eight feet further on.

An hour before day break, Derek time-jumped.

*

He stumbled to a stop on a gravelled drive and stared up at the great house. The untidy conglomeration of turrets, crouching chimneys, glimmering windows and weather-beaten brickwork – and the wide porch that guarded the iron-studded oak door.

He entered the hall where walls, ceiling and floor were black, plus an immense black and white stained glass window which depicted Lucifer poised in space with his left foot on the world.

Two footmen, attired in black satin livery relieved by white powdered wigs and flowing lace cravats, stepped forward and spoke in unison:

'Welcome to the Master's house. May your sins be heavy and your conscience light.'

Derek answered briefly: 'I am the undead.'

The footmen bowed deeply. 'Then pass, undead. Your sins are heavy and your conscience light.'

Now out of the black hall and into an equally black corridor and then down a flight of curving steps and into a vast underground room which was brilliantly lit by red-frosted globes. Something like fifty red-padded chairs formed a half circle in front of a red draped altar; each chair was occupied by a silent person, all of whom appeared to be paying homage to a large black, gilt-edged throne on which sat an immense personage clad in a long white robe.

Derek knew who this being was – the great Lord Marcus, head of the Dracula family; eight centuries had passed since his physical birth, but unlimited experience and knowledge was stored behind the high white forehead.

Lord Marcus had the dark satanic beauty of Lucifer, immortal son of the morning. An almost terrifying study in black and white, lit by large black eyes that could sear a soul or extinguish life with a single glance. A mass of black gleaming hair that flowed over the snow-white brow, a straight nose and well shaped mouth, that was at this particular moment parted in an extremely sweet smile.

The body radiated strength that could not be restricted to muscles and sinews, but came from some inner reservoir and manifest in every movement of the long fingered hands, or a twitch of the black curved eyebrows. The voice was deep, melodious, apt to enslave the five senses and created the urge to worship.

'Come forward, my son.'

Derek walked forward until he had reached the clear space before the throne. He inclined his head.

'My Lord Marcus.'

The beautiful eyes that watched him contained a glimmer of amusement.

'You are feeling pleased with yourself. Not unusual for those who have but recently broken the chains.'

'I have come, my lord, to claim that which is mine.'

A murmur rose up from the motionless audience, then ceased when the master raised his hand.

'To claim is to suggest a right. No one in the hidden world has a right, only certain privileges. Those I can grant or refuse according to my will. If you desire to request a boon, say so.'

'I would claim the Princess Marikova as my own.'

The smile was bitter, the eyes took on a baleful gleam, the voice contained the barest hint of a sibilant undertone.

'The sister that is much loved! Whose whims are tolerated! The pampered beauty! The princess of the Draculain royal line! You, newly created partaker, *dare* to claim *her*?'

'I, when a weak mortal, took her in, succoured, aroused an emotion in her breast she said was love. Then, because of my kindness ...'

The master smiled, but did not interrupt.

' ...I was persecuted, hunted by the pack, driven into the grey wilderness of despair, until finally that which had been given me by the Lady Annanova, ripened under the rays of a full moon. I have earned her. I demand she be mine.'

The Lord Marcus's humour became so intense it threatened to emerge from his eyes as death-dealing golden spears.

'Such insolence arouses my more than slightly contemptuous admiration. But let me summon the lady and hear her opinion.'

A tall plump person attired in a long red robe called out in a loud voice:

'Her Satanic Highness the Princess Marikova is hereby requested and instructed to wait upon the Great Lord Marcus.'

She came from behind the altar, dressed in a white shirt and tight-fitting blue satin shorts and matching ankle socks. She looked young and appealing. She turned and bowed low to the Lord Marcus and spoke in the lilting voice that Derek remembered so well.

'You summoned me, my lord. I wait upon your pleasure.'

The master extended a hand. 'Come and stand beside me for I delight in your presence.'

She took his hand and allowed him to draw her to his side, where she stood looking down on Derek, the master's arm around her slim waist. The Lord Marcus kissed the palm of her hand and spoke softly.

'Look well on the face of this being who has but recently been elevated to the status of undead. Would you belong to him?'

Marikova smiled so sweetly and looked upon Derek almost lovingly.

'I would he belonged to me, my lord. He would make a pretty toy for me to play with when the black depression of eternity turns my mind into a sunless forest of conjecture.'

The Lord Marcus turned his eyes upon Derek.

'Are you prepared to worship from a humble position? Such a practice was once called chivalry, I believe.'

Derek the man would have agreed. Derek the vampire looked proudly up at the master and spoke what he knew to be the truth.

'Male – no matter the species – can never be subjected to the will of the female. When all the protests have been uttered, the theories ranted, the bras burnt, the tears shed, the slogans shouted – then will the basic truth make itself heard. Eternal Woman bows her head and whispers with tremulous voice, "Master, thy will be done." '

Lord Marcus produced a brilliant, beautiful and evil smile and pinched his sister's left (always the left) arm.

'But when the female is a princess of the Dracula line. Surely you will receive her at least as an equal?'

Almost sadly Derek shook his head. 'When female comes to

male, she must lay down all superiority, be it of birth, beauty, or intellect. The wife must walk in the shadow of her lord. That is the way it always has been and will be forever more.'

The High Lord Marcus nodded slowly. 'The fellow speaks no less than the truth, although even I would not have found the courage to utter it. Little sister, you have been pampered and spoilt beyond redemption. Now, go forth and be trimmed by this great being into a more humble shape. Such is my will.'

The Princess Marikova left the shelter of her brother's arm and came to Derek the Vampire and knelt before him. She crossed her wrists and laid her hands upon his feet and uttered the words made sacred by tradition.

'Your will be my will, your road my road, your wish my command. May I become as the grass beneath your feet, the air which fills your lungs, the essence which nourishes your body. Great Beldaza be praised.'

Then the Vampire turned and left the temple, followed by his slave the Princess Marikova.

The sky was overcast, a soft breeze whispered secrets to the sighing trees when Derek and wife time-jumped into eternity.

III
Karl

Typescript of tape recording taken by Veronica Burnside

May 30th 1987: Hello, my name is Veronica Burnside and I've decided to keep a sound diary, which is much more fun than keeping a written one, because it might well be that someone will listen to my voice and hear what happened to me years after I'm dead, which will mean a bit of me will live on.

First of all, I'm eighteen years, seven months and two weeks old, which is pretty old. I mean it only seems yesterday that I was thirteen and even then I thought this must be the old age of childhood, which only goes to demonstrate what an unique sort of mind I've got.

Another thing the unborn generations that may hear this recording will be interested to know: I'm confined to a wheelchair. A riding accident was the cause. Prince, my darling pony, didn't quite make it over a low hedge and I landed in the wrong place. I've had two operations and they do say a third might mean I'll be able to walk again. I hope so. My best friend Carol Makepiece says I'm much too pretty to remain chairborne all my life, for, let's face it, no young man is going to be all that happy about dating a semi-cripple.

My chair is hand-operated; that is to say, I have to turn the wheels by pushing them round with my hands, which in the beginning was pretty tough on my hands, but now I guess they're getting hardened, although I don't get out and about much. Mainly from the back door, across the lawn to the tall garden wall.

I sit and watch that wall for hours. It fascinates me. Well, it was built in 1583. Before the battle of the Armada. Makes me feel very young indeed.

June 1st 1987: Carol called this morning and brought two boys with her. Harry Winchfield who's quite nice looking although he has red hair and Ken Miller who is really quite ugly, but interesting to talk to, which is more than can be said for lots of other boys of his age. Harry Winchfield for example. Kept combing his hair and suggesting he might be interested in me if I could get out and about.

All three pushed off around ten-thirty.

Daddy brought me a darling little puppy that loves to jump on to my lap and lick my face. I'm going to call him Brutus after my favourite Shakespeare character. He'll be company. Well I don't get much. Mummy and Daddy are away most of the day and Miss Crawford who comes in to get my meals and tidy up hasn't an awful lot of time to spend with me, and even if she had there's not a lot we can talk about.

June 2nd 1987: Ken Miller came back this afternoon to see me. What do you know! Seems he got the afternoon off from the architect firm he works for, because he'd put in a lot of overtime for which he's not paid. And he spent the entire afternoon with me.

We had a lovely long chat, mostly about people and things. He says everyone has a terrible sadness in them because they are longing for a world they left behind when they got born here. I know that sounds far-fetched, but rather wonderful. It makes all of us much more interesting. Immortal beings who jump from one world to the next on being born or dying. If I knew for certain that was true, I wouldn't mind dying a bit. Well, who would? It's the thought of being blotted out that's horrible.

Anyway, Ken is a bit above average and has got a little more in his head than football and pop music. He says he's coming tomorrow, if he can make it. I rather hope he does.

June 3rd 1987: I wheeled myself down to the newspaper shop this morning and stocked up with magazines and chocolate, although Doctor Hughes said I mustn't eat many sweets or I'll get fat, not being able to walk about. It rained after lunch which may have been the reason Ken didn't come as promised. I expect he didn't like to call at the house. Well, it's so easy to slip down the side passage and across the lawn, but ringing the front door bell ... He's a bit shy. Eh! Tape recorder, don't get the idea I'm going soppy about a boy who has only called twice – and only once under his own steam. No way. OK. Maybe I was just a wee bit disappointed that he didn't ring the bell when the rain stopped me going out into the garden this afternoon. But that's all.

June 4th 1987: Thursday. Half day closing in the village so I had to wheel myself to the greengrocer before one o'clock, seeing I wanted some apples and dog food for Brutus. And you won't believe this, but Ken was waiting for me outside the newspaper shop and insisted on pushing me home.

No nonsense this time. I invited him in and got Miss Crawford to make a pot of coffee (she looked down her nose a bit) and some half decent sandwiches. Ken explained that he couldn't come yesterday because the senior partner in his firm wanted him to take some plans down to Swindon of all places and he didn't get back until quite late.

After lunch – if you can call coffee and sandwiches lunch – we went into the garden and for a while sat staring at the wall. When I told Ken it was built in 1583 he said he could see that by the size and colour of the bricks. He's awfully intelligent and well read.

He's actually read all of Dumas's historical romances and the *Count of Monte Cristo*. I thought I was the only young person to have done that for miles around.

For your ears only tape recorder. He kissed me just before he left. A real kiss. On the mouth I mean, but he blushed dreadfully after he'd done it.

June 5th 1987: Gosh, I'm het up today. That's an Americanism, isn't it? Het up I mean. I've seen too many American films on TV. But let's settle one important thing right away. Again for your ears only tape recorder, but I do believe I'm in love. OK, I know what I said the day before yesterday, but one can live an entire lifetime in two days. Of course I must be mad. I've only known him properly for less than a week, but suddenly – at three o'clock in the morning actually – I realised he meant all in all to me.

Nothing to do with physical nonsense. If he wanted to bed me down, I wouldn't object, but that's only a tiny bit of what I feel. Our minds contact, strike sparks, make poetry and send quivering messages along the avenues of time.

Aren't I making with the words?

If only … if only … I wasn't stuck in this wheelchair.

June 8th 1987: Not a word have I recorded for two entire days. Well, so much has been going on. Yesterday it was Sunday and Mummy and Daddy said I could invite Ken to tea. Yes, I know that's dated stuff – invite your intended to tea! But the parents are dated. You wouldn't believe! Anyway he came and was so polite and charming. Mummy said he was a very nice boy and no greater praise could be given to any man.

But later after he had gone I saw Mummy eyeing me with a sort of pitying look. Know what I mean? I guess she thinks with me in this chair I can't hope to hang on to a permanent boy friend. But she's wrong. I know she is.

Ken is going to wheel me all the way to the park this afternoon.

See!

June 9th 1987: A marvellous afternoon. Well, all but. When we went down the High Street Harry Winchfield and a couple of other boys I didn't know, stopped to chat and Harry got to be … well … personal. Nasty insinuations. Pretended surprise to see Ken as a nursemaid. Said: 'She can't run away – you've got it made.' And they all giggled and I could see Ken was dreadfully upset. I mean he's shy enough for God's sake. Pushed the chair so fast it's a wonder we didn't run someone down.

For the rest of the afternoon conversation was hard to come by, until I came right out with it – I said: 'Does it embarrass you to push my chair in public where all your friends can see you do it?'

He denied it of course, but I noticed we came back the long way so as not to be seen in the High Street.

The necking session was rather short, but of course it's a bit awkward with me in this chair and nowhere for him to sit. Different in the garden facing my old wall.

June 11th 1987: Ken rang to say he couldn't make it last evening. Seems he had to go to Swindon again. I rather hoped he'd ring me when he got back, but I suppose it was too late. But I'll see him this evening, and maybe if the weather remains fine we can sit in the garden. We could go to my sitting-room and although Daddy wouldn't worry, Mummy ... Well she's the squarer of the two. Probably keep coughing outside of the door, then coming in to ask if we wanted a cup of tea or something.

June 12th 1987: I'm going to call you Tapsy. Seems a good name for a tape recorder and I can now think of you as a person. A Confidant.

So, Tapsy – it had to rain, didn't it? And Mummy had to steer Ken into the living-room and although both she and Daddy kept out of the way most of the time, there was always the possibility either or both might come in at any moment.

Ken sat miles away and I couldn't so much as touch him and I wanted to so much. I did. I know I shouldn't tell you my most innermost thoughts like this, Tapsy. I mean, suppose Mummy were to find this tape and play it back? I am going to hide it behind the tallboy bottom drawer. It runs for three hours so I won't have to start a new one for simply ages.

Well, I'm going to confess something now, Tapsy, that would make Mummy's hair fall out were she to hear it.

Last night I managed to wriggle to the edge of my bed and sit up stark naked and view myself in the wardrobe mirror.

Know something, Tapsy? I'm not half bad. In fact I'd say so long as I keep still I'm not all that far from the winning post in the nudie stakes. Thanks to Miss Crawford's daily massage my legs may be useless but they're still in good shape. And I do mean shape.

Breasts full without being over big and don't tell me men don't put quality before quantity. Slim waist, nicely rounded shoulders – I twisted round to have a good look – a flawless white back that flows down nicely to mature buttocks. And all that is going to waste.

Well – get this, Tapsy – it's not going to much longer.

Mummy and Daddy are going to a Mason do tomorrow night – Saturday. Well, I'm going to proposition Ken. Maybe not in actual words, but he'll be both blind and deaf if he doesn't get the message. And if he hasn't the strength to carry me upstairs, I can go up on the chair lift as usual. Will tomorrow night ever come?

This must be the way to break down all barriers. It must be. It must be.

June 14th 1987: (*Incoherent words intermingled with sobbing cries on tape, until –*) Tapsy, I want to die. Really, really die and become nothing. Absolutely nothing at all. Be blotted out forever. I'm saturated in misery, that bit of me that is *I am*, is one burning pain. I suffer from its reflection on walls, ceiling, the clothes I wear, the food I do not eat, my parents' eyes, even Brutus's drooping tail. He tries to comfort, but a punishing god stands over me and stares down with pitiless eyes.

But, Tapsy, I insist on telling you what happened. Adding my own punishment to that already inflicted. It can be briefly told.

Last night the longer I waited for Ken to turn up, the more I fantasised, until it seemed as if I had created a fraction of the future to my own design. In that future I knew Ken had loved me with all his being since that first meeting in the garden, and desired me so much, that when I gave him the green light, he all but fainted with joy. Do you understand? What I most wanted was an accomplished fact.

Tapsy, I was shameless. I rang him to say the front door would be on the catch and he was to come straight to my bedroom. I'd be in bed. I rather gave the impression the doctor had ordered me to retire early. There was a half formed fear he might call off his visit if I was ill, but I squashed that by saying I must see him. Anyway, he must have got the message.

Then ... then ... I rode ... rode ... the lift chair upstairs, wheeled myself into the bedroom, stripped naked, then ... then ... lay on top of the bed.

The pain of waiting was so delicious, because I knew it would soon be assuaged and after the raging fires of passion there would be a wonderful soothing peace.

I heard Ken close the front door. Then his footsteps muffled by thick carpet mounting the stairs. Then he was on the landing calling out, 'Veronica, where are you?' and I remembered he would not know which bedroom was mine. I answered, 'In here. The door is open.' Then closed my eyes.

I honestly don't know how long a period passed before I opened them again. Only a few seconds I should imagine; but in fact of course it was that vast desert of time that separates an innocent girl from an embittered woman.

Ken was looking down on my naked body with horror-bright eyes, then he shouted – yes – shouted, 'You must be mad! Don't you realise your body is half dead?'

He ran from the room, actually fell down the last few stairs, so great was his haste to get out of the house.

Who can tell into what red hell my sightless soul will roam? I walked into my red hell with eyes wide open and clearly saw every implement of torture. Shame and thwarted desire sear the soul with scars that time will never heal. I belong to the dead, let demons come to fetch my breathing corpse whenever they please.

June 22nd 1987: What a brilliant actress I am. Within twenty-four hours I have donned a mask. No ... no ... a suit of armour that hides my gaping wounds most effectively. When Mummy asked, 'Why hasn't Ken been round today?' I answered, 'Because I've given him the heave-ho.' Then she said, 'What a pity, I thought he was such a nice boy.'

I think Daddy may have guessed something near the truth, because he didn't ask any questions at all, but watched me with something more than pity. Compassion. Who knows, he may even have had a few words with Ken. If so, did Ken tell Daddy the truth? Told him the truth? Told him exactly what happened?

Tapsy, I'm not going to tell you any more.

There's really nothing more to tell.

August 21st 1987: Tapsy, it's me, Veronica. I'm back again.

The mood is upon me to once again pour out bile and listen to it sizzle on tape.

I love to hate men. Let's expand on that. I love to hate,

period. I love to read, learn, be told about something horrible that has happened to one of that hideous sex. I have created several fantasy dreams in which I torture a man – no, he doesn't look a bit like Ken – and take great joy in his screams. He's usually on the rack and although I never tear him to pieces, the thought is there. Oh, yes.

I wonder sometimes if I could turn that fantasy into reality, would I really behave in the same way? Probably not. The entire business would be distasteful. Even vulgar. And I cannot endure vulgarity.

The specialists have finally decided there is no point in my having any more operations. I will never walk again. Chairborne for the rest of my life.

The other day I saw Ken walking – yes *walking* – with a very pretty girl, brunette with deep blue eyes and a pouting mouth. May they grow to hate each other.

I have my hate to keep me warm.

Tapsy, why is it the only really peaceful periods I enjoy is when I am seated at the bottom of the garden looking at the Tudor wall? Indeed, I sometimes think that this is the place where I'll spend more and more time, until eventually I will never want to leave it.

August 22nd 1987: A snake has entered my Eden.

A young man has taken to sitting on top of my Tudor wall and looking down at me. I told him to go away. He grinned. An insolent grin and said the wall was his property and he would sit on it whenever it so pleased him. I toyed with the idea of throwing a stone at him. A nice sharp stone. But I had a feeling he would throw it right back – and hit the target.

I really hate him. Really ... really ... hate him. Well, he's about my age and so beautiful. I can imagine girls falling backwards in droves when he dishes out that insolent grin that uncovers his magnificent white teeth. Glowing white skin and waving thick blond hair that is almost white. And yes – green eyes. I try not to look at them direct, for they seem capable of looking into your mind. Silly. He's well developed, well endowed with muscles I'd say, under that white shirt and blue trousers he wears all the time.

I don't know how he gets on top of that wall, must have a

ladder on his side, I suppose. One good thing, it would be a hell of a jump if he ever thought of coming down on my side.

August 23rd 1987: He's always there now. Well, not when I arrive, but the very moment I get settled down – he's on top of that wall, grinning down at me. I am toying with the idea of getting Daddy to buy me an air rifle. Maybe putting two pellets into his white hide may have a discouraging effect. The trouble is finding a good reason why I should want an air rifle. I could make a catapult.

August 24th 1987: He has given himself a name. Karl du Vallon. Du Vallon! The family name of Porthus! Remember – of *Three Musketeers* fame. It would seem he owns the big house next door, although his family estates are in France. Enormously rich one gathers, which accounts for the arrogance, the pampered, spoilt, over-indulged air that is part and parcel of that beautiful body. Maybe it might not be such a bad idea to encourage him to come down from my wall, singe his pretty wings in the fire of my hate, so that I may delight in his cry of anguish.

I wonder – would he regard my body as half dead?

It might be worth while trying to find out.

August 28th 1987: Dear Tapsy. I am back after a four-day lapse with much to tell. The beautiful thing came down from my wall and I was more than a little put out by the way he did it.

He jumped down. As I sit here talking into this silly little mike, I swear he jumped off a forty foot high wall. Landed on his toes, rolled over on to his left shoulder and leapt to his feet, I've never seen anything like it, not even by an animal. When I expressed surprise – awe – he merely smiled and said it was the result of special training.

Yes, I had been encouraging him. Daring him to come down, you might say, and he made quite a thing about being invited by a person living in our house. Some old continental custom I suppose. But once here, he soon made himself at home. Sat at my feet and looked up into my eyes – and I made him look away. Threatened to go indoors if he didn't. Did what he was told.

He began to sweet talk me. Yes, he did. Told me how very pretty I was and what lovely hands I had – tried to hold one – I snatched it away and lightly slapped his face. Not hard – I don't want to frighten him away – yet.

Strange, but I've never paid much attention to my hands before, but now I keep examining them. Got Mummy to buy some hand cream. Pink stuff, enriched perfumed hand cream, containing lanolin it says on the tube. Know something, Tapsy? I have got lovely hands. That's worth knowing. Fully alive lovely hands. Not half dead.

Come to think of it so are Karl's, the boy from over the wall. His hands are beautiful.

I suppose you could say he is beautiful all over.

Cruel, vicious, terrible masculine beauty.

How I would like to ruin it. Blast it with old age, cover the face with sores and scrabs. Rot those marvellous teeth. Cripple those hands, then let him live for a hundred years.

August 31st 1987. Bank Holiday: Too many bank holidays. Means that lots of people are turned loose on the streets and if I go out in my chair they all stop and stare at me. I heard one woman say, 'What a shame, you poor pretty dear,' which I rather liked. Did I mention that Daddy has brought me a chair driven by electricity? Well he did. Last week. I could have had one long ago, but I was afraid of running into someone. Now I don't care if I run into any number of people. Particularly men – but let's not go into that again.

Karl – why not give him his name? – has become my favourite toy. Sits at my feet almost every afternoon and doesn't seem to mind a bit when I pull his hair and insult him. Sometimes I let him hold my hand and even kiss it, at others I won't talk to him and slap his face quite hard if he persists.

But recently I have detected, or thought I detected, a strange kind of smile that never reaches his eyes. Rather reminds me of a cat watching a mousehole. Relaxed, the epitome of patience, prepared to endure discomfort, knowing a satisfying reward must come his way sooner or later.

Well, he won't appreciate the reward he'll get from me. I'm going to torment him out of his tiny mind.

September 1st 1987: Tapsy, can you even guess what he said to me today? I bet you can't. He said – wait for it: 'How would you like to walk again?'

Just like that. Believe you me, I got really angry and lashed out at him with all my strength. My fingers sank into his cheek, but they didn't seem to have any effect. He didn't even blink. I said, 'You callous bastard. There's no way I can ever walk again. And well you know it.'

He smiled gently and never had I hated him so much. My very blood seemed to boil with hate. When he spoke his voice was different; more mature, deeper, enhanced by a faint accent.

'I only know you can walk whenever you wish. All you have to do is merely ask.'

I could only suppose he meant that to be some kind of sick joke, so I spun my chair round and returned to the house.

September 6th 1987: Mummy must have come home early and watched me with Karl from the living-room window. Last night she came into my room when I was in bed, and taking my hand in hers said, 'Darling, that young man, don't think I'm interfering (they always say that when they do), but do you think you should encourage him? I mean he is so good-looking, and that means he has the pick of all the girls around – and darling – I don't want you to be hurt again.'

I replied. Told the truth as I knew it: 'I don't encourage him. He comes of his own accord, even though I'm sometimes unkind to him.'

But she wasn't convinced. 'Darling, I'm much older than you and know from bitter experience that unkindness is often merely defensive action against a growing regard. A need for more intimate attention.'

I clasped hands to my burning cheeks and all but screamed my denial: 'No, I hate him. As I hate all men. I can't bear him touching me. I shudder when he comes near me. I do ... I do ...'

She took me into her arms and she was crying too. Really crying over me, the always-to-be nagged daughter. She whispered over and over again: 'You must send him away, dear. You must send him away ...'

But I won't ... I won't ... until I've tormented him out of his mind.

September 8th 1987: He's done it again. Told me I can walk if I only ask. I really think he must be mad. And yet – I must be going mad too – because I find myself wondering if perhaps – maybe – he could be right.

To walk again ... To suddenly get out of this chair. Mummy is right. I must stop him coming over the wall. I must ... I must ...'

September 9th 1987: Tapsy – he did it. Or maybe he made me do it – walk. And what a cruel creature he is. Let me remember exactly what happened. He came over the wall just after three o'clock. Jumped down as usual and I've got so used to him doing that I no longer marvel. He squatted at my feet and looked up at me with that disconcerting patient, amused look, and suddenly, without my really understanding what I was about to do, I said, 'Please, Karl, please give me the power to walk.' And he said simply, 'You've always had the power. Walk.' And I got up from my wheelchair ... I got up from my bloody wheelchair and walked ... walked... Walked to the bloody wall and back, then collapsed into my chair, without being able to move so much as a toe.

I burst into tears and struggled like a trapped wild thing to get up again, but the chains of paralysis held my legs in bondage, so that when I went limp from sheer exhaustion, I looked up into his smiling face and spat at him.

'You promised I would walk if I asked you.'

His voice bubbled with mischievous amusement. 'And you did. But I did not say for how long and you never asked.'

My anger and grief merged and became hysteria. The urge to reach the tormentor, then bite, scratch, hit, could not be realised, for he kept well beyond the range of my hands, while his soft, goading laughter drove me deeper into the morass of madness.

I drove the chair straight at him, but he rolled over on to one side, then lashed out with his feet, and the chair lay with one wheel spinning, with me clawing the grass with numb fingers.

He stood over me and never had he looked so beautiful or his eyes so satanic.

And God of mercy, if you exist, never again allow me to savour the bitter-sweet cup in which love and hate are blended, or take perverse pleasure from the urge to crawl to his feet and pay homage to the Prince of Darkness. And yet ... and yet ... why do you permit me to lick crumbs from the floor of hell, for did I not at that moment of subjection come to understand that suffering is the apex of living, while complete contentment is the prelude to death.

But Karl, my beautiful master-slave said:

'My dread sire took the essence of life from those who fell prey to his fangs. I take the essence of immortality from those who come willingly into my embrace.'

On the ground, helpless, quivering with desire – for I knew not what – I still managed to offer a tiny token of resistance.

'Never will I come to you of my own free will.'

He bent down until his face filled the universe.

'Then you have no wish to walk again?'

To curse again was futile, to struggle an act of gross stupidity, so I lay on my side and wept tears of despair. Then I was gently raised up, my wheelchair set again on to its wheels, I seated in it, before lips brushed my forehead – and a voice called out to me from the top of the old Tudor wall.

'When you wish to come to me, then you will walk forever.'

And he was gone. Not so much disappeared, but ceased to exist in that particular place. There was a subtle difference which at that time I did not understand. When I entered the house Mummy and Daddy were waiting for me in the hall and never will I forget the look of dread on their faces.

I was wheeled into the sitting-room and pushed into my usual place by the window, then noticed the stranger who stood by the fireplace. Tall, dark, lean as a hound trained to follow a trail since early puppyhood. Even to my untutored eyes, he could be no other than a hunter.

Daddy made the introduction. 'Veronica, sweetheart, this is Chief Superintendent Pickering. He's commander of the local – B Squad. A sort of special branch of the special branch – as I understand it. Superintendent, this is our daughter Veronica.'

The superintendent inclined his head. 'Miss. I'll get down

to essentials right away. The B Squad – known among the lads as the Bleeny – are specially trained, which is how it should be, seeing that they have special duties to perform. Not to beat about the bush, Miss, we track down and destroy Bizarres. Monsters of every form, but mostly vampires. Partakers of blood. That's why our official title is the Blood Squad. Follow me, miss?'

I nodded, although only about half of what he said soaked in.

'Splendid. I could see you were a bright young lady at first glance. Now, you've a certain person living next door that answers to the name of Karl du Vallon. Our informants say you've been seeing quite a bit of this person. Perhaps you'd be so kind as to confirm this.'

I cleared my throat. 'I know a young man who is called Karl.'

'Ah! Just so, miss. Only he's not so young. In fact I'd say he's pushing three hundred and fifty-five, give or take ten years or so.'

I shook my head, having swallowed more than my share of the bizarre for one day. 'No. He's very young. Not much older than me.'

Now the superintendent was waving a finger at me, even I swear playing at being coy. 'You must take my word for it – he's all but immortal. And there's something more you'll find it hard to believe. He's the son of Dracula. True. There's quite a few of the count's offspring around.'

How strange it was to gradually come to understand that this objectional man was stating nothing less than the truth. Then to realise that I had always known Karl was not an ordinary mortal. And now, when forced to look upon the naked face of truth, I didn't give a damn.

Didn't give a damn that the beautiful boy from over the wall was a second generation vampire. Whatever happened to sweet innocent little Veronica?

'Of course,' the superintendent was saying, 'we have to divert the pack. Four of the B's – pardon the language, ladies – that's taken twelve of our chaps out over the years. Kind of royal guard, you understand. Look after the family. We're launching a mock raid on Wittering Grange, the vam's headquarters, that will occupy the pack for about an hour; time for us to put paid to Karl. With your help, miss.'

My mother started to object. 'She's too young – and hooked on him. You can't use my daughter as a Judas.'

Pickering swung round and glared at my mother and in my brain the desire for revenge and the need to serve fought a never-ending battle. I listened to the grim hunter, the blood squad leader whose mission was to destroy the most unique life form ever to walk this planet. The magnificent, evil, beautiful, hideous creature who with a single thought could enable me to walk again.

I smiled demurely. 'Don't be so silly, Mummy. Of course I'll help. Karl has insulted me several times and he kicked my chair over. Superintendent, just tell me what I have to do.'

He dragged a chair forward and sat astride, the back facing me. His eyes raked my face, while he spat out words with a vehemence that suggested total dedication to his calling.

'He's Karl du Vallon, ostensibly a member of an old Picardy family; in fact son of Count Ivad Dracula and the Countess Marikova, both staked in 1896. He is therefore a second generation vampire – a vamling. He has a wonderful body that can only be destroyed by decapitation and or burning. Cremation is the safest and surest way, but I am going to be honest with you, Miss Burnside – we'd like to capture him alive. We've one or two boffins who'd like to find out what makes him tick. Then, maybe, we'd stand a chance of getting at the rest.'

All men are either fools or rogues and this one was both.

I said, 'Suppose you tell me what I have to do.'

His eyes narrowed and he snapped back a question.

'Suppose you tell me what you're prepared to do.'

I ignored Mummy's whimpered protests and Daddy's violently shaken head and explained what I was prepared to do in a cold precise voice.

'I will go to him, being certain of a welcome, for he has ordered me to do so. Then, so he tells me, he will grant me the power to walk.' I raised my voice when Daddy began to protest. 'I know he can for he has already done so, but only for a short time.'

'Then,' said Mr Pickering, 'you will be useless for our

purpose. Any being who can perform such a miracle will have your full allegiance.'

I assumed what I hoped was a sweet smile.

'Why? Had he made his miracle permanent, then he would have been entitled to my gratitude. But he didn't – he tormented me with the promise of a permanent cure if I went to him of my own accord. Very well, I will go to him freely, but take with me whatever is needful to render him helpless.'

Pickering leaned forward. 'A garlic net will paralyse the nerve centre and he'll be like Samson after his close hair cut.'

'Let me see it.'

He slid from the chair and opened a violin case that lay on the sofa. I had a glimpse of steel rods that tapered to a sharp point at one end, a heavy hammer, then a plastic bag fitted with a zip fastener. He laid the bag on my lap and I could see the finely woven net inside.

'On no account open the bag before you're ready to chain him,' he explained. 'The merest smell of garlic and ...' He did not finish the sentence and indeed there was no need to do so. 'When the opportunity comes – pull back the zip fastener, hold the bag by one bottom corner, then one jerk of the wrist and the net will float down over him. The very moment the mesh contacts any part of his body, he'll be paralysed from the neck downwards.' He took a silver whistle from his pocket. 'Blow this, just once.'

I looked down at the plastic bag and silver whistle and marvelled at the strange byways that branch out from the broad highway of life. Then a question slid up from a seething sea of conjecture.

'Why do not you invade his house with your full squad? All armed with a garlic net each. Surely one white body could not defeat a dozen dark ones.'

'If but one of us came within twenty feet of that house, he'd – do something. Disappear, change form, swamp us with a flood, bring us down with an army of rats, drive us mad with a swarm of flies. Only someone who can get near him can toss the garlic net. At this moment you are the only person that I know who can approach within throwing distance.'

I nodded my entire agreement. Karl du Vallon, vamling, heir of a dark line, the rampant masculine supreme, on you I will take the ultimate revenge. After – then will I invite death to seal my lips with the final kiss and go down into the abyss gleefully shouting my triumph across the wastes of eternity.

The superintendent was undoubtedly pleased with my decision, looking forward to some form of promotion if he succeeded in nailing a prominent member of the Dracula family. Mummy and Daddy looked very distressed – especially Mummy – and I? I was basking in a wide awake dream of revenge.

Like Delilah delivering Sampson into the hands of the Philistines, I would deliver Karl du Vallon into the coils of the Blood Squad torturers who would take him apart, piece by piece merely to find out what makes him tick.

Maybe if I do a neat job they'll let me watch.

September 20th 1987: At long last I return to you, Tapsy, my confidential tape recorder. Since I last spoke into your silly little microphone I've been down to hell and back and am in consequence much older. Thousands and thousands of years older. Mummy and Daddy are mere infants who weep and puke around the edge of my aura and sometimes I become more than a little impatient with them.

But they are not important. In fact I have learnt a great lesson and that is: People are not important. But the fruits of their work are.

Leaving a weeping mother, a glowering father and an exuberant superintendent plus an unknown number of B Squad members behind, I ventured into the house that stands behind my Tudor wall, silver whistle and plastic bag containing the garlic net, in my handbag.

Of course unless you're good at climbing walls, which I am not, the entrance is in the next street, by means of an iron gate which opens up on to a rather impressive cement drive.

I expected the place to be run down, I don't know why, but I did. Instead there stood a nice red-bricked house, with window frames and doors painted a cheerful light blue and a multi-coloured lantern lighting up a red tiled porch. I steered my wheelchair towards a single step and before I could ponder on how I was going to push the bell button, the door opened and Karl appeared.

He was dressed in a black satin tunic that buttoned up on the left side and matching trousers. I must confess black suited him and he looked more beautiful than ever. He smiled when he saw me, and bowing swept his left hand round in a gesture that indicated the open doorway.

'Enter, lovely lady. Rise and walk.'

I felt not the slightest doubt that I could walk, in fact had he told me I could fly I would probably have taken off. I heaved myself up from that chair and walked with the confidence of a long distance hiker across the porch and into the hall beyond.

The place screamed money. Expensive walnut panelling, thick pile carpet, furniture that had probably come from Harrods, plus an atmosphere that rightfully belonged to three centuries ago. The drawing room (I suppose that is what you would call it) was a dream in blue and white and equipped with chairs that took away some of my new confidence, for it seemed as if once seated in one I'd never get up again.

Karl did not act like a being who had just performed a major miracle, but pressed me to have some form of refreshment, which included spirits, beer, tea, coffee and a variety of cakes.

There were two questions I did not ask: What nourishment he took himself; would the major miracle be negated once I had brought him low?

I could not eat a thing, but did down a whisky and soda which had the effect of making my head spin. However I retained sufficient presence of mind to ask a very important question.

'Are you alone in the house?'

He nodded smilingly. 'At the present time. The family and retainers come and go, but there's a conference coming up and only I have decided not to attend. Also, I understand the B Squad have mounted a raid on our country house. That will keep the family and pack busy for a few hours.'

So, if I could successfully throw the garlic net over him, there was no one to come to his rescue. He clearly did not suspect that I, the humble female, the crippled prey that he could raise up and cast down, could possibly be used as a means of his downfall. When he was at the sideboard getting me another whisky and soda, I took the plastic bag from my handbag and unzipped the top. I held the bag by the left hand corner between thumb and forefinger. I was ready for decisive action.

Maybe it was the whisky, for after all I'm not used to alcohol in any form, but it did seem that slinging that fine, garlic stinking net over Karl du Vallon, son of the high and mighty vampire prince, Count Dracula, had nothing to do with me. Believe me, I watched my wrist jerk, my thumb and forefinger flick, then gasped when the net flew over Karl's head and settled about his shoulders.

Never will I forget the scream of terror-agony that came rasping from his throat. He flung his head back and emitted scream after scream, writhed on the floor, struggled to free himself from that net, but I'm sure the smell of garlic was paralysing him and sending him mad with either physical or mental pain.

I wanted to rejoice, take pleasure in his suffering, for that was the object of the exercise, but instead I was horrified at what I had done; wrung my hands and ran around like a beheaded chicken, not knowing what to do. Then I remembered the whistle and blew it with all my might and main, for at least the B Squad would know how to alleviate his pain, and to me, at that moment, that was all that mattered.

They smashed windows and came pouring in from every direction, doing an extraordinary amount of damage, most of it unnecessary.

How they descended on to the helpless vamling, pulled him screaming to his feet, pulling the net tighter, until Superintendent Pickering arrived and ordered he be flung flat on to the floor, where he wriggled while emitting muted cries.

I ran to Mr Pickering and grabbed his arm with both of my hands and tried to shake him.

'Please don't let him suffer,' I pleaded. 'Please help him.'

The superintendent looked at me with some surprise, then seeing I was standing, in complete amazement.

'I understood you were unable to walk! Do you mean he actually can ...?'

'Karl du Vallon cured me, as I knew he could. In return I betrayed him. I thought it was what I wanted, but I didn't know it would be like this. Maybe it's necessary to confine him ...'

'Take him to pieces, Miss. We've got to add to our knowledge about vamies. And don't worry too much about him suffering. He can in time overcome all discomfort and even heal wounds by sheer mental power. We can't be too careful. Given half a chance and he'll hypnotize my chaps, anything up to a dozen at a time. I'd put nothing past him. See, he's quietening down now. He'll start up again when we come to move him. Disturbs his concentration, but that can't be helped.

'In the meanwhile, Miss, I'd like to thank you for making his capture possible. You'll find HM Government will not be ungenerous in a discreet sort of way. And – and congratulations on your miraculous recovery. An ill wind that blows no one any good and all that.

'Just one thing more. I'd be obliged if you would travel to London and make a full report there, detailing your full relationship with the vamling. Our commander will want to question you. Most essential.'

Tapsy, I can't express the stress that almost drove me out of my mind during the night and part of the following day. Firstly Karl screamed again when they came to move him into a blue van, but Mr Pickering insisted his distress would lessen as the journey to London progressed. Then I was beset by the fear that he would change me back into a cripple so soon as his full powers returned, always supposing he was allowed to recover at all. And that tormented my conscience like a nest of wasps on a raw wound. They were going to dissect him, take him to pieces, destroy that beautiful body piecemeal.

I rode in a police car with Mr Pickering and we followed hard on the tail of the van in which Karl lay, still confined in the garlic net.

I don't know exactly where we finished up, but I believe it was in the vicinity of Victoria Station. We glided under a long archway and pulled up at an immense double door that was reinforced by iron bands and equipped with two black handles.

They carried Karl into the building on a kind of stretcher with removable railings on both sides and each end, and although he moaned it did seem he had the pain caused by the garlic net under control. As the superintendent was fully occupied and no one seemed to be paying any attention to me, I followed the stretcher through a number of narrow passages, until we came to an open space that was two parts surrounded by black iron doors criss-crossed by silver bands.

I seemed to remember reading or being told that a vampire cannot pass through or over silver.

Certainly Karl released a gasping cry when they carried him into one of the small cells.

Me – I hid behind a pillar while wondering what they would do to me if I was discovered this far into what had to be a top security building. Put down, I supposed. Extermination or whatever terms they have for murder in the B Squad. But I was not seen, Tapsy, and when the men had disappeared down another passage I crept to the door leading to Karl's cell and pushing aside a panel that covered a peephole, looked fearfully inside.

Karl was still lying on the stretcher, which had now developed four short legs, looking blankly at the door. The moment he recognized me a growl of rage emerged from his gaping mouth. A growl that gradually dissolved into words.

'When I am free from this stinking net, there'll be a reckoning.'

I stammered my lame excuses. 'I never wanted anything like this, I swear. If there's anything I can do ... absolutely anything.'

For a while I thought he had lapsed into unconsciousness for he was so still and silent, then I heard his voice again, speaking laboriously.

'Telephone ... 246 8091 353 ... Sector 29 ... red emergency.'

I repeated the numbers and words over and over again for I suspected they represented my salvation, and eventually got them committed to memory.

Then came the problem of getting out of the building and finding a telephone. I said goodbye to Karl and again expressed regret for my part in his capture, but he made no reply for I think he had put himself into some kind of trance. I went back down the passage, mentally repeating that telephone number and message and wondering what it all meant, but not really caring so long as it was the means of setting Karl free.

Fortunately I was back in the main building before I met Mr Pickering, who had apparently been looking for me. He frowned and consulted his watch.

'Your interrogation should be well under way by now. Where the hell have you been?'

'Looking for the ladies' cloak room,' I replied with a calmness that amazed me. 'And I've still to find it.'

'If you'd asked, I could have saved you and myself a lot of trouble. You will see a door marked Ladies over there. Will you kindly be as quick as you can, as the Commander hates to be kept waiting.'

I ran to the door marked Ladies thus giving a demonstration of a lady in dire distress, hoping it might contain a telephone, but it didn't. It did house a hard-faced middle-aged female who had muscles in lieu of curves, who watched me with beady eyes when I made a quite unnecessary visit to a cubicle, then washed my hands and did a few repairs to my make-up. Not a lot, just a touch of lipstick, but enough to produce an unwelcome comment.

'You shouldn't be using that muck at your age and with your natural complexion.'

I didn't like the way her eyes did a mental stripping job and made a bolt for the door. I found Superintendent Pickering again studying his wrist watch and making tut-tutting noises when I appeared, then with an abrupt, 'All right, follow me,' turned into the passage that I knew led to the cells, but veered into a right hand fork that I had not noticed. We stopped at a mauve door decorated with tiny bright green carnations that framed each panel.

Mr Pickering coughed, then tapped gently on the top left hand panel. A high-pitched voice called out:

'Enter.'

I did not expect such a gorgeous retreat in this place of grim purpose. The mauve door was most certainly in keeping with pea-green walls, bright pink ceilings and shimmering silver window curtains. And the personage of indistinguishable sex who sat behind a baroque desk made from polished silver pine.

He had blue tinted silver hair that hung down to his shoulders, a plump face that looked grotesquely young under a thin coat of sun tan make-up; while bright green eyes that glittered from a nest of puffy flesh, reminded me of a rather vicious, self-indulgent lethal snake.

But I would have given much for his light green suit, pink shirt and blue flowing tie. His footwear I could not see, his feet and ankles hidden behind the desk, but I was certain it would do him credit.

He spoke with a high-pitched voice and occasionally emphasized a point by waving a limp wrist.

'Come in, chicken. Pull up a nesting box and let's hear the cackle.' His wandering gaze hardened when it alighted on me. 'What have we here? As nice a piece of minced leg these eyes have seen for a long time. Grabable, spankable and shagable for those who have the right equipment. But I'm told you have a song to warble, a ditty to hum. My old luggies want to hear. Open that delicious beak and give out with sweet music.'

'The commander,' Mr Pickering interpreted, 'would like you in your own words, to tell him how you came to meet the vamling and carry on until the time you brought him down. Just keep to the facts.'

That was just as well, for it they had questioned me on my emotional ups and downs, everything I told them would have been suspect. Even while I relived the moment when Karl appeared on top of the Tudor wall, I could not be sure what my feelings for him were.

His granting a few moments of being able to walk, then snatching that precious gift back again was an act of supreme cruelty, but I was – thanks to his extraordinary power – able to walk now.

There again keeping him enmeshed in a garlic net which so clearly caused him great agony, was also an act of supreme cruelty, reminding me that I had once read that among the monsters that might exist anywhere in the universe, none could challenge the monstrosity of man.

'Chickie,' the commander interrupted my account, 'I'm enthralled. My luggies are soaking up your melodious-sung words. But what did he say about his kith and kin? The bouncing bos-wam of the loving family group? We don't know what they can do. Probably a lot and all of it nasty.'

I couldn't remember if he had ever mentioned his family.

You, Tapsy will, for everything I've told you about him is on your tape. I knew he was a son of Dracula, but couldn't remember how that little nugget of chilling information had come my way. And I'm certain there had been mention of a Lord Marcus – or had there? Could it be every living creature knows about that diabolical family, but can't translate that knowledge into words?

So I said, 'I don't remember anything he said about his family, but we all know about them, don't we?'

The commander groaned. 'Out of the milk-dribbling mouths of babes and sucklings, which don't mean I agree with the principle, although I agree there may be *something* in the theory. Carry on, dazzling one; your eyes alone would do something to my ghoulies, if they were that way inclined.'

I told them about the final miraculous cure, then my feelings when the garlic net transformed a lordly vamling into a screaming figure that must excite pity in anyone who was not a dedicated sadist.

The commander made a wry face and looked upon me with cold distaste.

'Thank you very much, chickie. So I am a dedicated sadist, am I? I'm most humbly grateful for having my complicated character explained to me. Indeed I am. Super, dear, how do you feel about that? Does your penny get a hard on when a vamy gets its come upperence? I do believe I've said a funny. Come up – ... Get it?'

'I think, sir,' Mr Pickering tried to explain, 'the young lady is expressing her natural pity for any suffering, no matter how merited. This is what makes us love the ladies, sir.'

'You speak for yourself, dear. I'm not all that taken by them. I can remember the howling vam of Brighton. She had a round mouth that could suck the whatsit out of a thinny and soaked up twenty gallons of bloody-ruddies in a single night.'

'Not all females are vams, sir,' Mr Pickering pointed out.

The commander expressed surprise. 'Really! I suppose you're right. Trouble is I'm so dedicated to my job, I see fangies when only eye-toothies exist. I mistake tomato juice for bloody-ruddy, and the gasping sigh of gratification for a howl of repletion. Who would hold high office, Pickering?'

'My heart is heavy for you, sir,' Mr Pickering admitted. 'But, sir, to continue with the interrogation ...'

The commander turned his peculiar green eyes in my direction and something like a sneer bared his beautifully capped teeth.

'The pretty little dear who couldn't walk, but now can. Must have captured vamie's heart. Then did the dirty on him. How woman-like. True to life.' He came round from behind the desk and bent over me. I almost gagged when a wave of perfume enveloped me; all but screamed when his dreadful eyes came within a few inches of mine. His voice sank to a harsh whisper: 'And now her nasty old conscience is giving her stingies and she'd like to help the lovely body. He has – hasn't he? What a pity it must be taken apart, but there we are. Now, tell me, how would you like to help him? Eh?'

A soft damp hand crept over mine, thumb and forefinger took possession of my little finger and began to slowly pull it back. At first I thought he was merely being nauseatingly playful, but when an excruciating pain forced a scream from my throat, I knew the fun would be all on his side. I struggled but there must have been muscles of steel behind that flabby exterior, for thresh around as I did, there was no lessening of the pressure on my little finger, until, just as I was certain it must break, he let go and walked back to his desk. He sat there for some little while watching me clutch and rub my left hand, then asked in a kind of lisping whisper:

'Tell your kind uncle – how would you like to help the lovely vamie? Tell me and if I'm pleased with what you tell me, I'll come over and kiss your finger better.'

My brain worked as it had never worked before, for I had to find an answer that would not bring him over to start the finger treatment all over again; and came up with one that was both simple and true.

'I would like to set him free, but I know it is impossible.'

The eyes were like green fire and the voice the angry hiss of a viper.

'If you had given any other answer I would have taken you to pieces. You may know more than you have told us, but if I ever find you have lied to me in the smallest way, you and I, chickie, will look forward to a bone-cracking time.'

Then the smile again revealed superb dental work and he lapsed into high camp.

'I know Chickie won't open her pretty beak and chirp about vamlings and bloodie-wuddie squads, for then I'd have to be a real meanie. And I'd so cry afterwards. I'm such a softie, aren't I, Pickering?'

The superintendent nodded gravely. 'After the last corrective session, sir, you were prostrate for six hours.'

The commander gave me a kindly, maiden-aunt look. 'So don't be cruel to me, Chickie. Never tell me lies, keep pretty beak closed and don't cackle about what you shouldn't. Keep rubbing your finger, it will keep reminding you how sweet I can be for some days to come.'

Mr Pickering inclined his head and taking me by the arm led me from the room. Outside, free from that baleful presence I exchanged fear for anger.

'That man is a greater monster than a houseful of vampires. He should be put down.'

The superintendent nodded. 'I entirely agree, but one must fight the monstrous with the super-monstrous. Believe me, Karl du Vallon will come to fear the commander more than the ghost of his infamous sire.'

'Can I go home now?'

He shook his head. 'Not until the commander gives us clearance. Then I'll lay on transport. In the meanwhile there's a room where you can wait.'

In fact a small cell not much larger than the one in which Karl was confined. It was furnished with a narrow bed and an armchair. Thankfully the door was left open and I was able to find the ladies' room again, where I bathed my swollen little finger, still watched by the old hag, who eyed the injury with a gloating smile.

Of course I took the wrong turning on my way back and began wandering through those innumerable passages, finding that all doors looked alike, mostly opening up on to cells similar to the one I had been given. Then I opened one door and found I was in a small office equipped with a desk, swivel chair and filing cabinet. On the desk was a telephone.

I shut the door, approached the desk, then stood staring at

the telephone. Was it connected to a switchboard or direct to an outside line? A switchboard might prove awkward – more fatal. If an alert operator wondered why a woman should be using this office so late at night and listened in – I could be back in the commander's hands within ten minutes.

Trembling slightly I picked up the receiver, ready to slam it down again if an operator spoke. To my great relief all I heard was the dialling tone. I pulled the number out of the rag-bag of memory. 246 8091. I dialled with meticulous care, heard the ringing tone at the other end which ceased abruptly and was replaced by a quiet, cultured voice saying: '246 8091 speaking.' The message seemed to be blazoned before my eyes in letters of fire. I uttered it slowly, not wishing to be obliged to repeat it.

'353 Sector 29. Red emergency.'

I fancied I heard a sharp intake of breath before the voice said, 'Thank you. We are grateful.' then rang off. I quickly replaced the receiver and left the office with speed and caution, peering down the corridor before emerging and closing the door quietly behind me.

This time luck favoured me for suddenly I wandered into the right passage, for there was a fire extinguisher that I remembered being opposite my cell.

I lay on the bed and closed my eyes, remembered how I had so hated Karl and realising that I now pitied him; and did not the old adage state that pity was akin to love?

To love a prince of the house of Dracula: a being endowed with wonderous powers, all but immortal; the antithesis of human, even though his appearance duplicated man; to allow one's senses to become enslaved to such a creature must result in black despair.

But the wayward heart is the Achilles heel of every mortal and not one can avoid the suffering it leaves in its wake. Happiness is the ounce of gold we try to mine from a ton of ore.

I must have fallen asleep for it was the screams and the sound of gunfire that brought me back into full awareness.

I leapt from the bed, ran to the door and looked out into the passage. Three uniformed guards were retreating backwards, firing revolvers, their faces masks of terror. I could not believe anyone could look so frightened, but when I looked beyond them the reason for ultimate terror became clear.

Deformed giant dogs in broad-brimmed hats and long overcoats. Creatures with tapering jaws, round black mouths, black, red-tinted eyes and pointed hair-tipped ears. They ran forward in a crouched position; moving with incredible speed. I could see three bodies sprawling on the floor behind them.

I cannot be certain if the guards were so agitated they were firing wide or if the bullets were actually hitting these creatures and having no effect. I counted six of them, but know now there were many more in the building, and one B Squad man after another threw their empty guns away and took to their heels. Tapsy, if I could only describe in every detail the terrible climax. If those things – madvams – the pack which guard the Draculain family – had moved fast before, the moment the guards ran they bounded forward, seemed to glide through the air and the one that led had reached the last guard in a matter of three seconds.

Again I can only suppose the madvam struck the guard with one of its long arms, although I could detect no movement, for he suddenly screamed a dreadful hoarse shriek of black despair and crashed to the floor. Another went down almost immediately, but the third was dispatched in a way that I still can't understand.

The leading madvam flung arms round the running man, hugged him – and appeared to *pull him into its own body*. It sounds impossible and indeed it should be impossible, but I saw what happened with my own eyes. A six foot tall, heavy man was completely absorbed by the body of the thing which pursued him. The entire incident could not have taken more than five seconds, and the madvam did not pause or falter but continued to race forward to seek new prey.

Mr Pickering came running from round a corner, a large revolver in his right hand, looking like a man who does not understand or why. He snarled at me.

'Get back into that room, girl. So soon as we get reinforcements in here, bullets will be flying in every direction. Apart from which those bloody things are killing everyone on sight.'

I didn't mention they had already passed me, although the

trail of bodies should have told him that. A uniformed guard came running up the passage and after saluting the superintendent, said, 'The commander requests and orders you, sir, to guard the prisoner at all costs.'

Mr Pickering grimaced. 'Tell the commander that was my first consideration, although if what remains of my chaps can hold out before reinforcements arrive is a matter for serious thought.'

Both men left and I decided that the superintendent's instruction was a good one, so promptly went back into the little room, after transferring the key from the front of the door to the inside and locking myself in. The firing and screaming was renewed, but now some way off, in the vicinity of Karl's cell I assumed.

I don't suppose more than five minutes had passed before I heard the sound of running feet and Karl's voice saying, 'Hold him tighter, but don't kill him. I want him alive.'

I decided against going out and showing myself, for I could not be certain if he would regard the service I had done him sufficient recompense for betraying him.

A few minutes later there came the sound of other footsteps, heavy, suggesting hob-nailed boots that pounded the cement floor as their owners doubled through the passages. They passed my door and it was then that I summoned the courage to come out. I was in time to see the tail end of men dressed in black uniforms jogging into a side passage and thought I could do far worse than follow them.

They led me to a battlefield. In front of what had been Karl's cell, there were anything up to fifty bodies, some appeared to have been transformed into skin-covered skeletons. One was minus its legs. Nowhere did I see a madvam body.

Superintendent Pickering was leaning against the open cell door, his face the colour of raw putty, his hands shaking so violently he could not hold the glass someone was trying to give him.

'They took the commander,' he kept muttering. 'That – that thing has got the commander.'

At that moment I knew that I loved Karl du Vallon. Be he vamling, monster or some kind of god, I could do no less than love anyone who had removed the commander from my life. I could only hope that he wouldn't be set free ever again. But frankly I did not think it to be very likely.

Then it struck me that no one was interested in what I did. The commander gone, Mr Pickering clearly a spent force, I had only to withdraw and trust that no record of my interrogation existed. The B Squad seemed to favour action rather than paper work.

Again it was a matter of following a well marked trail of bodies until I reached the entrance. I hired a taxi to take me home, then got Daddy to pay the fare.

Oh, Tapsy. I'm so frightened and unhappy. More unhappy than frightened.

September 20th 1987: There has been no mention of what happened at the B Squad headquarters in the newspapers. And no one has bothered me. I did not tell Mummy and Daddy the full truth and explained my swollen little finger by saying I had shut it in a car door. But what they do know has aged them dreadfully. In a way I feel guilty.

The house behind the wall appears to be empty.

September 29th 1987: Mummy was taken to hospital yesterday. And Daddy looks dreadfully ill. He keeps looking at me reproachfully and saying, 'You no longer love us. In your heart you wish us both dead, so you can do ... whatever it is you want to do.'

That's not true ... not true ...

October 8th 1987: Daddy collapsed in the street and I don't think he'll come home again. It's an awful business visiting two different hospitals, and I try to do them on alternative days. Waste of time really. I mean there's little to talk about and Mummy keeps crying and going on about what a nice boy Ken was and shouldn't I look him up now I can walk again. What a hope! When I look *him* up, he'll be grateful to be confined to a wheelchair.

And Daddy! That look! As though he knows more about me than I do myself.

Tapsy. I do believe I am beginning to hate him. I really do.

October 10th 1987: *Tapsy. He's back. Karl was on top of the wall.* Oh, mighty Beldaza, I'm so happy. Tonight I'm going to join him. I'm really going to become a member of the family.

Tapsy – how lucky that Mummy and Daddy aren't here. No one to interfere. My soul is my own – for a little while.

IV
Gilbert

The wind sang of despair round the house and deposited gale wuggles in the old chimney pots. Now and again it dealt windows and doors a mighty buffet as though trying to force an entry.

Former Sergeant Major William Wildeforce wondered how many slates would be missing tomorrow morning, thereby involving him in further expense, as though the place hadn't cost him enough already.

Wildeforce had served in the Queen's Light Infantry for twenty-one years, which entitled him to full pension at the age of forty-four, that when added to an income derived from investments left him by his grand-father, meant he could live quite comfortably doing whatever he wished.

Buying old houses for example, renovating them, then selling for a handsome profit: that had occupied him for the past two years – until he acquired Heron House.

It stood on the top of a cliff, the front windows acting as frames for a complete seascape, so long as the viewer sat on a chair and did not bob about too much. This unusual phenomenon did much to persuade William Wildeforce to retain Heron House and live in it himself. But a wind that often howled in from the north sea played havoc with roof slates and had been known to blow in window panes.

Strangely for a man who had spent a lifetime surrounded by other men, Wildeforce never felt lonely. In fact he derived certain satisfaction from this newly acquired solitude, making him realise that he had always been a private person, who had been forced by his chosen profession to lead a gregarious existence.

But on a stormy night such as this one, he had to admit

some congenial company would not have come amiss.

The crash of a fallen slate made him grimace, the bedlam of sound which was comprised of sea pounding rocks and the wind, was nigh deafening.

The house he knew to be solid. It was built of massive stone blocks and the foundations went down some thirty feet, providing roomy, cool and dry storage space. He had been informed that below the cellar was a series of passages that ran down through the cliff, constructed in the days when smuggling was rife on this stretch of coast.

But now, on this particular night when the worst storm for twenty years roared about the old house, a flaw suddenly developed in the cliff; a massive lump of chalk broke away and crashed into the boiling sea below. This weakened the main cliff face and a shuddering crack went racing under the house, loosening a mass of rock rubble that had been laid down two centuries before; this fell into a great cavity that had not been there when the house was built, resulting in part of the cellar floor collapsing.

William heard the crash and thought for a moment the house was about to tumble down around his ears.

He went down the cellar steps and saw by means of the electric bulb that still burned, a cloud of dust, through which could dimly be seen a gaping hole that seemed to go down a long way. When he clambered down some little way he found the foundation was still intact and what the subsidence had uncovered was a series of underground rooms.

They were mostly filled with rubble, but he was able to make out former chambers roughly twelve feet by eight, each one connected to the next by open doorways. It would undoubtedly cost a lot of money to remove all the rubble and even more to restore the original floor.

He did nothing that night, merely shut the cellar door so that no more dust could mar the spotlessness of the upper rooms, which he maintained in a rather alarming military neatness. But next morning he endured an uncomfortable and dirty experience clambering over lumps of fallen masonry, slipping into piles of grey dust, while looking for the opening to a passage he was certain ran down through the cliff to the beach below.

He did not find the opening, but he did uncover the body of a young man.

He lay on the ruined remains of a couch, partly dressed in the rotted remnants of what could have been a shroud or protective sheet. His face, hair and hands were coated with dust, and William just could not understand how the lad – he could not have been more than seventeen – came to be under his house.

Then a hand moved. He touched it. It was warm.

*

Ex-Sergeant Major William Wildeforce knew all about reviving those who had been given up as dead, so he stripped the slim body, washed it in warm water, then, after making certain there was a fairly strong pulse beat, dressed it in a pair of his pyjama trousers that were far too large.

A very good-looking youth, he decided. Rather too good-looking; in fact beautiful might be a more apt description: Smooth white skin contrasting with glossy black hair, thick matching eyebrows and full red lips, all of which would have done justice to a girl, but was most certainly wasted on a boy.

Then the boy opened his eyes and for no reason the sergeant major thought of cornflowers growing on a grassy bank in a country lane; the boy spoke in a slightly husky voice, somewhat enhanced by an indefinable accent.

'So, I am! The point is – where?'

William creased his face into what he hoped was a cheerful grin. 'In my house, lad. I found you in a hole in my cellar and carried you up here. In my living-room. So far as I can see there's nought wrong with you and once you've got the unexpired portion of the day's rations inside you, well, you'll be ripe and ready for a day's route march.'

The light-blue eyes surveyed him with rather irritating amusement. 'Ah! You have told me in a fashion where. What about when?'

William toyed with the word concussion, but he gave a simple and so far as he knew, truthful answer. 'By my watch which was synchronized with Big Ben this morning, it's fifteen hundred hours.'

The full lips were parted in a smile that revealed brilliant white teeth. There was a suggestion of a chuckle before he spoke again.

'I mean what year in the Gregorian Calendar?'

William stared at the youth for some little while, then asked: 'You want to know what year it is, lad?'

The smile widened and most certainly became an impudent grin.

'If you would be so kind. And the day – and the month. Then I will be able to get my bearings.'

'It is Good Friday, lad. April 17th 1987. Can you really have forgotten the year?'

He sat up and muscles rippled under smooth white skin. 'Not so much forgotten as mislaid. Did you mention nourishment?'

William stood upright. There was not much wrong with this young man and it would soon be time to find out where he came from and return him there.

'You're welcome to what I have, lad. Tinned stewed steak, carrots and green broad beans, followed by spotted dick swamped in hot golden treacle. Or would you prefer condensed milk?'

The young unlined face assumed a rather sulky frown.

'You haven't a black pudding?'

The sergeant major frowned in turn. 'That I haven't. Blood pudding! That's not food for a self-respecting Englishman.'

A deep sigh, followed by the ghost of a chuckle. 'But I'm not an Englishman. I will try to keep down the stewed steak.'

William decided to take umbrage. 'Don't force yourself, lad. Just tell me where you come from and I'll drive you there.'

A large, well-shaped soft hand was laid on his. The hand of someone who had not done a day's manual work in his life. The equally soft voice caressed his ear.

'Pardon. I did not intend to offend. But my constitution is such I find it very difficult to keep solids down.'

'Well, that being the case I've some tins of soup, tomato, ox-tail, mushroom ...'

'You wouldn't have any enriched mince?'

'Enriched ...?'

'Never mind. Tomato soup will look right.'

William grunted, not being able to entirely dismiss the notion the boy – in army parlance – was extracting the urine, and said brusquely, 'Tomato soup it shall be. If you feel up to it, come with me into the kitchen, where we can talk. You can answer a few questions.'

It did not take very long to open a tin of tomato soup, pour it into a saucepan, then stir gently. The boy perched on a tall stool and watched the operation with some distaste.

'Now where did you come from, lad?'

'Yesterday. Actual site – here.'

William stirred a little faster. 'I want straight answers. Not double talk. I'm old enough to be your father and some to spare. That means I'm entitled to a little respect. Get me, lad?'

Now there could be no doubt. The eyes were mocking.

'I understand your words and their import. But I have spoken the truth. By yesterday, I actually mean the distant past. The actual location where I was put into hibernation by my most lamented father, was the site of this house. Or beneath it if you wish to be exact.'

William stopped stirring. 'Distant past! How long were you down there?'

'So far as I can reckon ninety-one years. My father sought me out on his last visit to England, but when he found the B Squad was hot on his trail, put me to sleep, before sealing me up in one of your secret rooms. That would have been in 1896.'

William recalled his sergeant major voice back into active service. 'Don't tell me the old story, lad. And I've warned you about taking the mickey – extracting the urine. Unless you want me to dig out my old swagger cane, don't give me any more bull. Now, I want to know where you live and how the hell you came to be in my cellar.'

The beautiful eyes positively glittered with sardonic amusement, but his voice was that of a repentant child.

'I did not intend to irritate you, sir, but I cannot improve on my explanation, which I have given you. Let us say I have no memory of that period which includes your lifetime, or even possibly that of *your* illustrious father.'

'I never knew my father,' Wildeforce said bitterly. 'He

disappeared the day I announced my imminent arrival and was never seen by my mother again. Well if that's the best you can do in the way of explanation, you'd best be on your way. After you've had this soup which I've taken the trouble to prepare.'

The young man sipped hot tomato soup with extreme caution, and several times rubbed his stomach as though to circulate the liquid. Eventually he emptied the bowl, pushed it to one side, then patted his head.

'My head is becoming wozzy. This I believe is the result of hot liquid sending steam up to my brain. I cannot but help think that essential fluid will have to be a must in the near future. But now, sir, do you insist that I leave your home?'

William experienced a softening of purpose. After all the boy was not much more than a kid, who a short while ago had been covered with dust and unconscious in his cellar. Could he really turn him loose, suffering from concussion, which no doubt was responsible for all this rambling about his age and his father burying him under the house.

'Haven't you anywhere to go, lad?'

'Please, my name is Gilbert. That is to say my English name. And how shall I address you?'

'Eh – Wildeforce. Mr Wildeforce.'

Gilbert bowed. 'In answer to your question, Mr Wildeforce, I have nowhere to lay my body down, save the empty space beneath your house. And I have no one who would wish to claim me. I place myself at your mercy, sir.'

William scratched his head and tried to bring some kind of military order out of the civilian-like disorder in his mind. He didn't want a scatter-brained youth invading the privacy of his domestic Utopia. On the other hand he had a thwarted father instinct that years of military service develops in most senior NCOs and he wouldn't feel happy unless he could hand the boy over to someone who would be responsible for him.

'Look, there must be a mature person who more or less is responsible for you. You can't be more than seventeen – and don't let's have any more nonsense about ninety one years – a joke's a joke, but repeated too often it becomes a bore.'

'I will be seventeen if that so pleases you. And I do believe Great Uncle Manfred and Great Aunt Griselda are within two hundred miles, somewhere in a south-easterly direction, but they will not want to take charge of me. They didn't my cousin Zena, but she's a big girl now. And of course there is the Lord Marcus and the pack. Yes, they will seek me out sooner or later. In the meanwhile I am yours to dispose of as you will.'

William allowed his brain to relax, his resentment to dissolve, the tiny spark of fear to be extinguished – for the time being – and admitted that it would be a nice change to have some youthful company.

'Well, you can stay for a day or two, until you've found your feet, so to speak, or someone claims you.'

A smile transformed the young face into that of an angel – of one kind or another.

'You are indeed very kind, Mr Wildeforce, and I am indeed very grateful.'

Officer material, William decided. Sooner or later a ruddy great car would drive up and Sir this and Lady that would be demanding the return of their wandering boy. In the meanwhile ...

'You've still not explained to my satisfaction how you came to be in that hole.'

Gilbert never did explain that phenomenon – not to William's satisfaction.

*

Days passed and William began to realise that before Gilbert's arrival, he had been lonely. He had not been aware of this state of being, that some people maintain is a fatal disease, until it had been remedied. Not that the boy was of any use around the house, being incapable of even making his own bed, but his very presence seemed to generate interest that was not without an element of excitement.

One incident disturbed the tranquillity that William had come to value and started his enquiring mind on a trail of conjecture that never reached a positive end.

He insisted that Gilbert accompany him on an early morning jogging session, having retained the military belief that regular exercise is essential if one is to maintain a healthy body. They invariably ran across the downs, along a cart track that marked the limit of Willow Farm, then came back to the main road.

Willow Farm kept a large, rather savage dog that was normally confined to a running leash which did not stop the brute from barking and straining to get at any passerby.

One morning just as William and Gilbert were jogging along the track, the dog in a frenzy of rage bounded forward, causing the leash, which most probably had been weakened by innumerable other attacks, to snap.

William saw the great animal – it was a German Shepherd dog – bounding towards them with some alarm, but he remained calm and laid a hand on the young man's arm.

'The worse thing we can do now is to run. Stand by me and stare the brute out. It may not work, but it's about the only thing we can do. If it does attack aim a kick at the balls.'

The boy growled.

There was neither the time nor inclination to investigate this behaviour at that moment, for the dog cleared a low hedge and came for them with lather-dripping jaws, its eyes blazing with hate.

Not for the first time in his life William Wildeforce felt a wave of that fear that can so easily erupt into unreasoning panic rise up from his stomach and flood his brain. In the next second he could well have disregarded his own advice and broken into a mindless run.

Gilbert went down on to all fours and growled again. The hair on the back of his neck stood upright, his spine seemed to bend into a pronounced curve; when his head jerked round his eyes were red, blood-red, as though all the pigment had been removed, thus exposing the blood vessels.

The dog all but fell over when it stopped its mad rush forward, then, after a moment or so spent in staring at the crouching boy, it released a terrified howl and tore back to the hedge which it forced its body through, so great was the need to swiftly increase distance between it and the source of so much terror.

Gilbert stood up and wiped foam from his lips.

Without a word spoken, they resumed their slow steady jogging and presently came back to the house, where William made a pot of coffee and opened a packet of bacon. Later he watched the boy eat his sparse breakfast – fried black pudding and a few scraps of near raw liver, before asking, 'What the hell are you? A throw back? A madman?'

Gilbert spoke without looking up. 'I am a vamling. Or if that is too much for you to take in – the son of a super being. There were a lot of them around at one time. Read your Mosaic bible. Then the meat-eaters grew in numbers and at first adhered to our ways and religion. Then came the various Christian creeds that declared we and our ways evil. They slaughtered those they did not understand, perverted that which did not confirm their dogma. Do not again ask me what I am. Instead accept me for what I appear to be.'

William ate his bacon, crunched his fried bread, drank his strong sweet coffee. 'Would you harm me?'

'Only if you threaten my existence. Then I would summon the pack. So soon as I am acclimatised I will journey to the court of my Lord Marcus, assuming he is still head of the family and incumbent of the Draculain throne.'

They had washed up before William spoke again.

'Why did your father bury you under my house?'

'Not bury, hid me in one of the underground rooms. Then he gave me deep, deep sleep so I would not need nourishment. This was to save me from certain destruction – and as you can see he succeeded. But not for himself. Him they put down, together with my mother.'

'Will anyone come looking for you?'

'The pack and the family sooner or later, yes. Otherwise only if certain people find out I exist. Then *they* will come with their violin cases, the ideal container for stakes and other destruction equipment. But after all this time I must have been wiped from human records. Even the great Lord Marcus may not lower his gaze to observe that I still partake from Beldaza's bounty.'

William wiped his hands dry on the wiping up towel.

'Today we will work in the garden. This afternoon we'll look for shells on the sea shore. Tonight we'll wander the star lanes.'

Gilbert smiled gently and looked upon his newly acquired foster father with narrowed eyes.

'Your mind is losing its thick overcoat and soon the soul of a poet will shiver in the cold dawn of creation.'

*

The next few months became Eden-time for William Wildeforce and he tasted that special brand of happiness that is rarely granted to mortal man. Gilbert became a canvas on which could be painted the ideal picture of the dream-son; the companion who would gild the drab approaches to old age. The creation formed from the bright hues of eternal youth.

But no Eden is complete without its serpent.

The man with slate-coloured eyes stepped out of the shadows and smiled ingratiatingly before asking, 'Mr Wildeforce?'

William tried to escape from the street lamp light, but the short thin figure was now between him and the wall.

'That's me. What can I do for you?'

A hand came out and caressed his arm, the voice sank an octave; the weasel-like face radiated friendliness; invited confidence, intimate secrets that would be forever locked in the brain. For a while William thought he was confronted by a well-programmed computer that could drain his own memory bank dry. The voice seemed to speak in a hissing whisper.

'Could we go somewhere private. I need only fifteen minutes or so to convince you.'

William breathed a little easier. A door to door salesman. A commonplace nuisance and one that could be soon dismissed. Not what he had dreaded at all. He could even afford to be kind.

'All right. What is it you're selling?'

The slate-grey eyes grew a little brighter.

'Treachery.'

The single word exploded in his mind and sent cold tremors coursing through his entire body.

'What?'

The voice and eyes worked in unison and robbed him of free will.

'We believe in always following the narrow path of truth, although this does sometimes delay that all important signature on the contract. But, sir, we do – are in fact noted – for our perseverance.'

Evil dressed in a smiling face. Temptation delivered by a suave voice. William wanted to run and never walk under a naked sky again, but he was powerless to do or say more than:

'My house is nearby. Will you follow me?'

The man nodded. 'That was my intention.'

Walking was not an action, but a mishap resulting from a crippled will; opening the front gate, failing to make the stranger take the lead, submission of the most degrading kind; unlocking the front door and this time succeeding in motioning that undersized figure into the hall, the ultimate surrender.

In the living-room the small man seated himself without waiting for an invitation, then after fumbling in an overcoat pocket presented a white business card. William read:

BOUNTY HUNTERS LTD.
  Best prices paid.
  Presented by:
  B. Rodent.

He sank into a chair opposite his uninvited guest and breathed a question.

'What is it you require from me?'

The smile broadened and revealed large yellow teeth.

'I would prefer, sir, to reverse that question – what do you require from us? We really do pay the best prices. Particularly when you have such a marketable commodity to sell. A commodity that is at this moment trotting some three miles to the south across the downs. Our detector van picked him up – on the screen of course. Don't worry, sir, an associate will give me the whistle when the commodity comes into view.'

William struggled to leave his chair, but B. Rodent flicked a forefinger and it was as though he had been punched in the chest. He experienced difficulty in speaking.

'What the hell is it you want from me? That boy ...'

The face came nearer until the eyes became great red-flecked grey pools that reflected an alien sky. The voice now came in on a foul smelling wind that had blown over the cess-pits of hell.

'Not boy, sir. Not boy. Rather a young-looking ancient, if the very concept of time could be applied to his race. Or if you prefer – a powerhouse with an unwearable exterior.'

'I ask again – what do you want with me?'

The face retreated a few inches. 'Since you put it like that, sir, let me draw a picture. This commodity can be disposed of marketwise in a variety of ways. The B Squad will give quite a bit, but not enough. Official sources never have what you might call unlimited funds. Too many knives cutting the same cake. Then there's the Inter-Dimension-Slavery Corperation. Another matter entirely. Get them interested and one dribbles, if you get me. Promise them a trouble free delivery, no interference from the pack – has he told you about the pack, sir? Might as well give up if they get on to your track. But as I was saying – troublefree delivery and the IDS won't quibble over a few million. And I'm not extravagating. I extravagate not.'

'You want me to sell Gilbert to you?'

B. Rodent permitted himself a pale smile. 'Gilbert! That's the name he's using now? Well, what's in a name? Sell has a rather nasty ring when connected with a being that looks like you and me and can spit just as long. I prefer commercial disposal, sir. We dispose, they commerce. More gentlemanly. Now, have I got you interested?'

William fought to free himself from the reptilian stare and succeeded in so far as he was able to express disgust and indignation.

'You want me to sell the lad – yes lad – he will always be that to me – to sell him into some kind of slavery? I intend to notify the police ...'

Two hands came out and gripped his knees and exerted such pressure he all but screamed, but the physical pain was nothing compared with the searing agony that blazed across his mind.

The voice now seemed to come from two dimensions.

'We never worry the official mind. Whatever disagreements disturb the usual tranquillity of our commercial enterprise, we settle them among ourselves. Hume interference is not permitted. Ever.'

The fingers relaxed their grip, the agony in his brain abated, his courage, which flowed from an ever bubbling stream, forced him to renew the attack.

'I will do nothing to harm the boy. I will not be a Judas.'

The face expressed hurt surprise. 'A Judas! You'll have no

reason to kiss him, sir. Just say a few words at the right time. Nothing more. And we pay – or my clients – pay well for good honest treachery. A blank cheque you might say. So much money you won't have to think about it again. Shall we say a million multiplied by a million – then add two noughts?'

'Absolutely out of the ...'

The face advanced again. 'Before you come to a rash decision, sir, take a few days to think it over. If you find sleeping on it a bit difficult, don't count sheep – count banks. Every man has his price. If I've rather under-estimated yours – just add some more noughts.'

A shrill whistle came from beyond the curtained window.

B. Rodent rose.

'I will leave you now, sir. Look for me at every sunset. But – no dilly-dallying. Leave it too long and I'll have to make other arrangements. Arrangements you may not like. Be seeing you, sir.'

William did not remember him leaving. Indeed after the lapse of a few minutes he began to consider the possibility that there had never been an under-sized man with slate-grey eyes who had made an outrageous proposal. Rather, could not he William Wildeforce have invented such an obnoxious being to give substance to the thoughts that had seethed at the very back of his mind, these past weeks.

For could there be any doubt that Gilbert was an exceptional being – creature – who must be wanted – sought after – by someone – an authority – organization – somewhere – who might be willing to ...?

'Love the boy,' William whispered. 'I will never by word or deed even wish to do him harm. Never.'

Truth, like a grey venomous snake crept across the floor of his mind and spoke with his voice. 'You will spend the rest of your life regretting an act of treachery, but unlimited wealth is balm that will soothe the smart of outraged conscience.'

The door opened, closed, then Gilbert came into the living-room, where he became rigid, head jerking from side to side, as he sniffed the air. He spoke softly:

'A stranger has been here. He has left an alien stench behind.'

William marvelled at the speed in which his brain reacted.

'Yes, a salesman. Farm machinery. He was a foreigner of some kind. Italian possibly.'

Gilbert relaxed slightly, but his eyes flashed from one item of furniture to the next. They stopped at the chair in which the stranger had sat. 'For someone who has no need of farm machinery, you entertained him for a long time. I can see his illuminated form that has yet to fade from that chair.'

William shrugged and again could only marvel at his own ability to deceive. 'I was bored and the fellow helped pass twenty minutes or so. Did you enjoy your run?'

Gilbert with one graceful movement sank into the chair and ran his hands over the arms, before closing his eyes and breathing deeply. Carefully produced thoughts took on sound and became words.

'He ... came ... from ... a ... long ... way ... off ... but ... he's ... not ... far ... away.'

'Plough Farm, I should imagine,' William suggested. 'For hell's sake, forget the fellow.'

His eyes were again unveiled and now they reflected the memory of those dreams that sometimes relieve the total darkness of eternal sleepers. The voice carried a hint of self-mockery.

'You must bear with me, Mr Wildeforce, but I can never quite subdue the urge to view the out of the ordinary with instant suspicion. Before I awoke to find myself your adopted son, there was always the need to trust only my own kind. Now, I cannot describe the joy – yes joy – a word we of the hidden world rarely if ever use – the joy of being able to lower all defences and place complete trust in another life form.'

Conscience blazed up into a searing flame and resolutions, oaths and mere promises subdued it to a spluttering spark, while temptation became a bright red ball that went bouncing towards a black bleak horizon.

William meant every word. 'We can trust each other – and that is a very unusual situation indeed.'

'In your world,' Gilbert said almost sadly, 'the expression public duty is often used as an excuse for sublime cruelty.'

William Wildeforce's lease on his particular Eden was given an extension. For the first time in his life he enjoyed an intimacy with another being that was no less enjoyable when he sometimes paused to realise it had grown from an unknown base. He had come to accept Gilbert for what he appeared to be, not what he really was.

Their conversation covered stony ground and produced a meagre harvest, yet there was a certain beauty to be derived from the fragile blooms of trivialities. All the fruits in Eden were sweet, but after a few weeks William began to wonder how the apple of betrayal would taste.

He fought temptation with every weapon in his armoury. Fair play. Loyalty. Friendship. Decency. Playing a straight game. Words were easy to come by and *duty* would keep popping up whenever the mind tried to relax. The memory of that morning when Gilbert had growled and indeed taken on the characteristics of a dog, suggested that just maybe he should be placed in the hands of someone – or some organisation – that could restrain him.

'I do love the lad,' William whispered to an elm tree that stood well back from the cliff edge and had over the years taken on the attributes of an old friend. 'But I must think of what is best for him. And no one has come forward to claim him – unless you count that fellow from Bounty Hunters. And suppose he had another turn like the one when he faced that dog. I'd be helpless.'

But when they sat facing each other across a table playing draughts, all such thoughts fled like dead leaves before an autumn wind and William wished with all his heart that B. Rodent was present so he could send him running with an emphatically expressed refusal of his infamous proposal ringing in his ears.

On such occasions was the planet earth a wonderful place, set in a glorious universe and William basked in a warm feeling of satisfaction and came to the conclusion he was of the texture from which gods are made, for surely to resist overwhelming temptation in the sacred name of friendship, had to be a near divine act.

But some malicious god must have picked up that thought and sent a peal of sardonic laughter echoing across the vault of heaven, for the next morning William received a letter from his stockbroker that stated a block of shares that had contributed to the main source of his private income had been wiped out; the following night a gale sprang up and removed most of the slates from his roof. In consequence rain did something horrible to the bedroom ceilings. And to make matters worse he had been careless in the payments of the house insurance.

The next night Gilbert came home with blood on his shirt front and the police called to warn William to keep an eye open for a savage dog that had attacked and brutally killed a sheep.

'Practically drained it of blood,' the young policeman added with undisguised relish. 'Never seen anything like it before.'

A day or so later William found B. Rodent bathing his feet in a pool left behind by the tide. The little man looked up and gave the ex-sergeant major a tired smile.

'Ah, sir! I was hoping to run into you. Save me coming up to the house, which would not have been all that wise. The subject that beds down in your spare room has a keen nose and other senses that we know little about. And there's a nice sunset for a stroll and a chat.'

'I have nothing to add to what I said last time,' William said with at least seventy-five percent conviction. 'So don't waste my time or your own.'

The little man wiped his feet on a large red handkerchief.

'That's being a bit hasty, sir, although I must admit our deal will have to be adjusted if we don't come to an irrevocable decision soon. Mind you I do find that gentlemen are apt to drag their feet, so to speak. That's why the ladies make the best clients when one goes all out for a treachery deal. Promise them deathless beauty and my word, they'll hand their husbands over ready tied and gagged, with half the medicine cupboard in their stomachs. But you, sir, are clearly an honourable gentleman, and if I may be permitted the pun – I honour you for it. Even if your little friend has rather blotted his copybook – a fine old phrase that, sir – you still stick by him.'

'No proof that Gilbert killed that sheep,' William protested.

'Oh, he killed it all right. You take my word for it. The full moon got to him, see. Doesn't often get vamlings that way, but being interred – fine word that, sir, better than buried – being interred all that time must have sort of sharpened his appetite.

'Forgive me mentioning what must be a painful subject – how's your bank balance this morning?'

William Wildeforce almost gave in to an impulse to strike that mean, little, weasel-like face, indeed had already clenched his fist for that very purpose, but the iron restraint forged by years of military training finally prevailed. Instead he clenched his teeth, shook his head and glared before replying.

'My financial matters are strictly my concern.'

B. Rodent tied a shoe lace with slow precision, then tilted his head to admire the perfect bow. 'That is true, sir. Very true. But I can't help thinking to have your slate wiped clean of all money worries, would be a great relief. Sir, admit, I only speak the truth.'

William clamped hands to his ears and cried out so loudly a flock of seagulls went flapping out to sea, while making the morning hideous with their lost-souls cries. 'I'll not listen. I'll not listen.'

B. Rodent chuckled. 'That's what Adam said when Eve explained the joy that comes from eating nice juicy apples. But he did hear. There's no way of blocking the ears when truth is determined to get in.'

'I'll run,' William threatened. 'I'll run out on you. Then I won't have to listen to your …'

'Words that make up the treachery sentence, sir? But what's the point? All I do is tell you what to do, should you ever decide to make yourself rich and healthy for as long as your body is your own. After that …? Maybe nothing. Now, sir, I know I'm wasting my time – of which I have plenty – for it don't take much savvy to see you're a man of iron. There's no way I'm going to talk you into selling your pretty young friend down the river. So, humour me, sir, then I'll have done my best and will be going about making a little adjustment to the deal.'

'Well …'

'Only take five minutes. And you needn't listen if you don't want to.'

William made a great business of expelling his breath as a vast sigh of exasperation.

'Very well, if you insist. In fact it might be interesting to hear you talk.'

The little man bared his yellow teeth in an enormous grin and waved his hand in the direction of a low, squat rock.

'Let us be seated, sir, for to rest the body is to refresh the brain. And if your excellent brain is refreshed, sir, anything may happen.'

'Not what you hope,' William retorted, seating himself, then grimacing when he realised this meant B. Rodent would be seated beside him. The representative of Bounty Hunters Corporation rubbed sand from his shoes with a pocket handkerchief before speaking in a slow deliberate voice.

'All you have to do is walk with your friend in the sunlight, then when I emerge from – somewhere – say in a loud voice: "This body I deliver to you in its entirety." Nothing more.'

William's laughter was forced. Brittle and artificial.

'And my reward? How will I receive that?'

'The sum agreed – plus the noughts – will be yours the moment the transaction is complete. Swiss bank accounts. Don't worry on that score.'

'And you expect me to consider such an outrageous contract?'

B. Rodent wrinkled his forehead and widened his eyes.

'I, sir? I thought that was clear. I do not expect you to consider it. I have given up. But I'm always on hand if needed.'

'And that's all?'

Mr Rodent rose and brushed sand from his trousers. 'That's all so far as I'm concerned, sir. Our contract – which has yet to be signed – has been adjusted. And let me say this, for remaining loyal to your vamling friend, I admire you and wish you all good fortune. But when the iron of adversity bites deep, spare me a thought.' He performed a deep but ironic bow. 'I salute the captain of an immortal soul.'

He turned on his left heel and walked away as smartly as clinging sand would permit and disappeared round a bulge in the cliff. William went home and spent the rest of that day avoiding worrying thoughts.

*

The iron of adversity did bite deeper.

Like Job William was sorely afflicted. Although he did not suffer from a plague of boils, an unexpected attack of rheumatism made walking a trial and a painful stye made a sudden appearance on his left eye.

His income did not drop further but a flock of bills united to launch a mass attack before which his bank account melted and for the first time in his life he was forced to wonder if he could make ends meet.

And Gilbert became awkward. He took to remaining in bed all day and wandering abroad all night, returning early next morning with bedabbled shirt front and stained mouth. And when William raised his voice and pronounced such words as – ingratitude – baseness – taking without grace – never giving – he became the object of spiteful rage, feline eye-scratching, and other manifestations of displeasure that stopped just short of physical attack.

And the mature, level-headed, no-nonsense ex-sergeant-major stood a little way from the begging-to-be-hurt creature he had become and mourned for the passing of the peaceful years.

When Gilbert crept from the house at sunset and wild life screamed along the seashore and far across the downs, William attempted to obliterate the lonely hours with the contents of the whisky decanter, a weakness up to that time he had always scorned in other men. This resulted in black fits of depression and the mind freezing awareness of another dimension that bordered on the one in which he had been born.

Death peered over his shoulder as he sat on the floor, head lowered, hands clasped round knees that trembled when he tried to relax; he heard the patter of insubstantial feet down in the hall and creeping up and down stairs. Horror can only exist in the black mist of ignorance; knowledge can only produce an anti-climax. Because William Wildeforce lacked knowledge, even in a half-drunken state, his soul became saturated in fear, that in the bleary-eyed aching, foul-mouth reality of early morning, turned to quivering hate.

On one such morning he faced Gilbert in the pale pink light of a rosy dawn and allowed his secret mind to control his tongue. 'If you were not here I would feel the relief that follows the removal of an aching tooth.'

Gilbert smiled most charmingly. 'Yes, but there would be an unsightly gap that could never be filled.'

William took a firm grip on the straw of reality and looked long upon the beautiful face that seemed enhanced by a rose-tinted mist. Truth erupted and for a moment he saw with an eye-searing clarity.

'You are growing strong on my weakness.'

Now a hint of sadness came into the clear eyes and the low voice made an effort to explain the great, unending tragedy.

'Life feeds upon life and man's last act will be to tear the heart from his own breast. His machines will inherit the earth and thus bring down the House of Dracula, for the life force of a million machines will not sustain a legend for a single day.'

William shook his head. 'I do not understand – or want to – people who play with ideas. To me life is a parade ground where every move is governed by standing orders. And I grow weaker while you grow stronger.'

'I never take more than you can afford to give.'

'You are merely a parasite.'

'And you a fool. A freak storm uncovered me. You revived me. You always have the power to dismiss me. But your limbs welcome the chains, your eyes the tinted glasses.'

William shouted and his voice started a series of little echoes throughout the house. 'Don't preach at me. I won't be talked down to by *something* that looks like a pretty boy with a bad temper. Something that should be confined for its own good and that of decent human beings.'

Now he had a startling reaction. Anger, rage-fires reflected in enlarged eyes; the beginning of a transformation – a shifting of the hair line, the merest broadening of the nose – a rasping undertone to the voice.

'Decent human being! How can this rare creature exist when you all unite to kill it – one fine day or foul. Say self-righteous human-being. They grow in rich profusion on the dung-hill of civilization.'

He stopped and looked with stark intensity into William's eyes.

'And you? What secretly invited wanderer strayed into the barren waste of your mind, when you first saw me? What kind of love blossomed under the sun of your regard? The love of a father for the long lost son? Or the lover you dare not think about?'

Anger exploded and became rage. Rage expanded and became a state of being that could not be described in the crude language created by the descendants of apes. And no other emotion could exist in the hothouse in which the brain shimmered like a bright red jelly on a table with rickety legs.

William opened his mouth and made the basic sound that escapes from the throat of that being who is prepared to kill – in one way or another – that creature he most loves.

Gilbert slowly withdrew until his back was pressed against the opposite wall; there he looked upon his benefactor with expressionless eyes.

William replaced the basic sound with the spoken word.

'You perverted little bastard! Never suggest anything like that again, or I'll kill you. I'll do my best to kill you.'

Gilbert now stared at some spot on the floor.

'Your destiny lies in the dust, only you can pick it up.'

William covered his face with his two large and capable hands and wept like a lost child who has wandered too long along the road to eternity and knows there is no way back.

'What must I do? What can I do?'

A hand brushed his hair, a voice whispered in his ear.

'If there is any doubt, then do what you must do.'

*

When William rose on the last day he found the sky had been washed white, then rinsed with blue. Outside a chill breeze wrapped him in a shroud of transparent gauze and in a single moment sent his memory gliding back to the beginning of all things without bothering to record the journey on the active part of his brain.

Gilbert presently came to join him, dressed in a bright blue roll-neck sweater and a darker blue corduroy trousers. He looked very young, beautiful and vulnerable.

He addressed the sun. 'Do what you will this day, but only after very careful thought.'

They walked and jogged a long way and looked down upon the sea from a great height. Gilbert said he could see the soul of a sailor being tormented by a mermaid who had bound him to a rock. Then he pointed to a formation of jet black birds and asked William to describe them.

'I don't know. Ravens maybe. Or rooks. I'm no expert on birds.'

'They are not birds at all. But little witches wearing black conical hats and long matching gowns, riding on broomsticks. The young of all species often see them, but forget what they have seen when they reach adult years. You live in a wonderful world, but only see, never observe. That is why your race is doomed.'

When they arrived back at the house Gilbert prepared breakfast, which was something he had never done before, while William opened his mail. Bills had taken on the appearance of do-it-yourself paper darts each one equipped with a poisonous tip. Letters began with Dear ... and ended with ... Otherwise ... The stench of misery rose up from the breakfast table and transformed fried eggs into the likeness of dead man's eyes.

'Will you not,' Gilbert asked, picking daintily at his usual fried black pudding and half raw liver, 'invite me to take a walk under the noonday sun?'

William jerked his head round and almost choked on a portion of crisp bacon. 'I had an idea you were not all that keen on walking in bright sunlight.'

A beautiful all-embracing smile. Love, friendship, warmth, the promise of eternal happiness shone from those wonderful, clear eyes.

'You have helped me grow a strong, British Army backbone. Now I only blink in sunlight. Soon I will be able to stare at it with wide open eyes.'

'Please don't come if it will at all discomfort you.'

He mimicked William's precise way of speaking.

'*If it will at all discomfort you.* Discomfort means little to us. When it becomes unbearable we erase it. Banish it into Limbo where it whimpers in solitude. Are you beginning to understand our shadow-English? There is a meaning hidden behind each word. Don't try to translate them all at once, or your poor little sanity will break.'

But now William could only think of the terror-joy that would accompany them on a walk under the midday sun and the guilty glittering reward that would be his afterwards.

'*I will buy this ... that ... everything ... I want a million million plus three noughts ... so I need never have to think about money again ... and I will do a lot of good ... lots and lots of good ...*'

The young voice shattered his thought line.

'Well, am I to walk with you under the blazing sun?'

He looked up, the decision taken. He felt very strong.

'Of course. It will be an experience for both of us.'

*

The sun was a ball of white flame on a flawless blue field. The air shimmered with heat, the sea reflected it from a gleaming rippled surface. Bluebottles hummed the summer song and aroused sleeping memories of golden summers that lived and died long ago.

Gilbert did not show the slightest sign of discomfort, whereas William found he was soon soaked in perspiration and his hands and head were by no means steady. And he could not dismiss the notion he walked over a hollow ball that was hidden under a thin carpet of grass and wild flowering plants, while above him a blue roof acted as floor to a place where innumerable universes were made, and strange beings peered down through holes, that at night occupied the sites of yet to be created stars.

A red and white butterfly fanned his cheek, then flew on to burn out its short life in a continuous output of energy, and Gilbert murmured, 'A fire elf,' but did not offer any further explanation.

Occasionally William caught a glimpse of a drifting figure that appeared as a head with long, white hair attached to a trailing white veil. Its mouth was perpetually open and perhaps did emit a kind of whistling cry, but that might have been due to the ever murmuring breeze that rose up from the sea far below.

Without a word being spoken they veered left and presently came to the road that curved gradually inland, to serve farm and meadow until it gave birth to sprawling towns that one day would reach ugly maturity as unsightly cities. Hideous fortresses designed to subdue the already depleted forces of nature.

B. Rodent slid out from behind a cement lamppost. He rubbed dry hands and bobbed his head several times.

'Good day, Mr Wildeforce, sir – and friend. What a lovely day this is to be sure. A golden day, sir, to conduct a golden transaction. A clean, no-nonsense, satisfaction on two sides, transaction. I am glad, sir, you have seen your way clear to coming to a sensible decision.'

'I haven't,' William uttered a protest, rather than a denial. 'You're taking far too much for granted. Far too much.'

B. Rodent hunched his shoulders, blinked his eyes and rubbed his hands so furiously William imagined them evaporating until all that was left was bone rasping bone. The voice was now like air blown through rarely used organ bellows.

'I do beg your pardon, sir. But I did think we had a deal – of one kind or another – under way. I mean, you bring your friend on a long walk under the sun, I can only surmise you are prepared to say the contractual words, for the agreed sum of a million million, plus three noughts, which is at this very moment deposited in a Swiss bank, the needful documents and pass book in my pocket, sir. All that must be done is done – save for the words to be spoken. Just imagine, sir. All that money? Never need worry about the horrible stuff again.'

William gave Gilbert a frantic glance. 'Why don't you say something? Speak, curse me, plead, anything. But don't just stand there looking like a young king who has just renounced his throne.'

B. Rodent assumed a puzzled expression. 'I didn't get that one, sir. What has a young king renouncing his throne to do with our transaction?'

Gilbert spoke for the first time since they had left the downs.

'He is beginning to think in hidden world language.'

B. Rodent expressed pretended or real horror. 'Don't do that, sir, I beg of you. Once you get the hang of that hideous jargon, that has no words as such, just unformed thoughts, you'll learn secrets that will haunt you to the very end of non-existent time. Better bury your head in black fire.'

Gilbert spoke again as he thoughtfully looked at a square black car that had come to a halt some hundred yards down the road.

'Can we continue with the transaction? The sun will not remain overhead for ever.'

The little man with the face of a tired weasel nodded vigorously.

'Your friend, sir, calls us both to rights. We must say yea or nay. Are you willing to say the words that will sell the merchandise – to wit one body of exceptional value, for the sum agreed?'

William turned his back on Gilbert. 'I cannot remember what I am supposed to say.'

B. Rodent narrowed his eyes and added a sibilant tone to his voice. 'Come, come, sir, that won't do at all. Once I've told a prospective client the words, they're etched on his brain. No way can he forget them or me repeat them. No way at all. So you just get your thinking cap on and trot out the right jargon so I can turn you into a billionaire.'

William jerked out one word, spluttered, and thus earned himself another rebuke from B. Rodent.

'Speak up, sir. Never be afraid to let every being in the cosmos hear what decision you have had the courage to make. Let your voice ring out, sir. Make galaxies tremble and suns explode. Shout, sir and become the richest man on earth.'

William took his irrevocable decision. He announced that decision in his best parade ground voice:

'*This body I deliver to you in its entirety.*'

The agent of Bounty Hunters Corporation expelled his breath as a vast sigh of relief. 'Now, sir, that didn't hurt one little bit, did it?'

'No,' William agreed, not daring to look at Gilbert. 'Does that mean I'm now …?'

'The richest man on earth? Indeed it does. Let me hand the signed documents over, for to be frank they've been burning a hole in my pocket for several days now.' He pulled a thin leatherbound book from his breast pocket and took out several papers.

'You'll find cheques here for the sum agreed – a million million – plus three noughts – together with the pass book and deeds that make it all legal and above board. I feel quite dazzled looking at a billionaire, sir. Frankly we've never parted with such a sum before, but it has been a pleasure to do business with you. A great pleasure.'

William, while enjoying the excitement natural to a man who has just received his first billion pounds, did wish Gilbert would go away – or be taken away – instead of standing still as a statue, looking at the square black car which was now disgorging four sinister-looking figures. They gave the general impression of being large and very ugly dogs wearing broad-brimmed hats and long overcoats, that despite the intense heat covered them from neck to ankles. As they drew nearer William experienced a thrill of horror when he saw the tapering jaws, the black wet nose, the pointed, hair-tipped ears, the crouched stance that made them bound rather than walk along the road.

'The pack,' B. Rodent murmured, 'come to collect the body.'

Now William discovered there was no way he could avoid Gilbert's concentrated stare. The beautiful eyes were still lit by an enchanting smile, the smooth hands outstretched as though wishing to embrace his betrayer. William turned and addressed B. Rodent in a trembling voice.

'In the name of mercy, man! Do I have to be present when they take him away?'

The little man created a slight frown. 'Take who, sir?'

'Him. Gilbert. The person – being – the one I have sold.'

B. Rodent substituted his frown with a laugh.

'There does seem to be a little misunderstanding, sir. You haven't sold the truly exceptional body of His Satanic Highness. No, indeed, sir. You have sold your own exceptional body.'

William felt his own world slipping slowly away. The world of trees, grass and murmuring leaves; the place in time and space where those forms called people hide their true faces beneath carefully created masks and one only caught a glimpse of the grotesque in an unguarded moment. He screamed as the pack moved closer.

'No, it was him that I sold. You said it was him you were buying. You did.'

B. Rodent tried to look contrite. 'I must sincerely apologise if I am responsible for this terrible misunderstanding. But don't you remember? I mentioned having to make a small adjustment to our contract, due to the delay when you could not come to a prompt decision. The adjustment was changing both seller and buyer. His Satanic Highness has now purchased you. Or I should say His Satanic Highness and family.

'But you promised to make me a billionaire.'

'And so I have. The money is under your name in a Swiss bank and you have all relevant documents. True, I cannot think of any way you can spend a penny of it, but for as long as you live – and I will not dwell on that prospect – the money belongs to you.'

The pack shared their labour load. They took an arm or a leg each and frog-marched William to the square black car and dumped him on the back seat. Just before they slammed the rear off-side door, Gilbert leaned over the speechless, bulging-eyed man and kissed him full on the lips.

B. Rodent chuckled as the car drove off and dared to nudge the vamling prince in the ribs with his elbow.

'There was no need to kiss him,' he said, 'they knew who he was.'

Gilbert smiled gently. 'Yes, but I wanted to be certain who I was.'

V

Louis

Letter from Hilda McCarthy to Liza Russell, May 15th 1987

c/o Mrs L Brand
23 Sea View Avenue
Broadstairs

Dear Liza,

Just a line to let you know I am extending my holiday by at least two weeks. Mrs Brand – my landlady – is quite agreeable, as the season has not really started yet and there are no bookings for my room for at least three weeks. I think I should tell you that the reason for this extension is – well partly – due to my making a new friend down here. His name is Louis Longchamp and to be frank – as I can be to an old friend like yourself – I find we have so much in common. Similar tastes, books, films – the better ones and those made before 1960 – music and a complete hatred for the present government.

Please, Liza, don't get the wrong idea. This is friendship pure and simple and the fact that this new friend happens to be a man, is beside the point. We met at an outdoor exhibition of modern paintings and Louis very kindly explained the finer details, which without his help I would have most certainly missed. During the ensuing conversation it came out we were both down here by ourselves, and – well – as Louis so aptly put it – 'why not be lonely together?'

We've been together every day since and I have to be frank, I've never had such a wonderful time. Not even when Daniel was alive.

I've told Louis about you – how you're my best friend – my only friend – and he's looking forward to meeting you. Isn't it amazing he only lives a few miles from us – at Hampton Court actually.

Well I'd better finish off now as Louis is waiting to take me to North Foreland Lighthouse, then to lunch afterwards. I'm saving an awful lot of money. He pays for everything. When I objected – well one has to – he said nonsense and when he took his wallet out I noticed it was simply crammed with fifty pound notes. From the way he talks I get the impression he's very well off.

Give my love to Tiddles,
Hilda

Letter from Liza Russell to Hilda McCarthy, 17th May 1987

18 Kingston Gardens,
Twickenham

Dear Hilda,

Thank you for your letter dated the 15th.

Well, the way you carried on about this new friend of yours took my breath away. I can only hope from what you tell me he's everything you'll eventually think he is. But take my advice, Hilda, soak him for a few lunches and dinners, let him have a little kiss and cuddle in one of those glass-sided seating arrangements they have down there, if you feel so inclined, although I would have thought at your age you'd have something better to do; then call it a day. As my mother used to say, you can't beat a nice warm fire, a purring cat, a friend to have a chat with, then a manless double bed, when the years begin to draw in. If you get my meaning.

I might as well mention after all that, that I found Arthur Minns ringing your doorbell two nights ago. When I gave him the good news – you were away for at least two more weeks – he got into a hell of a stew because you hadn't written to him. Not so much as a postcard. I must say, Hilda, I never knew things had gone that far between you two. You never told me if they have.

Tiddles is eating well, but I think she misses you. I found her mewing in the hall when I opened the door yesterday.

Don't stay away too long and be very careful of this Louis.

Lots of love from your friend,
Liza

Letter from Hilda McCarthy to Liza Russell 20th May 1987
c/o Mrs L Brand
23 Sea View Avenue
Broadstairs

Dear Liza,

Thank you for your lovely letter.

Arthur had no business ringing my doorbell and complaining because I hadn't written to him. I mean – I've had a couple of coffees with him and a chat about *1984*. Nothing more. Some men are so silly and if you just try to be a wee bit friendly, think that's an invitation to come share bed and board. Honestly, he makes me sick. Arthur Minns, I mean.

That's what I like about Louis, he's a real gentleman and never even tries to take advantage. I mean, whenever he asks me out anywhere, he always adds: 'If you've nothing better to do.' And if I said – 'yes, I have,' which I never have – I know he wouldn't be in the least put out.

Rather exasperating sometimes.

I must tell you what he looks like. Do you remember Ronald Colman? Well, if you don't, you must have seen him in *The Prisoner of Zenda* on TV. Well he looks like Ronald Colman, only taller. And the same kind of voice only it's got the merest hint of a foreign accent. And Liza, when he puts his hand under my elbow to help me up the steps and sort of half whispers in my left ear: 'May I hope to see you tomorrow?' Liquid fire ...

Good heavens! How I am raving on! One would think I was infatuated by the man, which I most certainly am not. As you say, dear Liza, at my age – forty-three on the 30th – I have something else to do than play slap and tickle with some man – no matter how attractive he might be. We went to the theatre last night, and saw *Pygmalion* performed by the local rep. Not at all bad, but of course missed the music, forgetting it wasn't *My Fair Lady*.

We had late dinner afterwards in a little restaurant facing the sea and Louis told me how Charles Dickens so loved Broadstairs and lived for a while in Fort House – which is now called Bleak House – so silly don't you think? – which does look like a small fort. Much extended since Dickens's time Louis said.

It is really very sweet of you to look after Tiddles, Liza. And I am most awfully grateful. You must allow me to wine and dine you – as Louis would say – when I get back.

Must finish off now. Louis wants to take me out to the Goodwin Sands while the tide is still out.

Fondly and forever yours,
Hilda

Letter from Liza Russell to Hilda McCarthy May 23rd 1987

18 Kingston Gardens
Twickenham

Dear Hilda,

Thank you for your most interesting letter.

Dearest, please don't misunderstand what I am about to say, which is for your own good. I mean, dear, we have a rather special friendship and for that reason I can dare give advice and even criticize – in the nicest possible way of course – a line of conduct that might land you in an awkward, even dangerous situation.

Hilda, dear, from your letters it is becoming clear to me you are becoming too involved with this Louis. You are indeed.

Look – I am going to be awfully, awfully frank now and you'll most probably hate me now, but bless me in the future.

It would seem this Louis is a real dish. Well, if he looks like Ronald Colman only taller, he must be. And he sounds as if he is a lady killer into the bargain. Now, to me, Hilda, you are the most beautiful person in the whole world, because I know the *real* you that lies behind – please don't get all hurt and angry, Hilda – behind the rather homely exterior. Before you tear this letter up, go and look into the nearest mirror and ask yourself a really honest question: 'What have I got a dishy lady killer could possibly want?'

Well, darling Hilda, you have a very nice flat which would fetch a nice sum and a respectable little fortune tucked away in stocks and shares.

Hilda, don't you really think it's about time you came home and let poor old Liza comfort you? I do. Oh, I do. Please think over what I've written and try not to hate me. I couldn't bear that. If I really thought you hated me I'd most likely do away with myself.

Before I forget Arthur Minns has been round again. Wants your holiday address. Of course I refused to give it to him.

Why do you get yourself implicated with these men? I thought we had decided we could do well without any of them.

All my undying love,
Liza

Letter from Hilda McCarthy to Liza Russell May 25th 1987

c/o Mrs L Brand
23 Sea View Avenue
Broadstairs

Dear Liza,

Thank you, thank you very much for your very, very kind and most thoughtful letter. It is such a source of happiness to me to know I have a friend who is not afraid to tell me the whole, unvarnished truth. Indeed, I was not aware of the full extent of my 'homely appearance'. As I believe Robbie Burns put it: 'See ourselves as others see us.'

Do you know what I did after reading your so kind letter – I went into the bedroom, as you advised, and took all my clothes off, stripped starkers and stood in front of the wardrobe mirror. And I was not all that displeased with what I saw. And I think my sight is as keen – if not keener – than yours.

No one could fault my breasts – despite my *age* – which according to you merits a seat by a nice warm fire, a purring cat on my lap and a kind, thoughtful friend to chat to before retiring to an empty double bed. Or am I supposed to share that with the nice, kind thoughtful friend. May I suggest in the nicest possible way, that you, Liza dear, do some soul-searching. And have a good look at your reflection in a mirror.

Although, as you say, Louis may have designs on my worldly wealth, I could see no reason why he shouldn't lust after my body as well. I took the trouble to measure my vital statistics and do you know what I came up with? 38. 35. 37. Not bad for an old crock like me. We can only wonder if you have the courage to take a tape measure to yours, Liza dear. My skin is white and smooth, no sign of wrinkles round eyes and mouth. I know of no one else in *our age group* that can say as much.

Did you know Arthur Minns was raving about my eyes when we had coffee together last? Large and cornflower blue he called them. Louis over dinner last night – 'Auburn hair that frames your heart-shaped face. And very little tinting. Teeth my own and in good trim. Not many old things like *us* can make that boast.

I can't write anymore. I'm going dancing with that fortune hunter Louis who keeps his repugnance for my homely face under admirable control.

Your one time friend
Hilda

Letter from Liza Russell to Hilda McCarthy May 26th 1987

18 Kingston Gardens
Twickenham

Dear Hilda,

I have not slept since receiving your cruel letter. How could you even think such awful things about someone who always thought she was your best friend. Dreadful, hurtful words that should never have come from your pen. All because you deliberately – I repeat – deliberately misunderstood my good intentions. I really do believe you have always wanted to grossly insult me, and used my – if you hadn't been so blinded by *hate* for me who has the misfortune to love you – letter that was simply saturated with good intentions, as an excuse to pour out bile upon my super-sensitive soul.

We are finished of course. Absolutely. I will continue to feed Tiddles and clean out her dirt box until you come home, but no more. Please don't write or try to communicate with me again. It would be like drawing a sharp knife across a raw wound.

I wish you well with your *new* friend Louis.

My best regards despite all that has happened.

Liza

Letter from Hilda McCarthy to Liza Russell May 31st 1987

c/o Mrs L Brand
23 Sea View Avenue
Broadstairs

Dear Liza,

I was very upset after reading your last letter, but after much thought and deliberation cannot view yours of the 23rd with other than pain. I'm sure this is very silly of me but I just can't do otherwise. I have written to Arthur Minns and given him this address so you should not be bothered by him again. If you are at all interested, Louis is taking me to see his family tomorrow. It would seem they have an estate hereabouts. He gave me a lovely gold bracelet for my birthday, which you may remember was yesterday.

Regards
Hilda

Letter from Liza Russell to Hilda McCarthy June 3rd 1987

18 Kingston Gardens
Twickenham

Dear Hilda,

This is to acknowledge your letter dated May 31st.

I am not in the least interested where Louis took you and what he gave you for your birthday. I should have hardly thought it wise to give Arthur Minns your present address. If I know him he'll be down there trying to cut your *new* friend out and generally making a nuisance of himself. But perhaps that is what you want. Have two men fighting over you.

But still that is your concern.

Sincerely
Liza

Letter from Hilda McCarthy to Liza Russell June 10th 1987

The Imperial Hotel
The Parade
Broadstairs

Dear Liza

You will note the change of address. I really just couldn't

stay with Mrs Brand any longer, so I moved into the Imperial Hotel. I shall probably stay here for another two weeks – maybe longer. I did not intend to write to you again, especially after the vile insult in your last letter, but I don't like to be at daggers drawn with anyone, least of all with someone whom I at one time held in some esteem.

Besides – there has been some trouble – and I must tell someone about it or I'll go mad. Arthur Minns turned up at Mrs Brand's house four days ago and created an awful scene. I was just going out to dinner with Louis; me in the white off-the-shoulder evening gown – the one you said made me look quite seductive – and Louis in a really well-tailored dinner jacket; when that awful little man suddenly appeared from nowhere and started shouting. Something about me toying with his emotions. Can you imagine? I've never, but never encouraged that man to believe my feelings for him were anything more than casual friendship.

Louis of course behaved like the perfect gentleman he is. Said in that lovely voice of his: 'Will you kindly not embarrass the lady [me], sir. At this time she happens to be my guest.'

That made Arthur really wild. You know of course he's rather coarse on occasion. Well, it's only to be expected, his father kept a fish and chip shop down in Camden Town. That is a fact. Daniel's father knew him. Arthur called Louis a tarted-up ponce. I've never known what a ponce really is, but it must be something very rude, for Louis from being awfully white – which he generally is – went sort of grey and glared at Arthur until I thought his eyes would spit fire. Then he leaned over him and said in a dreadful harsh voice: 'Tonight you are filled with wine and false courage, tomorrow night you will be empty of everything worth having.'

I don't know what he meant by that, but I think Arthur did, for he shrank back and suddenly looked quite old and said to me in a little pathetic voice, 'I never thought you'd do this to me, Hilda. I really didn't,' then slunk off like a rejected dog.

I didn't really enjoy the rest of the evening for I kept remembering Arthur's face and the way Louis spoke and looked at him. I'm still very happy being in Louis's company, for he is really so charming and handsome, but at the same time I'm not all that joyful. What with his family and this awful scene with Arthur. I haven't told you about his family. He took me to see them on Monday ... But you won't be wanting to hear any more of my troubles.

My very best regards
Hilda

Letter from Liza Russell to Hilda McCarthy June 12th 1987

18 Kingston Gardens
Twickenham

Dear Hilda,

Thank you for your letter dated June 20th. Your affairs of course are no longer of any concern to me, but I did warn you. Give Arthur Minns your present address, I said, and he'll be down there causing trouble. Far be it for me to say I told you so – but I did. You have only yourself to blame. And as for this Louis – handsome is as handsome does, as my dear mother used to say.

I'll not lay myself open to insult again by giving unsolicited advice – but personally I would chuck both of them and come on home.

But you must please yourself.

Best wishes in so far as they are for your own good,

Liza

P.S. Belatedly – many happy returns of your birthday. The gift I had for you I threw in the dustbin. Wrapping and all. Stupid really. If I had taken it back to the shop I'd most likely have got a refund.

Letter from Hilda McCarthy to Liza Russell June 14th 1987

The Imperial Hotel,
The Parade
Broadstairs

Dear Liza,

I've just got to write to you and hope you will find it in your heart – sooner or later – to forgive if not forget my awful letter of May 25th. The fact is, Liza, I'm sorely troubled and all mixed up and think maybe I'm going mad. I saw Arthur

Minns yesterday slinking along the front and I do mean slinking – like a fox that is being hunted by a lot of angry chicken farmers with shot guns. When he saw me he broke into a shambling run and I just had to catch up with him. He looked simply awful. All white and drawn and sort of shrunken. He shuddered when I touched him and said in that common way he has sometimes: 'Keep 'im off me.'

I can only assume he was talking about Louis, but why he should be so frightened of him I just can't understand. Then he ran away and I haven't seen him since.

Liza, I'm going to tell you about Louis's family and if you don't want to read it, don't. Use this letter to line Tiddles' basket. But I must tell someone.

The family estate is way out in the country and is called Wittering Grange and it really is eerie. First of all, we came to a pair of immense iron gates guarded by a dreadful-looking old man with white hair that looked like bleached snakes. He had no teeth and grinned at me with black gums, then flung the gates open as though they weighed nothing at all. Then we drove up a tree-lined drive and came at last to an old house that was a mass of turrets, crouching chimneys, deep embrasured windows and tiny red bricks. You reached a great iron-studded door by means of three black marble steps and went into a hall where all the doors, walls and ceilings were painted black. A black and white stained glass window had a picture of Lucifer (I think that's right) with his left foot on the world.

Two footmen dressed in black satin and white powdered wigs and flowing lace cravats bowed to Louis and said together:

'Welcome, Prince Louis, may your sins be heavy and your conscience light. Glory to the Lord Marcus.'

My heart bounced up to my throat then down again. I mean, I guessed Louis was someone important, but I never dreamed he could be a prince. Right, maybe a foreign prince that isn't like one of ours, but still ... I mean if he were to get around to popping the question and I was to say yes, then I'd be a princess with people bowing to me and royal highnessing me all over the place. Not bad for a girl whose dad mended windows round Teddington way.

There again I wasn't all that happy about the heavy sins and light conscience part, but dismissed it as some royal protocol business that was part of the tradition his family wallowed in.

Then I met the king-pin – the head of the family – the great Lord Marcus, the one they all bowed to. A great black and white brute whose eyes gave me the shakes, for I could swear they burnt a hole in my head and were peering into my brain.

The family drank thick red stuff from large balloon glasses and smacked their lips in a most disgusting fashion. In fact I was the only one who ate anything – roast beef, potatoes and Yorkshire pudding, followed by roly-poly pudding with hot jam poured over it. Very nice indeed. But I was rather put out when one little creature who looked as if he had horns poking through his thick black hair, which had to be ridiculous, after watching me eat with marked distaste for some while, clasped hands to his mouth and ran from the room, then made being-sick noises in the hall.

And how they kept looking at me as though I was something they hadn't seen for a long while. Thankfully we didn't stay all that time, just for dinner and a big argument that Louis had with the Lord Marcus afterwards. All about taking some place over as I understood it and how something called a meat-eater with special essence would be so useful, but frankly I was more worried about a horrible little man with a greenish face who kept pinching my arm to take all that notice.

On the drive back Louis didn't say much and for some reason I found myself worrying about Arthur Minns, wondering why he was so frightened of Louis and why he should say, 'Keep 'im off me,' I mean he was an awful pest, but I wouldn't like to think something dreadful had happened to him.

Well, I've let it all pour out and I expect, Liza, you have long ago torn this letter up or twisted it into a spill to light the gas ring. But in case you haven't, let me say this: I'm really and truly sorry about that letter and wish I hadn't written it.

It's up to you to decide if I'm to be forgiven and our former relationship resumed – if you understand me. I'm thinking about coming home soon. Very soon.

If I can.

Your rather sad and just a wee bit frightened,
Hilda

Letter from Liza Russell to Hilda McCarthy June 17th 1987

18 Kingston Gardens
Twickenham

Dear Hilda,

I read your letter dated June 14th with mixed feelings.

It's all coming out as I thought it would, and that is after making allowance for your hysterical nature and the tendency you have for dramatizing even the most mundane event. The truth is of course you are already getting fed up with your glamour boy and just can't find the courage to bring the entire business to an end. It does sound – if I am to believe what you say – he has some weird relations. Lots of people have. I seem to remember your Uncle George wasn't the kind of person one would willingly introduce to polite company.

The only sensible decision you've made yet is to come home soon. Of course I don't know when *soon* will be and how firm your *intention* is. Frankly I'm not all that interested. I know. To err is human, to forgive divine, but Hilda you must know I'm not in the tweeniest bit divine. The dreadful things you wrote in your letter have seared my very soul and I honestly can't find it in my heart to forgive yet. *When* you come home I do think it might be well if we don't meet or talk for some while. Maybe an exchange of notes pushed through our respective letter boxes might be in order, until such times as we either decide to have a full reconciliation – (which at this moment I feel to be most unlikely) or – perhaps wisely – make a complete break. In that event I am certain we can both (I know I can) behave like civilised intelligent people and pass the time of day should we meet in the street or lift.

I feel rather sorry for that poor little fool Arthur Minns. He's clearly besotted with you and I cannot help feeling that you have behaved rather brutally in so blatantly encouraging him. I always thought he was rather unbalanced and now from what you tell me, it would seem he has gone right over the edge.

You know, there are times, when I think I am the only rational person on this planet.
Put a note through my letter box *when* you return.

Regards that are intended to be kind,
Liza

Letter to Liza Russell from Hilda McCarthy June 20th 1987

The Imperial Hotel
The Parade
Broadstairs

Dear Liza,

I did not know you could be so cruel and heartless. No matter how much I may have hurt you by my unwise letter, there can be no excuse for such calculated unkindness. I am really very upset, which when added to the feeling of approaching menace that cannot be explained by rational thinking, has the effect of driving my confused mind into a kind of madness. I find myself accepting the possibility of something happening to me, in much the same way as a person marooned on the top of a tall burning building, comes to believe that jumping into space is a quick and easy way down.

Yet, I ask myself, what have I to worry about? Louis is charm itself, even though I cannot believe that gleam in his eyes means he has come to love me. Poor homely me – remember? Most certainly he is not after my poor little financial assets, for he is very rich. And his strange family even more so.

Shall I tell you what really worries me? Ever since my early teens I have always let my brain plan ahead. Usually when I am making up in front of the dressing table mirror. I will do so and so today – and tomorrow such and such a thing will take place. This time next week I will ring Mrs What's-her-name.

I can no longer do that. The brain refuses to even consider the future, as though it can sense a black wall of nothingness, or a future so horrible it must not be even thought about, if sanity is to be maintained until the last possible moment.

Of course you will say I am over-dramatizing, allowing an undisciplined imagination to run wild. I do hope you are right.

But during the day and evening when I am with Louis I am right as rain. His personality seems to drug mine so that fear and foreboding are banished into a painless void.

I have not seen or heard from Arthur Minns and can only hope he has gone home. Yes, you are most possibly right – I did act brutally towards that silly little man, for I did encourage him – at least sub-consciously – to inflate my ego. What strange creatures we women are, particularly when we reach a certain age. There was I simulating indignation because Arthur was showing all the signs of imitating a clinging leech, when that was what I was hoping he would do, even if I did not really like him.

Better be worshipped by a beggar than ignored by a king. And you, dear Liza, what kind of satisfaction are you deriving from pretending to be still very hurt and unforgiving? Tell me, do you still pull the wings off blow flies, then watch them running across the table vainly trying to fly? That was your favourite pastime as a child I seem to remember. But now of course you play with much larger victims.

When I finally slip into the slough of despair, you will find brief happiness in pushing my head under. Later of course you will be tortured by remorse and spend the remainder of your life doing good works at the local church.

I am writing this by the window and have just seen Louis running up the front steps. He looks so handsome and distinguished. Some woman has stopped and is now staring at him. They all do. Going into a restaurant with Louis's hand lightly cupping your elbow is equivalent to a triumphant entry into ancient Rome. The only trouble is I don't know which of us is the conqueror.

Don't bother to answer this letter if I've flicked too many raw wounds. I shall fully understand.

Hilda

Letter from Hilda McCarthy to Liza Russell July 7th 1987

The Imperial Hotel
The Parade
Broadstairs

Dear Liza,

As you can see I am still at the same address – The Imperial.

You have taken advantage of my suggestion that you did not answer my last letter, but I do sincerely hope you will not ignore this one.

Liza, I can't get away. Surrounded by hotel staff and the holiday crowd which is now packing the place, I am as much a prisoner as some poor wretch doing solitary confinement in Dartmoor. Louis is with me even when he is miles away visiting his dreadful family. His eyes are black holes leading to another universe, his mouth the gateway to a particularly vicious kind of hell.

Liza – lips, hands and voice can raise a flame of unendurable pleasure, which so quickly turns to freezing horror.

Teeth in the neck ... His sink deeper ... deeper ... and fire races through the veins and I can hear his tongue splashing liquid against the roof of his mouth and in his eyes I can see a distant view of a misty valley which runs between fire-tipped mountains, with that awful Lord Marcus riding a black horse in the scarlet cloud-covered sky.

It has been such a relief to have written all that even if you do decide I've gone right round the bend.

Another thing – the people in this hotel are more than a bit peculiar, although I'm not all that normal myself. They all seem to be continually talking to each other, without making any sound. As though I am living in a strange dream. All dreams are silent are they not? And I have a feeling they are all watching me, without so much as one head turned in my direction.

Do you know I'm so desperate I tried to telephone you yesterday evening, but the lines must be down or something for all I kept getting was a man's voice saying, 'Last train to Limbo one minute past dark hour.'

I must really make a real effort to get away. This is so silly. Liza, please contact me. Ring – do anything ...

Hilda

Telegram sent by Liza Russell to Hilda McCarthy c/o The Imperial Hotel, The Parade, Broadstairs, telephoned 06.45 hours July 8th 1987.

TRIED TO TELEPHONE YOU NO JOY AM COMING DOWN TO BROADSTAIRS BY 0900 HOURS TRAIN BE PACKED READY TO LEAVE LIZA

Letter from Liza Russell to Hilda McCarthy July 8th 1987

18 Kingston Gardens
Twickenham

Dear Hilda,

What bloody mad game are you playing? I went down to Broadstairs this morning as I promised in my telegram and went straight to the Imperial Hotel, only to find you are not registered there. The desk clerk remembered my letters being delivered and which he placed on the collect letter board. They apparently all disappeared sometime during the morning. This surely means you go there to collect them, but are living somewhere else. My telegram had been delivered, but that too had gone.

I found Mrs Brand's house and she told me you moved out on June 8th. She hasn't seen you since. She remembered this Louis of yours quite well. She thought he was very handsome, but in her opinion rather sinister. It would seem his eyes did something dreadful to her spine.

Hilda, by the tone of your letter and the fact you pretend to be staying at the Imperial Hotel, when you are somewhere else, tells me that either something very dicey is going on or you are really deranged. Now read what I am going to write very carefully.

Get in touch with me at once. Either by telephone or telegram, or if both for some reason are not possible, by express letter. If I do not hear from you by some way or another, I am going to contact the police. You have until the 10th. That is to say the day after tomorrow – Friday.

Yours, very worried,
Liza

Letter from Hilda McCarthy to Liza Russell, July 9th 1987

>The Imperial Hotel
>The Parade
>Broadstairs

Dear Liza,

Has the entire world – including you – combined to drive me mad? I received your telegram and *sat for the entire morning in the IMPERIAL HOTEL foyer waiting for you to turn up*. Even after Louis insisted on giving me lunch in the hotel restaurant, he gave instructions to the desk clerk to let me know the very moment you arrived. But you didn't. Liza, you must have gone to the wrong hotel. Louis says there isn't another Imperial in Broadstairs, but one of the smaller establishments may have called itself something similar and you could well have been mistaken.

But it is very odd about the telephone. I've tried to ring you from the phone in my room and keep getting what must be the railway station for this man keeps on about the last train to Limbo leaving one minute past dark hour.

Half of me still wants to leave and the other half can't bear the thought of being parted from Louis. But, Liza, I seem to be getting weak and frightfully thin.

Which reminds me. I saw Arthur yesterday evening. I was sitting on the balcony which commands a clear view of the beach, when I saw what had to be a skin-covered skeleton trudging through the sand. Hat down over the ears, torn shirt and frayed trousers flapping in the strong breeze, he looked like a walking scarecrow. But there was that personality over-print that often enables us to identify someone we have not seen since childhood, which told me it was Arthur Minns. Suddenly he turned and broke into a shambling run back the way he had come and just after he had disappeared, I saw Louis approaching the hotel. He laughed when I told him about seeing Arthur and teased me on my overwhelming effect on men.

Liza, I am still determined to come home and will, I promise you break free from this hold Louis has on me. Please forgive me for so hurting you and please try to recapture a little of that regard you once had for me. I still can't get over your visiting Broadstairs, thinking you were in the Imperial and me looking for you all morning. Then there was the matter of your letters and the clerk remembering seeing them. Honestly, it's all beyond me. Unless ...!

I am not going to get all fanciful again. I'm not, I'm not ...

Please get in touch with me again – soon – at once – the fact is dear Liza, I'm so very frightened. I am ... I am.

Yours forever,
Hilda

Letter from Liza Russell to Hilda McCarthy July 11th 1987

18 Kingston Gardens
Twickenham

Dear Hilda,

I think we both must have been driven mad. Hilda, I was in that foyer at the Imperial Hotel – the one and only Imperial Hotel – on Wednesday last – I questioned the staff, went to see Mrs Brand, then came back to the Imperial where everyone denied ever seeing you. The only reason the clerk knew your name was because he had seen it on the letters I sent you. And the telegram. Hilda, don't try to put me off by a cock and bull story. I have just rung the Imperial – less than five minutes ago – and the manager still maintains no one of your name or appearance is staying there.

Hilda, please stop this playing about and tell me *where the hell you are*. Or better still, do what you say you want to do, come on home. This is a civilized – well almost – country and no one can be unlawfully stopped from going wherever they wish. Tell this Louis weirdo to go take a running jump. Look, send me a wire if you still can't get through on the telephone and I will hire a car and come and fetch you. Maybe you're sick, I don't know. I'm beginning to feel a wee bit panicky. Oh Gawd! *Tell me where you are. Come on home. Do something positive.*

Your very worried,
Liza

Letter from Hilda McCarthy to Liza Russell July 13th 1987

> The Imperial Hotel
> The Parade
> Broadstairs

Dear Liza,

Thank you, oh, thank you for your letter. Yes, that's a wonderful idea – hire a car and come and fetch me. Don't worry about not finding me this time. I am at the Imperial – I am. It's the largest hotel which faces the front and I will be sitting on the front steps from nine o'clock onwards. My luggage with me. And Louis will not talk me out of it. This morning I told him I was going home and he didn't object the least bit. Even offered to drive me home in his car. But I'd much rather be with you. With him there would always be the suspicion that just maybe he would take the wrong turning and we'd finish up at Twittering Grange.

I keep noticing strange things lately. There's a clock tower over an arrangement of glass-sided seats in the pleasure gardens. Well, that clock is going backwards. The little and large hands are moving backwards and that is giving the silly impression that the day is moving backwards too. The sun rises at nine p.m. Sets at six in the morning. The clock in the hotel foyer is misbehaving as well.

Liza, darling, wouldn't it be awful if I was rushing backwards in time? Getting further and further away from each other. But I mustn't think that way.

Louis has just come into the room – he never taps any more – not to be wondered at I suppose. But I must close now.

I'll be on the steps tomorrow morning, I promise. Oh, I do hope this letter reaches you in time. I couldn't send you a wire, I tried, but just couldn't raise telegrams on the phone – or get through to you. Tell you what – if you don't make it tomorrow, I won't panic, but do the same thing the day after. On Wednesday. Can't wait to see you.

> Hilda.

Letter from Liza Russell to Hilda McCarthy delivered by hand to the reception desk of the Imperial Hotel, Broadstairs. July 15th 1987.
0900 Hours

Dear Hilda,
This situation is really mad and I've just about had enough of it. I not only came down here by car yesterday, but having waited for you to put in an appearance – as promised in your letter of the 13th – *took a room in the hotel.* – and I do not intend to leave until you stop messing about and come out of hiding.

Hilda, I've seen the hotel register and if you booked in here, then you must have used a different name.

As you seem to have received all the letters I sent you here, I am handing this one in at the reception desk, where I am given to understand, the clerk will put it on the 'Mail to be Collected Board' – the one covered with green baize and triangular tapes – in front of the lift. I am going to seat myself where I can watch the board and grab you or whoever comes to collect it.

Hilda, I am determined to solve this mystery, one way or another. I won't be made a fool of.

Hilda, for God's sake if you're in trouble let me know where you are. I'll do anything to help. Anything at all.

Your devoted friend,
Liza

Letter from Liza Russell to Hilda McCarthy, July 15th 1987. [Placed on mail collection board 11.00 hours. Imperial Hotel, Broadstairs].

Hilda, how the hell did you do it? I swear I did not take my eyes off that board, but suddenly my letter was not there. I've just got to believe I dozed off without realising it. Well, I'm standing by this one. No one is going to get by me. But no one.

Hilda, if you get this one and you are nearby for God's sake shout. Call my name and I'll come a-running.

Your very devoted and worried friend,
Liza

Letter from Hilda McCarthy to Liza Russell, [redirected from 18 Kingston Gardens, Twickenham, to the Imperial Hotel, Broadstairs July 15th 1987. Collected by Liza Russell from letter collection board at 20.15 hours].

Dear Liza,
    I'm so frightened and don't know what to do. I collected your letter dated today's date from the letter board and just can't understand anything. I sat on the front steps all day yesterday and Liza, you did not turn up. There is no way you could have got by me without my seeing you. And you are not in the register. And I've been in the foyer all morning as well. I am going to put this letter on the board, so if by chance you are in the hotel, you'll pick it up. I'll even stand by the board so that no one can get at that letter without pushing by me.
    Louis is getting a wee bit cross with me and says I'm being very silly and why don't I let him drive me home? There's not much point in him doing so if you are really in Broadstairs. Anyway, I don't believe he means it. I keep seeing members of his awful family coming and going out of the hotel and they all give me a quick glance as though to see if I come up to expectations.
    And lately there is a square black car parked in the vicinity in which are seated four dreadful looking creatures that make me think of a picture book I had as a child in which were depicted dogs dressed in big hats and long overcoats. I have a feeling they are watching me as well.
    I've been thinking of hiring a cab to take my things to the station and making my own way back to town, but I'm not sure if those awful things that look like dogs will let me. I can't dismiss the thought that I am very important to Louis's family, and they want me for some reason – in a very special place.
    Louis told me a while ago that Arthur Minns's body has been found washed up on the beach near North Foreland. Do you know? He chuckled and said poor Arthur was empty of everything worth having and I do believe I heard him say something like that before, but can't remember when or where.
    The clocks are all going backwards – even my wrist watch –

the one you gave me last Christmas – but that doesn't bother me anymore. Louis is changing and his smile is more gloating than loving and almost becomes a sneer when I talk about catching a train for town. He whispers in my ear: 'Pretty lady is catching the last train to Limbo, that leaves one minute past dark hour.' That's what the man on the telephone said – about the last train for Limbo leaving one minute past the dark hour.

Just before starting this letter I thought I saw you in the foyer, but it turned out to be someone who did not look a bit like you. Oh, Liza, what is going to happen to me? That black car is parked outside of the hotel now and I have a feeling one of those dog-shaped things is standing by my door ...

Liza, I think that when Louis made me move from Mrs Brand's house, he took me into – another place that is in the same place ... Oh, I'm not making sense and you'll think I'm over-dramatising again. But my poor little brain has been working day and night on what had happened to me and dimly – very dimly – understands.

Liza, could there be more than one version of the Imperial Hotel? And another version of Broadstairs – another version of our world? The hidden world? The one Louis has taken me to is going backward in *our* time. And shortly I am going to be forced on to a train that will take me to another hidden place called Limbo.

Liza, there's nothing either of us can do. Louis and his family can go anywhere they wish – you and I only to where we are allowed or taken. Lord Marcus and Prince Louis rule the timeways ...

I cannot understand how our letters get through, but I do not believe they will much longer. Maybe the wonderful, fabulous, soul-destroying and most evil Louis has overlooked one little loophole. Pray that it remains open so that some other poor wretch in my position can maintain a form of contact with the world that gave them birth. But I cannot hold out much hope. Louis knows we are corresponding.

Oh, Liza, if only we could be together again – with claws sheathed.

Yours forever
Hilda

Letter from Liza Russell to Hilda McCarthy handed into the reception desk Imperial Hotel, Broadstairs at 18.30 hours. Disappeared one hour ten minutes later.

Dear Hilda,
I am willing now to accept truth no matter in what guise it comes to me. I have reported you missing to the police and a search is being made for you everywhere. A plain clothes policeman is on duty round the clock in the foyer of this hotel, watching the post collection board. I can only hope he has more luck than I did. So far as I was concerned, one moment my letter to you was on the board, the next it had disappeared.

Hilda, I have a practical, no-nonsense mind. As a child I never believed in Father Christmas, as an adult I could not accept the concept of life after death. Now I find myself forced to believe that a dear friend has somehow been abducted and taken to another dimension. Such knowledge undermines the basic concepts that form the foundation of my being. Already I can feel the grip I have on this form of existence, slackening. Soon – very soon I will be dead. Let us hope that in some unforeseeable future we will find ourselves together at a yet to be imagined destination.

Believe me, dear Hilda, my thoughts will be with you for so long as whatever laws that control the universe permit me to be a rational, remembering, thinking individual.

Liza

Letter from Hilda McCarthy to Liza Russell written on Imperial Hotel notepaper and in a corresponding envelope, which was found on the mail collection board at 0600 hours, 21st July 1987.

Dear, dear Liza,
I found your letter on the board – and one of the dog-faced creatures was watching it – the board I mean. Liza, the police won't find a trace of me, or the remains of poor Arthur Minns. But there must be a way back, there must be ...

But I must remain calm or you will begin to think I've gone mad and start you looking for me all over again.

Liza, forgive me for anything I may have done and said to

hurt you, but a silly vain creature like me cannot always be held responsible for what she does or says. Yes, Liza we will meet again somewhere. On the road to eternity, perhaps.

But it is dark here and the moon is reflected on the sea and I can hear a solitary gull crying and can't help wondering if it is the soul of Arthur Minns calling vainly for help. The four dog-faced creatures are in the room with me, not doing anything but staring with unblinking eyes that are black with red-red sparks in them ... sparks that might become flames if I move or do something I must not ... And Louis is seated on the bed looking so handsome and wonderfully evil ... And I'm terrified for it's time to go ... to go and catch the last train to Limbo and I will never see the moon again let alone the sun which will never rise ... Good ...

*

Note: All the letters and one telegram that were exchanged by Mrs Hilda McCarthy and Miss Liza Russell were found in room 16A first floor the Imperial Hotel, Broadstairs, laid out on a bed. There is no explanation at the time of going to press how they came to be there. No traces of Mrs Hilda McCarthy or Mr Arthur Minns have to date been discovered.

Miss Liza Russell died on August 29th of a heart attack.